SENSATION

OFELIA MARTINEZ

READING CACTUS PRESS

READING CACTUS
PRESS

First Edition

Library of Congress Control Number: 2022916842

ISBN 978-1-954906-21-1 (paperback)

ISBN 978-1-954906-16-7 (eBook)

ISBN 978-1-954906-22-8 (hardcover)

SENSATION

For the allies
The ones who love, respect, and promote Latine cultures and peoples
The ones who speak up in the face of bigotry
You have a permanent invite to the carne asada

A WORD OF CAUTION

Sara and Ramiro's story is a gloomy one.

I'm a mood writer, and when I started writing this book, it was a particularly dark time in my life. Please read responsibly. I've started a preliminary list of content warnings on my website and strongly encourage you to read those at www.ofelia martinez.com/cws. I will continue to add to the list as readers bring more to my awareness.

CHAPTER 1

SPRING

I've been in love with Ramiro Jimenez since my junior year of college, and now his fiancée is dead.

I'm watching him, in love with him, and he's watching her, getting lowered into the ground in her beautiful white dress in her pretty mahogany casket, her engagement ring secure around her finger.

The tornado sirens that on any other day would send my heart rate through the roof stopped just in time for the service to conclude and allow the funeral procession to begin.

I've been terrified of that awful sound since I was a little girl, when I endured tornado warnings pretty much alone. Only, today, my heart is occupied with a grief so immense, the sirens are an afterthought.

I always thought the minute I graduated from college, I'd move as far away from the tornado valley as I could. Then I found my adoptive family when I was in college, and I couldn't imagine being away from them—every single person at this burial today—so I stayed.

Despite the love of all these people, spring is still the worst season of all in this place. It's rainy, gray, and those damned sirens go off at the worst times. Springtime in Kansas City always makes me think of Forrest Gump describing all the different types of rain. Today it was the sideways type for several hours. Now the raindrops are heavy, and the wind has died down a bit. They aren't pelting us sideways anymore, but the downpour is still heavy.

So heavy.

And despite all that, today, even the rain is an afterthought. I'm not cold, or scared, or annoyed at being wet. It's like none of us here care or can even feel the rain. We're all still numb, in shock.

This particular dreary spring day is the worst of them because today, I get to watch the love of my life bury his fiancée.

It's unrequited love. I'll make that clear now.

I met Ramiro when Carolina, my then-roommate and now best friend-slash-big sister, took pity on me and invited me to her home to spend the holiday break with her and her dad, Don Gustavo. Back then, Ramiro was the one deep in unrequited love for Carolina, whom he'd grown up with. So, in a way, he's already been through exactly what I'm experiencing with him.

But Carolina knew how he felt about her. And he has no idea about my feelings.

Nearly eight years is a long time to be in love with someone who will never love you back. I was only twenty when I met him, and I thought I'd outgrow it one day, but watching him today, with those big brown eyes, glassy as he holds back his sobs, hurts me more than anything ever has, and that's when I know—I'll never stop loving him. Even if he'll never see me as anything other than Carolina's annoying little sister—a gnat in his periphery.

After Carolina finally made it clear she'd never be in love with him, Ramiro had a whirlwind romance with a woman four years his senior, and they got engaged two months ago. He finally thought he'd found happiness.

They never made it to their wedding day.

Francisca Garcia died at thirty-four years old.

She hadn't been sick, and her sudden death at the peak of their love story crushed Ramiro way more than his heartbreak over Carolina ever had. It was an accident. A nighttime walk and an all-black workout outfit a driver couldn't see in the dark. She never saw her crossing the street, distracted as she was by texting on her phone, driving much faster than she should have been in a residential area. Francisca died on impact.

And I feel guilty.

Guilty, because more than anything, I wish I could allow myself to admire how handsome he looks today in his suit. I'm used to seeing Ramiro in what I swear is a uniform of jeans and a ribbed tank, all greasy from his work as a mechanic.

The only suit he had for today was the one he'd already bought for his wedding.

So here we are, Ramiro, dashing in his three-piece wedding suit, getting drenched in the rain as he buries his fiancée. I'd trade places with Francisca to save him this pain if I could.

Without thinking, I interlace my fingers with his, and on the other side of him, Carolina is also holding his hand. He doesn't flinch, or push me away, to my surprise. Today, we're the twin pillars propping him up, though Carolina and I are sobbing messes ourselves. We all do our best to keep it together.

We've known Francisca for years since she lived just down the street from Carolina's family home—and Ramiro's, who was Carolina's neighbor growing up. Though Carolina and I were never particularly close to her, this death still hits very close to home. Losing someone from our tight-knit community hurts more than I imagined, and not just because I feel this pain for Ramiro.

I'd gotten to know Francisca and her family over the years. We often invited them to our home—that is, Don Gustavo and Carolina's home. They also welcomed us as guests to their home when they had cookouts and birthday parties, and let's not forget invitations to watch the all-important soccer games.

Even when Ramiro fell in love with her, I didn't have it in me to hate her. Francisca was the embodiment of what Don Gustavo called de sangre livianita. During one of our Spanish lessons, he explained that when someone has light blood, it means they're easy to like, while someone with heavy blood, or sangre pesada, is a person who is hard to like. In reality, I saw how happy she made Ramiro—how he lit up when she walked into a room—and that made me happy, regardless of the weight of her blood.

Francisca must have had feather-light blood, though, because to know her was to like her. I understand why he fell in love with her so quickly once they started dating.

As they begin to lower the casket into the grave, Ramiro's grip on my hand tightens, and he croaks out, "Sara." I look up at him, blinking, surprised he called out my name. Not Francisca's. Not Carolina's. Mine. He said, "Sara."

I know what it's like to lose family and loved ones. Not to death but might as well be. That's probably why he said my name, knowing I understand what he's feeling with this loss. I squeeze his hand tighter and lean my head on his shoulder, hugging his bicep with my free arm.

"I know," I whisper. "I know."

A strangled sound leaves his throat, but he won't cry. I know he won't. Definitely not in public. Not even under cover of rain. In private? I'm not even sure he'll cry then, either.

Though only thirty years old, Ramiro Jimenez is a very proud, young Mexican-American man. Taught not to cry from his earliest memories by his father, who learned it from his father, and so on. At least that's my understanding of his upbringing.

I wish he would cry. He needs to. He can't bottle up all this pain.

This pain that is all around us. Pain reflected in Don Gustavo's eyes—who knows exactly what it's like to bury a loved one so young—and in Doña Pancha's tears at having to endure the pain of burying her child.

But the biggest pain in this tiny, wet patch of land today comes from the two little boys hugging their grandma, unable to stop crying because they'll never see their mom again.

On the day they bury their mother, René Garcia is ten years old, and Oscar Garcia only eight. Their father is still living, but he isn't here today and hasn't been for a single day of Oscar's life.

I don't think any of us can hear the priest's words any longer over Doña Pancha's wailing.

When the casket meets earth and the sound stops, Oscar finally looks up, and there's a wild look of panic in his eyes. He screams, "¡Mamá!" and lunges toward the opening in the grave as if intending to dive into it.

Ramiro's hands pull from Carolina and me, and he rushes forward to intercept Oscar. He barely grabs onto the back of Oscar's shirt in time and pulls him back before he reaches his goal.

"No!" Oscar screams. "Let me go!"

Ramiro's hand stays fisted firmly on Oscar's now drenched shirt, no longer under the cover of Doña Pancha's umbrella. Then Ramiro falls to his knees and spins Oscar around by his shoulders. He takes the little boy in his arms, and for a moment, Oscar fights it. Those tiny fists punch at Ramiro's sides, but Ramiro stays put in his embrace of the little guy.

All of us around them are stunned into silence because no one fucking deserves this kind of pain. Not Ramiro, and definitely not Oscar and René.

Eventually, Oscar stops fighting, and his cheek falls to Ramiro's shoulder, his sobs down to hiccups.

"I know, buddy," Ramiro says, rubbing his back. "I'm here,"

he says, just loud enough for me to hear over the rain. "I'll always be here." Ramiro lets his cheek fall to the top of Oscar's head. Fat raindrops roll down Ramiro's close-shaved head and onto Oscar's black, unruly waves.

If there's one thing I know to be true about Ramiro Jimenez, it's that he's a man of his word.

That promise he just made?

It transformed him into a single father of two little boys before my very eyes.

CHAPTER 2

The velorio, or repast, takes place at Don Gustavo's, a choice that made both Carolina and me very nervous when we heard the plans. In the end, it was Doña Pancha's choice, which we decided to respect, but I won't lie and say we aren't walking on eggshells around Don Calixto, Ramiro's dad, and Don Gustavo.

"Ramiro looks a lot like his dad, doesn't he?" I ask Carolina as I watch father and son, standing tall—eyes completely dry despite the surrounding sniffles.

Carolina looks up from her barely touched plate of food and follows my stare. "Yeah. Both are very handsome, though I think Don Calixto is a little better looking. I like the gray in his beard."

I roll my eyes at my friend. "Why do you always go for the older guy? If you didn't have such an amazing dad, I'd think you have daddy issues."

Carolina shrugs. "It's just the look, I guess. I know objectively that Ramiro is handsome, but I've never been attracted physically to his type."

My jaw drops a little. Not attracted to his type? The perfect, muscular, handsome type? Maybe our friendship works so well because our taste in men is so different.

As we watch, it's hard to ignore how Don Gustavo avoids any room Don Calixto is in and vice versa.

I've never fully understood the rivalry between Don Calixto and Don Gustavo, but Carolina reassures me it runs deep.

The apple didn't fall far from the tree, and for his age, Don Calixto is a very handsome man. His brown skin has deepened further in his recent Floridian retirement, deep brown eyes framed by the same long lashes that grace Ramiro's beautiful eyes.

But there's a hardness to him, and not only because we've just attended his daughter-in-law's funeral. Not an ounce of feeling has crossed his stoic expression. I only really ever saw him at the various neighborhood events and family cookouts before they moved away, so I'd assumed his coolness was a permanent state of being. I realize now, of course, it deepens when Don Gustavo is around, and hardens into a distasteful glare.

As I watch him at the velorio today, it's hard to miss his back stiffening whenever Don Gustavo steps into a room, followed swiftly by Don Calixto exiting said room. They're cordial with each other, but it doesn't seem to extend beyond that.

Apart from the age difference and Ramiro's slightly taller frame, the only distinguishing factor between father and son is Don Calixto's dark waves, neatly combed back, contrasted to Ramiro's neatly trimmed head, giving him a near-bald look.

From my spot sitting on a bench near the dining room, I watch as Don Gustavo approaches the buffet table, making Don Calixto drop the serving spoon in his hand and walk away immediately before his plate is full.

I'm not usually nosey—okay, maybe I am, a little—but it's been hard to miss the animosity.

"What happened?" I ask Carolina, eyeing the plate on her lap full of asado rojo, rice, and a few tortillas.

"What?" she asks.

"Between Don Calixto and Don Gustavo. Why does Ramiro's dad look like he wants to murder your dad? I heard they were best friends when you were growing up. Isn't that why they used to joke around that you and Ramiro would marry when you grew up, to join the families?"

Carolina scoffs. "Don't remind me. And yes, when my mom was still alive, she and Doña Rocio were best friends, and Don Calixto and Dad were too. They were inseparable. But after Mom died, Ramiro spent a lot of time with Dad and me. Taking care of us, you know?"

I smile. Of course, young teenage Ramiro would have done something like that.

"It really connected him and Dad. Eventually, he ventured into Dad's garage and fell in love with working on cars. Don Calixto hasn't been able to forgive my dad, which is ridiculous because Dad didn't even do anything."

"Wow," I say and grab her plate from her to steal a few bites.

"Hey, that's mine," she whines, and we allow ourselves a small giggle. So absent from this day, the laughter is like coming up for fresh air after nearly drowning. My chest is so tight from the pain and the crying. It's a relief to have Carolina by my side. And a bigger relief our little community all showed up for Ramiro and Doña Pancha today.

Ileana, who lives a couple of blocks over, brought a big batch of asado rojo, my favorite dish of hers—pork in red sauce. And Don Gustavo made rice and handmade corn tortillas. Sofia, our best friend, brought several bottles of tequila and whiskey from her bar to spike our coffees with.

Few of Ramiro's friends showed up since most of them are in the military and couldn't find themselves in Kansas City for this. Leo Moreno, his best friend from childhood, is in the Army, and so are most of the guys they used to run with.

Ramiro isn't alone, though. His parents flew in from Florida, and he has Carolina, Don Gustavo, and me.

I hand the plate back to Carolina—with only half her food remaining—and she keeps nibbling at it. "That's too bad, for such a long friendship to end over something so silly."

"It's not silly to Don Calixto. He had grand plans for his son to take over his law practice when he retired."

I snort. "Can you imagine Ramiro as a lawyer? Wearing a suit every day of his life?" I shake my head. As dashing as he is today in a suit, his large physique, square jaw, and bald head are much better suited to his usual jeans and tee or ribbed tank.

"I know. He'd be miserable."

"He did the right thing," I say.

"Tell that to Don Calixto," Carolina deadpans. "But yeah, in Don Calixto's eyes, my dad stole his son from his predestined future—"

"You mean like the predestined future that you'd marry Ramiro one day?"

Carolina laughs. "I'm sure Don Calixto is relieved I didn't let that happen. We'd all be family then, and he'd never escape Dad."

That wouldn't be so bad, I think, for our families to come together like that. If Francisca hadn't died and everything had gone to plan, Ramiro would have joined her family and surely distanced himself from the Ramirez household. Even though this outcome is tragic, I can't help but feel a little guilty to be glad Ramiro isn't lost to us just yet. Though Carolina may not be in love with him, I know she loves him as she would a brother.

Rocio has her arm laced through her son's as they walk to Carolina and me.

"Caro, mi niña, I'm so glad you're here," Rocio says. Her eyes are red-rimmed and swollen as she pulls Carolina in for a kiss. "Thank you for being here for my boy."

Hard to believe that not two weeks ago, Doña Rocio was helping Francisca with her wedding preparations.

"Of course, Doña Rocio. Please let me know how I can help in the coming days," Caro says.

"Yes, thank you," Ramiro says, but his voice is sullen, hollow, and somehow robotic all at the same time. He kisses Carolina on the cheek, she returns it, then he turns to me, doing the same.

When his lips grace my skin, I feel all my blood rush to my cheeks. Then I hate myself a little for the inappropriate reaction. This is the worst time to blush from the chastest of kisses, but it's the first time since I've known Ramiro that I've felt his lips on me. Though a kiss on the cheek is the proper greeting of respect, somehow, Ramiro has managed to avoid it with me since I've known him—until now, when he's in the presence of his mother, who would undoubtedly say something about his rudeness if he didn't.

After years of dreaming about those full lips on my skin, my body was bound to react, but I feel like the shittiest human ever at my involuntary response, given the circumstances.

I'm such an asshole.

Thankfully, he notices nothing, and neither do Rocio and Carolina, it seems. I gulp my soda, resisting the urge to press the icy glass to my face to cool it down.

I've completely missed whatever the three of them are talking about when Doña Rocio turns to me. "Sara, could I have a moment with you?"

I look between her and Ramiro, taken aback by her request for a private conversation with me.

"You can go upstairs to my old room," Carolina offers.

Ramiro unlaces his mom's arm from his and pats the top of

her hand. He takes my seat next to Carolina as I walk away with Doña Rocio.

As we leave to go upstairs, I allow myself one glimpse back at them.

Ramiro and Carolina absolutely look perfect together—like they were made for each other. I understand why their parents wanted them together.

Carolina is nearly as tall as Ramiro. Her shade of beautiful brown skin is almost as dark as his, making her amber eyes pop. She's elegant, graceful, poised—everything I'm not. A parent's absolute dream. A driven doctor who looks like a bombshell. Even if Carolina won't entertain the idea of dating Ramiro, watching them together and knowing that their shared history runs deep forces my thoughts away from my dreams of one day being with him.

"Close the door, mija," Doña Rocio says.

"Sure."

She sits on the edge of Carolina's bed, and I flip around Carolina's old desk chair to take a seat in front of her.

"Sara, I need your help."

As much as Ramiro avoided me over the years, Doña Rocio always included me in her family plans. Just as Don Gustavo invited me into his home, Doña Rocio did the same. She's done so much for me and been there for me when I've needed a support system almost as much as Don Gustavo. Up until her move to Florida, we spent a lot of time together. I'd do pretty much anything for the only positive mother figure I've had in my life.

"Anything I can do, Doña Rocio—"

She cuts me off with a wave of her hand. "None of this 'Doña' business. It makes me feel old." She smiles a bit mischievously, like she's being sarcastic.

I smile back. "Rocio," I correct myself. It's a constant battle we've had since it goes against everything I've learned, to not use the respectful form of address for my elders. "Anything I can do to help."

"Calixto and I have flights to head back to Florida in a couple of days. I wanted to extend my stay, but Ramiro is as bullheaded as his father."

"He won't let you stay and help, will he?"

"Of course not! Have you met those men? And Calixto is no better. He's raised his son on tough love, and if it were up to him, we'd leave Ramiro to sort everything out by himself so he can adapt to his new situation."

"You mean Oscar and René?"

Rocio nods. "Yes."

"You think he'll become their guardian?"

"He'll do anything he can to make that happen. I know my son."

"Okay." I take a deep breath. "What can I do to help?"

"Ramiro won't grieve, not like he needs to, but he also doesn't have the first idea of how to raise two little boys on his own. He's going to need help, and I think a woman's hand, especially for the boys, could be very soothing to them all."

"Errr," I scratch my head nervously. "Shouldn't Carolina be the one to—"

"She'll help. Initially, I'm sure. But you know what her schedule as a doctor is like. And yes, I know a nurse's schedule is also hectic, but you could try, couldn't you? To spend some of that time here? Help with the boys?"

There's no way to say no to her in this situation, is there?

How could I sit here and say, ma'am, your son can hardly stand to be in the same room with me? He avoids me almost as much as your husband avoids Don Gustavo. I'd sound like an asshole, which we've established already that I am.

And yet, I can't bring myself to deny his mother this little comfort before she returns to her everyday life.

"Sure Doñ—" I clear my throat. "Rocio. I'm happy to help as

much as I can. I'll keep an eye on them, and you're right. I can ask for a more regular schedule or the night shift, at least for a while. I've been at Heartland Metro Hospital long enough to feel comfortable making that request. I'm due for some vacation days soon, so that will help."

"Thank you, Mija," she says, palming the side of my face.

We stand, and before I can stop myself, the question is flying out of my mouth, "Why me?"

That mischievous smile is back, tugging at the corner of her mouth. "Some things are just meant to be," she says.

I look after her as she walks out of Carolina's childhood room, leaving me to wonder what on earth that could possibly mean.

CHAPTER 3

As Rocio predicted, Ramiro won't take the time to grieve. He went to work at the garage the day after the funeral and the next day after that. On Saturday, stir-crazy from being inside, he's leaving for errands he invented, but a delivery man greets him on the front porch, stopping his escape strategy.

"Is that for me?" I yell from my spot in the kitchen. I pull an apple from the fruit bowl and walk toward the front door to find Ramiro in the doorway, holding what looks like a package. "Ramiro?"

Silence.

"What is it?" I walk around him and find him staring at a box in his hands. His expression blank.

"Ramiro, you're scaring me." I gently tug at his elbow until he steps back so I can close the door. I lead him to the couch and take the box, placing it on the coffee table in front of him.

"Were you expecting something?"

He shakes his head. I lean over the table to peek at the box and set my uneaten apple next to it. The sender label states it's from Leonardo Moreno. "It's from Leo!" I say. I'm glad one of his best friends is thinking of him during this tough time.

"Yeah," Ramiro says. "It's from Leo."

"Well? Aren't you going to open it? Let me get you a knife."

I round the sofa, and head to the kitchen, pulling a steak knife from the block on the counter, then find Ramiro still staring at the box.

"Here." I hand him the knife, but Ramiro doesn't take it.

"Can you open it?" he asks and leans back, like he doesn't want to see what's inside.

"It's not spiders or something, is it?" I ask, only half-joking.

"No. I don't think so."

Great. Reassuring, I think, though I don't tell him that.

I slice through the tape and remove the packing paper inside, revealing another box wrapped in beautiful pearl-white paper with golden flowers and a white bow. An envelope is attached to the top.

A wedding gift.

Saturday. It's Saturday.

His wedding day.

How could I be so stupid? I've been known to be thoughtless, not from ill-intent, but because sometimes I'm just oblivious, especially when it comes to family stuff. But this really takes the cake. I should have known the minute I saw the delivery man that it might be a wedding gift that would need to be intercepted.

I can't begin to imagine what he must be feeling.

He would have been on his way to the church right now. "Oh, Ramiro," I say, and bring my hand to my mouth. "I'm sure—"

"It's okay. I know he's deployed. He probably couldn't cancel it after ordering it."

"I'm not even sure he knows yet," I say, following Ramiro's train of thought. Of course, his best friend would send a gift since he couldn't be here in person for what was supposed to be the best day of Ramiro's life.

Carolina and I have already called all the guests to break the news and assured them any gifts would be returned, but we never thought about his friends in the military.

Ramiro clears his throat. "Could you, uh—"

"Yes!" I say, springing into action. "I'll take care of it." I rush to re-stuff the packing paper into the box, and don't even bother taking out the card with well-wishes. I fold the box flaps back into place and hurry to ditch the box in the trunk of my car until I can figure out what to do with it.

When I head back into the house, Ramiro is standing. Silent. Stoic. Just like his father at the funeral.

"Ramiro?"

"I'm tired," he says. "I think I need to take a nap. Would you do me a favor?"

"Anything," I say.

"Pick up the boys from Doña Pancha's?"

I nod, and he heads upstairs to sleep.

That night, I help the boys get settled for bed and take care of dinner. Afterward, I head on over to Don Gustavo's, letting him know Ramiro will need a week or two for bereavement after all.

When I check in on them in the morning, Ramiro is still asleep.

He sleeps for three days straight.

Two weeks after the funeral, I decide to take some vacation time. Ramiro is drowning.

Doña Pancha is too frail to keep up with two boys, especially in all their grief. I don't think any of us understood just how much of a caretaker Francisca was for her mother, either. These past two weeks, Carolina and I have helped Ramiro as much as we could, and we're still stretched thin.

Ramiro is in a fog. He hasn't returned to work, and he tries, he really does, to get up in the morning and be there for the boys, but we always send him back to bed because he looks utterly exhausted.

Carolina and I have split tasks. She takes care of Doña Pancha's shopping and errands while her dad takes care of meals for her. I then go over every night and help her shower and get ready for bed.

Now that Carolina is back to her grueling full-time schedule, though, all the tasks have fallen on me.

Doña Pancha has finally accepted that she'll have to go to a nursing home, and this morning we went to visit three.

She didn't like any of them.

Tomorrow, I'll check out a few more, and I'll likely have to pick one myself and just take her since I'm doubtful she will be happy with any of them.

René spends his time outside when the weather permits, kicking his soccer ball around. He hasn't said an unnecessary word since the funeral, and mirroring Ramiro, he won't be caught dead crying.

I hear him through his bedroom door, and I'm glad that at least in private, René allows himself to grieve.

Oscar has had nightmares every night since the funeral, and I have to stay in bed with him until he falls asleep. I finally went and grabbed most of my clothes from my apartment and moved them into Oscar's bedroom, then relocated him to share René's.

I'd expected René to hate the idea of sharing a room with his little brother, but when I told him of the change, he just shrugged like he didn't care without saying a word.

I feel like I'm moving a mile a minute, trying to get everyone to function, but they're all ghosts, disembodied, untethered, and uninterested in my hectic agenda.

They all just need time, I remind myself.

I knock on Ramiro's bedroom door. "Hey," I say. "I'm heading to my apartment for a few more things I need."

Ramiro rolls over on the bed to look at me and does his best to smile. "Okay," he says.

"I'm leaving the boys here. Keep an eye on them?"

He sits up and massages the back of his neck, then cracks it. "I'm their temporary guardian. I'm the one supposed to be taking care of them."

"I know. But I like to help."

When I get back from my apartment, Oscar is watching a movie and René is focused on his phone with his headset on. I find Ramiro at the kitchen table, drinking a cup of coffee.

"Thank you, Sara, for helping so much. Really."

I reach my hand over the table and open it. He slides his forward and places his warm palm in mine. Under any other circumstances, Ramiro's touch would have left me completely speechless, but this gesture is intimate in a different sort of way—in an 'I got you' way. "You'd do the same for me. I wanted to tell you. I'm taking some vacation time from work—"

"You don't need to do that—"

"Yes, I do. We need to get Pancha into a safe home, and soon it'll be time for you to head back to work, and the boys have to go back to school—"

"I'm not going back to school!" René shouts. He must have taken his headset off when he saw me talking to Ramiro.

Then he storms off to his room and slams the door shut. Oscar flinches but stays put in front of the television.

Ramiro sighs down into his mug. "Shit," he says. "I don't know how I'm supposed to do this—"

I signal him to be quiet because Oscar is listening, and Ramiro nods.

His every thought is written on his face, so he doesn't have to say them, anyway. He's wondering if he makes a suitable guardian, a good dad.

We've had this conversation once already—briefly. The boys were indifferent about the engagement, and they hadn't fully warmed up to him by the time Francisca died, which only makes this more complicated. They must feel like they're being cared for by two complete strangers, despite them having known us for most of their lives. But that was all in their periphery. We were never regulars in their lives until Ramiro started dating Francisca.

When we took them to Ramiro's home instead of Pancha's that first night, they were devastated, especially René, but in the end, they understood.

The hearing for final guardianship is in a few weeks, and Ramiro's hat is the only one thrown into that particular ring. Then there was the promise he made Oscar at the burial, and we all know he is the only one who can have custody.

I pop some popcorn, and Ramiro and I go sit on the couch with Oscar.

"Want some popcorn, buddy?" I ask. He shakes his head.

"Not even with this?" I lift a bottle of Valentina hot sauce I was hiding, and his head turns to look at what I'm holding.

His eyes immediately brighten, then he nods. "Mom used to put hot sauce on our popcorn," he says.

I smile at him. "I know. She's the one who taught me this." Before we can go deeper into a conversation about his mom, I shift his attention. "So, what are you watching?"

"*Thor: Ragnarök.*"

I sigh. I hope this isn't the one where Thor watches his mom die. Just what we need around here. More dead moms.

Both Ramiro and I take turns grabbing handfuls of popcorn

from the bowl in Oscar's lap, stopping to lick off sauce from our fingers now and then.

I think about heading to René's room to talk to him, but he's made it more than clear that he needs his space. Barely any time passes before he joins us in the living room, wedging himself between Oscar and me so he can bum some popcorn.

Luckily, *Ragnarök* is actually quite funny, and we all find ourselves laughing at the Hulk's antics. Except for René. He still won't laugh. But I would have bet money, during the scene when the Hulk makes fun of Thor, that the corner of his mouth quirked up just the tiniest bit.

That night, when I put them to bed, Oscar insists on me reading him a bedtime story. When I finish, he's still wide awake, thoughtful.

I brush his black waves away from his forehead. He'll need a haircut soon, I think to myself. So many things moms do I never even thought about before. At least, things good moms should do.

"What are you thinking about?" I ask him.

He shrugs, and with a small voice, says, "Thor."

"What about him?"

"In *End Game*, The Avengers use the Infinity Stones and go back in time. Iron man sees his dad, who died, and Thor sees his dead mom. I was just thinking, how cool it would be to have Infinity Stones—"

"Infinity Stones aren't real, dummy," René interrupts from the other side of the room.

"René!" I snap. "That wasn't very nice. Apologize now."

René downcasts his eyes. "I'm sorry, Oscar."

"I know they aren't real," Oscar says, looking more than a little embarrassed, pink creeping up to his ears.

"Wanna know what I think?" I ask.

Oscar nods the tiniest nod I've ever seen.

"I think we all have Infinity Stones." I pause to smile. Then I poke his chest gently with my index finger. "Right here. I have a fan theory. I think Thor saw his mom in his heart, how he remembered her, didn't actually travel back in time in the real world, but traveled back in time in his heart and mind. She will always be with you, so long as you carry her here."

Oscar sighs. "Maybe," he says and turns on his side away from me, not convinced. I hold him until he falls asleep, then tuck him in. I go over to René's bed, and I kiss his forehead after tucking him in, too. He stiffens at the kiss like he has done every night since I started tucking them in. I thought it made him uncomfortable and asked him if he would like me to stop after that first night. René only averted his eyes and shook his head, so now this awkward tucking-in ritual happens every night.

I smile down at him. "I hope you know you have an Infinity Stone, too."

When I step into the hallway to close their door, I hear Ramiro's door clicking closed gently.

Was he listening to us?

CHAPTER 4

I smell bacon.

I hear a noise downstairs.

My eyes fly open, and I hurry to put on my slippers. I'm ecstatic, thinking Don Gustavo snuck in to cook us breakfast. He has a spare key in case Ramiro ever locks himself out. His parents gave it to Don Gustavo before they moved.

I smile. Don Gustavo's breakfasts are the absolute best.

When I get to the kitchen, it's Ramiro I find wielding a spatula, not Don Gustavo. He's wearing checkered pajama bottoms, his signature ribbed tank, and has a tea towel over his shoulder while he works. He's facing away from me, and it's so early in the morning, I'm not thinking properly, so I check him out.

Blatantly check him out.

Those broad shoulders that I've dreamed about so often. His deep cinnamon skin, taut over bulging biceps and triceps. It's no secret Ramiro likes to work out. The most tantalizing part of all, though? His ass.

His perfectly sculpted ass and those pajama bottoms draping off his rear at precisely the right spot.

And the man is cooking.

Cooking.

Apart from Don Gustavo, I've never seen a man cook before. My father sure as hell never did. Neither did any of my exes.

Yet here he is. The hottest man I've ever met in person, cooking breakfast for his family. It's a sight, let me tell you.

The coffee is brewing. I see bacon nowhere, so it must be in the oven, and Ramiro is rolling perfect omelets on a griddle. A second griddle warms up corn tortillas.

"That smells amazing," I say.

Ramiro spins on his heel and beams at me. Actually beams. A smile I haven't seen in weeks.

He looks rested. Finally. The dark circles under his eyes are nearly gone now, and he has shaved. He's also buzzed his hair, restoring his former tidy buzz cut.

"Good morning," he says with a smile.

"Got one of those for me?" I ask, eyeing the omelets.

"Got two of them for you," he says, handing me a plate. "Two minutes on the bacon if you want to wait."

"I only need one," I say.

He passes me a funny look. "I know how you eat, Sara. You don't have to be shy here. I want you to feel at home."

I laugh. "I'm not being shy or trying to help you save on the extra eggs."

"Then what's with the appetite change?"

"Apart from the fact that everyone's appetite has been meager for a while in this house, I haven't been running. When I don't go on my runs, I'm not as hungry during the day."

Ramiro's perfectly full lips purse together. "I'm sorry I haven't been much help. That's going to change. I promise. You shouldn't have to miss out on your runs."

"I know, Ramiro. I'm not guilt-tripping you. Everyone has had to adjust."

Sliding one of my omelets onto his own plate, he then reaches for the cookie sheet in the oven and places two strips of bacon onto each of our plates. "I actually wanted to talk to you about that," he says.

We have a couple of hours until the boys wake up, so this is a perfect time for a conversation. "About what?"

"How much you've been helping."

I frown. Am I overstepping? I wonder.

"Do you like it here? I mean, normally, not lately with how things have been?"

"Yeah. I do. And I really like René and Oscar too. We were sorta buddies before you even started dating Francisca, so it's not like we're uncomfortable around each other or anything."

"Good." He takes a bite of his omelet and chews slowly, like he's thinking. I try not to focus on his thick neck contracting when he swallows and that smooth skin just below his jaw I've fantasized about licking on so many occasions. "I kinda had a crazy idea," he says.

"Oh?"

"You got into a ton of debt to get your nursing degree, didn't you?"

I wince. I knew someone would ask sooner or later.

After the demise of the worst relationship of my adult life, I threw myself into work and school. I went back to get my master's degree in nursing, and I only graduated this past winter. And yes, I took out so many loans for that master's program, but my nursing job pays well. Not to mention, if I get the promotion to nurse manager I'm hoping comes my way with my new credentials, the plan is to pay it all off rather quickly.

"I'm not judging," Ramiro adds when I stay quiet too long. "Carolina only mentioned it in passing. It's not a big deal. I never told you, but I'm so proud you got your master's degree."

I will live off of that compliment for a month—at least. I never imagined he cared at all about me or my life. But he's been paying attention. Somehow. Through Carolina, probably.

"Thank you," I say and blow out a breath. "And yeah, I have loans, but I'm sure I'll be able to pay them off."

"Well, I'd like to propose a way for you to pay them off faster."

I take a bite of my omelet and a piece of bacon and listen as he continues.

"Move in with us—"

I snort, and the bacon goes down the wrong pipe, making me cough. Ramiro hurries to fill a glass with water and hands it to me. I chug it down desperately. My eyes widen, and when I stop coughing, I say, "What?"

"I can't do this alone. At least not at first. I have no idea what I'm doing. I need help, Sara. Just a year. It's all I ask."

"A year? I'm not sure I'm the best person to—"

"You are," he says. "They boys like you. Stability would be good for them. And I need you. I need you so much, Sara. Please."

He needs me.

"Ramiro, I—" I try to find the words and tell him why I think it's a terrible idea, but he keeps on talking.

"Just hear me out. All I ask is that you tag team with me for school drop-offs—and when René gets back on the soccer team, he'll need someone to drive him. I'll try to do most of it, but I know I can't do it alone. In exchange for your room and board, I just ask you to help me figure out our routine. The house is mostly paid for."

That I knew from Carolina. When Ramiro's parents moved to Florida for their retirement, they left Ramiro the home he grew up in. He's an only child, so they directed all their support to him. Ramiro tried to get a loan to pay them for the house, but they wouldn't hear of it. Both his parents were lawyers, and they didn't need the money from the house for their retirement. Instead, they wanted to give their son a leg up in the world.

Ramiro continues. "I'll take care of all the bills and groceries, and you and I just share the chores and work together to figure out the parenting thing."

Half my omelet is uneaten when I push my plate away, and that's not something that happens often. "Ramiro, I don't know."

"Would you please just think about it?"

I nod and watch him eat the rest of his breakfast.

Ramiro needs help. I know that. But even if he was in love with someone else not too long ago, I'm still in love with him.

Living with someone I love and can't have will undoubtedly be harmful to my heart.

Then there's René and Oscar to think about. They've never had anyone but women raising them their entire lives.

I decide it's the boys I need to make this decision for, not for Ramiro and not for myself. I must make it for Francisca and her sons.

CHAPTER 5

"**M**ake it a double," I tell Sofia after slamming down my first tequila shot and asking for a second.

From behind the bar, Sofia raises an eyebrow at me, her incredibly full lips pursing together. Then her eyes dart to where Carolina sits with her assistant Mandy, next to me at the bar, while she decides if she'll pour me a second.

"Okay," Carolina says, looking at me, "what's going on? You hate tequila."

"I need the shot to tell you," I say, not meeting any of their eyes.

I avoided telling Carolina all day at work today, and after a long shift, both of us still in scrubs, I begged her to come to Sofia's bar, La Oficina, to give me a little courage, but also to tell Sofia and Mandy at the same time so that I don't have to go through with this at three different times only to hear three different versions of the same objections.

My three closest friends couldn't be more different. While Carolina looks at me warmly with her amber eyes, Sofia's black gaze is inquisitive as she studies me. And Mandy—Mandy pops the bubble she just blew with her gum and spits it into a napkin before taking her own shot.

Mandy and I've become closer since Carolina started drowning in her work, and it often leaves me talking to Mandy instead of her boss. The short package she comes in is deceiving. Mandy makes up for her short stature with a loud, bubbly personality that says her presence won't be ignored even when she's standing next to statuesque Carolina. Mandy is also incredibly intuitive and quickly picked up on my feelings for Ramiro. Whenever Carolina mentioned him, Mandy swears she saw a reaction on my face.

Ultimately, Sofia sets the double shot in front of me, and I slam it, then chase it with a lime. I really do hate tequila. It goes down my throat like glass on fire. I've never understood how Carolina and Sofia love this stuff. Even Mandy handles it well, even though it's not her usual drink of choice.

I cough, and with my eyes glued to my empty shot glass, I decide to just blurt it out. Rip off the Band-Aid, so to speak. "I'm moving in with Ramiro and the boys." There. That wasn't so hard. What's the worst that my friends can say? That it's a terrible idea? Like I don't already know that.

After three seconds of shocked silence, all three of their responses fly my way at the same time.

Carolina screams, "What?"

Sofia lets out a loud bark of laughter.

And Mandy yells, "Get it, girl! Sad sex can be awesome."

I stare blankly at them, trying to decide whose comment I should address first.

Carolina repeats her question. "You're what?"

"I'm moving in with Ramiro."

Carolina closes her shocked mouth for a moment, then speaks. "Sara, I don't think that's such a great idea."

"Why not?"

"Your crush, for one," Carolina says.

"Oh my god, I don't have a crush on him,"

"Sure, and pigs fly," Mandy says, following a snort.

"And Addy lets me have a good night's sleep," Sofia jokes about her daughter.

Geesh. Who needs enemies with friends like these?

Guilt slithers through my mind. I didn't take a moment to ask Sofia how she's doing before I rushed my drink order. The black, asymmetrical bob without a hair out of place—Sofia's signature style for years—has long given way to light brown, messy waves, and the dark circles under her eyes are concerning. I can't imagine what she must be going through with a new baby, running a business, all while being a single mom. "How are you?" I ask Sofia. "Really. Do you need any help?"

"Oh, no, you don't," Sofia says. "I have plenty of help between Ileana and Lola," she says, referring to her bar staff who are her close friends. "And we're not making this about me. You're really moving in with Ramiro?" she asks, bending over the bar and resting her elbows on the counter.

"Yes. Just for a year. Help him find his bearings with the boys, let him take a moment to grieve a little."

"We can help him," Carolina says. "We can take turns. Dad will help too—"

"You know that's not enough. Your schedule is more hectic than mine. Doña Pancha has to go to a nursing home, and Ramiro's parents are in Florida. He needs help."

"Sara—" Carolina argues.

"He's drowning, Carolina. It's not like Sofia—"

"Hey, don't drag me into this," Sofia defends herself.

"I mean, he wasn't expecting to be a single dad. He didn't have a nine-month pregnancy to prepare him for these life changes. He'd planned to share the load with a partner, and I'm afraid he's not taking a moment to grieve. The boys need a functional adult taking care of their basic needs."

"I wasn't expecting to be a single mom, you know," Sofia

says, a bit annoyed.

I look at her with a gentle smile. "You know that's not how I meant it. You have a village helping you. Ramiro needs a village. I can be that for him." I don't tell them about my conversation with Ramiro's mom, Rocio. For some reason, the way she handled it, dragging me to a room to have privacy while we talked, told me Rocio didn't want anyone knowing the request she'd made of me at Francisca's velorio.

"I'm worried you'll fall more in love with him—" Carolina argues.

"I'm not in love—" I start to lie.

"Why does everything have to be about love?" Mandy jumps in. "Why can't crushes and sex just be about sex? Not everything has to have meaning."

I've always admired Mandy's sex-positive nature, how unapologetically she is herself and requires no permission from society to follow her heart at her own pace, and only when she says. She is the only driver of her own destiny. She'd never in a million years make the idiotic mistakes with men I've made. In short, I want to be Mandy Gomez when I grow up—or my own version of that.

Carolina rolls her eyes. "Fine. I'm worried your heart will get broken."

Carolina, it seems, is projecting from her own broken heart she is currently nursing from her almost-lover. I won't make her mistakes, though, even if she can't see it now.

Mandy rolls her eyes. Now that she's off-the-clock and in friend-mode, she seems to feel free to speak her mind. "That's what I'm saying. Separate the feelings from the physical." She pauses to demonstrate with the two shot glasses she pulls farther apart on the bar top. "Sex," she taps one shot glass, "feelings," she taps the other. "No need for your heart to get broken. Enjoy that hunk and let him plow you like a field of barley."

We all burst out laughing at the simile Mandy uses. Where

does she get this stuff?

"We can't all compartmentalize as well as you, Mandy," Sofia argues when our laughter dies down.

"I'll still help, you know," Carolina says. "I'm his village too."

"I know," I say.

"I'd help too, but I'm kind of …" Sofia starts.

I reach across the bar to squeeze Sofia's hand. "We know, hon. You're already stretched super thin. You keep taking care of my beautiful niece."

"Don't look at me," Mandy says. "I love you to death, but I have two full-time jobs. It wouldn't be genuine for me to offer to help when I don't have the bandwidth. What I can do, however, is steal my mom's albondigas tomorrow and bring you lunch."

I beam at Mandy, who understands food is my preferred love language. And I'd never dream of interrupting her passion for her second career as an artist, to which she's dedicated sweat, blood, and tears. "You're the best," I tell her. "That's all I need."

"Don't I know it," Mandy says with a wide, toothy grin. "I am the best. And that's my cue. I have to get up early tomorrow." Mandy kisses my cheek, then Carolina's, then does her best to hop on the bar—which is hard given how short she is—and barely manages a kiss on Sofia's cheek before she falls back on her feet from the jump, landing expertly on her skyscraper-high heels.

Sofia smiles at me and fills my glass for a third—and final —shot.

I slam the last tequila shot before we say our goodbyes and Carolina drives me home. My older sister is pensive and quiet most of the way there.

We're almost at my apartment when Carolina says, "You know, if you and Ramiro got together, I'd be okay with that."

I turn to blink at her. "What?"

"I don't know if you knew that, with our history, but it would actually make me happy if you ended up together. I always thought you'd be perfect for one another. I guess what I'm saying is, if you want to make a go of it when he's ready, you have my blessing."

"Trust me," I tell her, "The last thing on Ramiro's mind right now is dating."

THE LAST WEEK OF MY VACATION TIME IS THE MOST EXHAUSTING.

We settle Pancha into her new home, and so far, she doesn't seem to hate it. At least she doesn't complain. Ramiro and I make a plan to take the boys to visit her at least once a week.

Ramiro, Don Gustavo, and the boys all help me pack up my apartment in record time.

In all honesty, I'm not sad to leave it. This apartment has a lot of terrible memories for me. If I hadn't been working at Heartland Metro Hospital and taking night classes these past two years, mainly staying out of the apartment, I probably would have moved a lot sooner.

As they carry the last boxes to the moving truck, I take one last glance at the empty space. I focus on the counter where my arm was broken once, and my eyes brim with tears that I quickly sniff back before anyone sees them.

I run my finger across the length of the scar along my forearm.

That's another reason I loathe the spring. Storms make the healed bone ache, bringing back all the reminders of just how stupid I was.

I take a deep breath and reel in the tears before they spill.

"Never again," I whisper into the empty space before closing the door to that chapter of my life and stepping into a new one.

A better chapter, opening up in the lovely summer.

CHAPTER 6

SUMMER

The last few months of the school year for the boys are hellish. René keeps coming home with detention slip after detention slip—mostly for picking fights with other students. At his last parent-teacher conference, Ramiro was told they were making allowances for him because of his grief but that they won't extend to next year. If things don't change, he's likely to get expelled.

The school also suggested therapy.

Ramiro doesn't believe in therapy.

We almost fought over me trying to convince him to take them to counseling, but at the end of the day, he's their guardian. Not me. I'm just the sometimes nanny, sometimes housekeeper. I'll give them all time and try to broach the subject again because I agree with René's teacher. In fact, I think all three of them could benefit from a bit of grief counseling.

Though here I am, the hypocrite who never went to therapy even when I really should have. Carolina begged me at one point after my last relationship imploded in the most spectacular way, but I was too proud to admit I needed help. Maybe, if

I'm going to bat for therapy in the future, I should start by setting the example.

These are the things I think about when I'm running. I add scheduling an initial counseling session to my never-ending mental to-do list.

In happier news, our routine is running more smoothly. I even saw René crack a full smile when Doña Pancha said a particularly funny idiom in Spanish the other day. They tried explaining it for me, but it didn't translate well. I can't wait to be fluent in Spanish. I'd say I'm about sixty percent there, though my lessons with Don Gustavo have stopped since I moved in with the boys.

I add resuming Spanish lessons to the to-do list.

After a short three-mile run, I'm back at the house. It's Saturday morning and only eight, so I'm surprised everyone is awake already.

The first thing to hit me is the aroma of breakfast. I glance at the table, smiling at the two omelets with tortillas, avocado, and hot sauce Ramiro has started greeting me with on my run days. Then I look at the other uneaten dishes at the table, and my eyes drop to Oscar sitting on the couch. He's in his green Hulk pajamas that make his little red nose stand out even more. His eyes are puffy, and I know he's been crying. He says something as he runs up to me, and I take my headphones out to ask him to repeat himself.

"Hey, buddy," I say as he wraps his little arms around my waist. "What's this?"

He sobs into my stomach. "Sara! You can't run."

What? I'm so confused. "Why not?"

"You can't die!"

"What?" I unclasp his arms from me so I can look at him. Then I look up at Ramiro. He's in pajamas, too, his arms crossed over his chest, jaw tight. "What happened?"

Oscar is still crying, so he can't answer. Ramiro is about to speak when René answers.

"The twerp thinks you're going to die like Mom. She went on a walk that night because she said she needed to exercise to fit into her wedding dress. When he woke up early, and Ramiro told him where you were, he just ... freaked out."

"Oh, sweetie." I wrap my arms around his head and hold him for a while before leading him to the couch and sitting next to him. I hold his hands in mine. "I'm not going to die because I go running."

"Mom did. And she was just walking." He sniffles.

"That was a really, really, terrible but rare accident."

His eyes well again, and he begs. "Please, Sara. No more running. Or I can come with you," he adds, thoughtfully. "I can take care of you."

René yawns. "I'm going back to bed."

I look up at Ramiro to ask for help, but his eyes are a bit glassy, and I know I have to take care of this one myself.

"Listen to me, buddy," I say. "I'm a really, really good runner. I can't promise you I'll never die because we're all going to die some-day. It's part of life." I figure honesty is the best way to go about this, even if I'm sure this is the last thing Oscar wants to hear. "But I'm very safe when I run. I've been running almost every day before I go to work, only you didn't realize because you were still sleeping."

His eyes widen with panic. "Every day?" he breathes out, appalled at how reckless he thinks I've been.

I nod. "Yes. And I've been fine all this time, haven't I? I always come home."

He considers that for a moment. Then he wipes his eyes with his pajama sleeve. "Yeah," he says.

"See? I'll be just fine. I can even promise you I'll be extra careful. How does that sound?"

"Okay," he says weakly, looking down at his fidgeting hands.

"Do you feel better?" I ask.

He shakes his head.

"Would pancakes help?"

His little face snaps up to me, and he nods. "Maybe. If they have chocolate chips?"

I laugh, and Ramiro and I head to the kitchen to make the pancakes together.

"I'm sorry," he whispers. "I didn't know how to handle that."

"This is hard, Ramiro." He hands me the milk and eggs, and I whisk the flour. Just when we think we have a moment of normalcy, that maybe our routine is finally down, something will trigger René or Oscar, and it feels like we have to start all over again.

"Have I thanked you for being here with us?" he asks.

"You don't have to. I know you're thankful."

"I don't know what we'd do without you."

I laugh. "You'd have pancakes without chocolate chips, the way you grocery shop. Lucky for you, I bought some. They're in the pantry. Grab 'em?"

AFTER BREAKFAST AND A LONG SHOWER, THE HOUSE FEELS HOT. Too hot. I check the thermostat and try to adjust the temperature down. Nothing.

Great. The AC is broken, today of all days. This day has been too long already, and it's still early morning.

After checking my phone and confirming my worst suspicions, it's going to be in the upper nineties today, I grab my pair of short denim shorts and my bikini.

I hurry to do some picking up since I know I won't have the energy later when it really heats up. I'm in the living room dusting when Ramiro comes back from checking the mail.

"Whoa, whoa, whoa! What are you wearing?" He covers his

eyes with a stack of envelopes like he's seeing me naked.

I laugh. "It's just my swimsuit."

"Why are you wearing a swimsuit?" he asks, looking up at me again, lowering the envelopes from his face.

It's tough hiding my shit-eating grin when I realize he's struggling to keep his eyes on my face.

I don't have the biggest boobs. I like them well enough, and this bikini really does a spectacular job with them. So, I can't be too mad at him for acting weird.

Ramiro swallows as he awaits my answer.

"The AC broke," I say.

"Oh. Uh—I'll call to make an appointment for repairs."

"Thanks. In the meantime, should we maybe take the guys to the pool?"

I'd thought about taking everyone next door to Don Gustavo's, but I figure the pool will be a nice pick-me-up for Oscar after the morning he's had.

"That's a great idea," Ramiro says.

"Why don't you go figure out if they have swim trunks and gather our towels? I'll make some sandwiches and pack a cooler for lunch."

Ramiro is way too fast getting away from me, attacking his tasks with gusto.

Well, I'll be damned. I'd felt guilty when I bought this designer bikini last summer since it was way above my budget, but making Ramiro a little nervous just now was worth every last hard-earned penny.

When they all clamor down the stairs thirty minutes later, ready for the pool, I have our sandwiches ready. I lift the cooler and hand it to Ramiro, and that's when Oscar gasps.

"Sara!" He yells. "What happened to your legs?"

I look down, remembering the twin scars on the front of both my thighs. I don't wear shorts often, even in summer. It's usually capri pants, but that's hard to do on a pool day.

I was so little when I got those scars that they don't look nearly as bad anymore, but the slight discoloration and the twisting scar tissue from the skin grafts are still visible.

Great. I didn't even think about them. Just what Oscar needs, another reason to worry about me today.

"Oh, buddy, this happened many years ago when I was just a little girl. It's nothing for you to worry about."

"But what happened?" he insists, his curious mind wanting to know more. He gets closer to me to get a better look.

I sigh. I promised myself when I moved in, I'd always be honest with them. "It was a kitchen accident. Boiling water fell on my lap, and I had to have skin grafts—that's when a doctor fixes skin after a burn. That's why I have those scars."

Oscar moves close to me to study my legs. "Do they hurt?"

I shake my head. "No, buddy. They only hurt when I first got them. When I was little."

"Can I go to the deep end with Trevor?" René asks from inside the pool. After an hour of exhausting swimming and playing Marco Polo with Oscar, Ramiro and I are on lounge chairs next to the pool.

"Who's Trevor?" I ask.

René points to a boy now by his side. "My new friend. Trevor."

Ramiro and I have already verified that both René and Oscar can swim. Oscar isn't quite as strong a swimmer, but he's working on it.

"If Trevor's parents are okay with it, sure."

"That's your mom?" Trevor asks, trying to whisper, but it's a stage whisper. "She's so hot."

René rolls his eyes. And for some reason, he doesn't correct Trevor. He lets him assume, and then he defends my honor and dunks Trevor's head, his black curls vanishing underwater. "Stop looking at her," he says, but he's laughing when Trevor comes back up and splashes water at René's face.

"Can I go too?" Oscar asks.

"No, buddy. You need to stay close where we can see you," Ramiro says. We've agreed we'd take turns with our yes's and no's with them so that neither one of us is the jerk they hate or the favorite one. It's worked out well so far. Balance is key.

At least Oscar isn't too upset that Ramiro said no and goes back to play with a group of kids in the shallow end.

When the kids are out of earshot, Ramiro asks, "How come I'd never seen those scars before?"

I shrug. "I'm a little self-conscious about them, I guess. So, I do a good job hiding them for the most part. It's harder to do in the summer." I smile. He didn't even notice them when he first saw me in shorts this morning. He was too occupied trying to keep his eyes on my face.

"Can I ask what happened?" He's wearing sunglasses, so I can't see his eyes, but I know his gaze is glued to my thighs.

My smile fades. I take a deep breath and share the worst of my past. "I was six. My parents were gone. They left me alone quite a bit back then. I got hungry and decided to make some instant noodles. Six-year-old hands are still a little clumsy, though, and I spilled the bowl on my lap when I was setting it on the table."

Ramiro is so quiet; I turn to look at him.

His jaw is so tense, his cheek muscle visibly ticks. "You never talk about your parents," he says.

The truth is, though I've considered Ramiro a good friend these past eight years, we've never gone too deep. He always kept me at arm's length in his pursuit of Carolina. He was blind to any woman who wasn't her until Francisca caught his attention. I'm not surprised he doesn't know so much about me, even things that Carolina and Don Gustavo already know.

"I don't enjoy thinking about my childhood. They weren't good parents. There were a few child protective services close calls, but my mom was so beautiful and charismatic that she always convinced them the complaints were misunderstandings. She had that girl-next-door kind of look, you know? Blonde, blue-eyed, cardigan-wearing."

"But they weren't misunderstandings?"

I shake my head. "No. Both my parents have battled addictions most of my life. Everything under the sun. Alcohol, drugs, you name it. The accident happened when they'd been gone for nearly two days. Looking back, I realize they were probably trying to score, or on a bender."

"Two days?" Ramiro asks, appalled.

"They'd be gone much more than that over time. Anyway, I look a lot like my mom. All she'd have to do is clean up the house a little and pull her hair into a respectable low bun, and she looked like the perfect suburban wife, so she always got away with her neglect of me."

"I'm so sorry, Sara," Ramiro says. His jaw bulges, skin so tight I'm afraid for his teeth. The grip on the car magazine he's holding tightens, and part of a page rips under his thumb before he realizes he's clenching his hands and eases his grip.

I know that this seems unfathomable to him, who grew up in a loving household. But it was just my life. My normal.

"I'm glad they're not in your life anymore," he says.

Only for one moment do I allow myself to wonder if he said that because he's glad not to expose Oscar and René to people like that, but I know that's not Ramiro. He genuinely cares about me. I know that at the cellular level.

"I tried, when I was old enough to understand, to have a better relationship with them. I made excuses for them. They loved me in their own way. I know I had it a lot better than so many kids in similar situations. They never beat me or harassed me. The worst of it was watching them fight and scream, but they always left me out of it. It took me a long time to understand that neglect is also abuse."

"You haven't seen them since when?"

"College. When I met Carolina. I was still trying to get them both, especially Mom, into an addiction program, but she refused. Then I'd see how Don Gustavo called Carolina every other night before bed to see how she was doing. She received a care package in the mail once a month, with rolls of quarters for laundry, Mexican candy, that kinda stuff." I smile at the memory. I used to steal Carolina's candy when she was away at class. She told her dad about it, and he started sending extra for 'la güerita,' as he started calling me. "He'd show up randomly when he could to take her out to lunch. By our junior year, he'd take us both out to lunch when he stopped by campus. The comparison between my parents and Carolina's was unfair but striking all the same."

Ramiro smiles approvingly. "So, Don Gustavo gave you the courage to break away from your toxic family?"

I smile. "Yeah. And I hadn't even met him yet our freshman year. Here was this single parent, so involved in his grown daughter's life, he checked in on her often. Communication with my parents at that point was entirely one way. If I didn't call them or go to see them, there were crickets. Not until I saw what it was supposed to be like, did I realize I shouldn't invest time and love into people who don't invest back. So, I just stopped calling them. That was eight years ago. It hurt those first few years that they didn't think to check in on me—not once, Ramiro. Anyway, now I have this great new family who does. That helps."

"People like Don Gustavo?"

I nod.

"He's a great boss," Ramiro adds.

"This story has a happy ending, though," I say. He just looks at me, so I keep talking. "That's why I decided to become a nurse. When I burned my legs, I managed to call 911. When I got to the hospital, this pretty nurse, I thought, looked like an angel. She stayed with me the entire time until they located my parents. They were in another state. She treated me better than anyone had treated me my entire life. Her name was Becca. I remember thinking I wish she'd be my mom. Then, all the other nurses I met were so nice to me. That hospital room was the happiest I'd been in a long time, and I was in excruciating pain. The nurses played games with me and brought me cherry gelatin cups. And they all had these fun scrubs with cartoon characters on them. They worked so hard to distract me. That's all my memories are. I hardly remember the pain from the burn treatments. I decided right then and there, I wanted to be a nurse like them when I grew up. They were my heroes, you know?"

"I can't believe CPS didn't take you after that."

"Nurse Becca called them, but my mom got out of it, like she always did." I pause and take a deep breath. "I really don't like thinking about that time in my life. Mind if we change the subject?"

Ramiro nods. His face is a little twisted, his brows pinched together, but he says, "I'm sorry I brought it up."

AFTER A LONG, QUIET WHILE, I REALIZE I NEED ANOTHER COAT OF sunscreen if I'm going to keep sunbathing, and I work the lotion on my body. I sit up when I'm done, trying to reach as much of my back as possible.

I'm doing some serious contortionist act to achieve this when I feel a tap on my shoulder. I look up, and Ramiro is standing, hovering above me. The sun behind him leaves me with only a view of his silhouette. "What?" I ask.

"Hand me the sunscreen. I'll get your back for you."

Don't make this weird, Sara. "Uh, thanks." I hand him the bottle.

He crouches behind me and starts working the lotion onto my back. His hands stroke slowly, lathering me up. I'm one hundred percent sure he's already done when he passes every inch of my skin a second time.

My breath hitches in the back of my throat when I feel him tug under the strings holding my bikini top in place so he can get some lotion under there. It doesn't escape me that if he tugs the strings just a little more, he'll be undressing me. It's odd having him touch me like this after such a vulnerable moment with so many truths revealed. Then, there's the fact that his touch feels … like I'm safe.

"Done," he says from behind me after much too long and reaches over to hand me the bottle again.

"Thanks," I say, only a little breathless.

I don't know what that moment was, but for the rest of our time at the pool, Ramiro and I can hardly look at each other.

THE AC REPAIR SERVICE COMES TOMORROW. LUCKILY, ALL OUR rooms have ceiling fans, and we'll survive the night if we keep the windows open to let the air circulate.

It's still a bit too hot in the house, so I sit on the porch enjoying the starry night while Ramiro puts the boys to bed. We take turns doing that now, too.

The screen door creaks as he comes outside, his heavy steps making the floorboards creak a little too. "Can I join you?" he asks.

"Yeah," I say.

He sits next to me on the stoop and hands me an opened beer. The bottle sweats, and my mouth waters in anticipation. "My hero," I say, taking the bottle. "It's a beautiful night, isn't it?"

"Yeah," he says, taking a pull from his beer.

"Wanna know something?" I ask.

"Of course. I want to know everything."

I turn to look at him for a second, wondering what he means, then shake the question away from my mind and look back out in front of us. "It doesn't matter how old I get. I'll always love fireflies. Ever since I was a little girl, I've loved them, and I never quite outgrew it." There's a sea of them around the house tonight, and I stare dreamily at them. "I used to catch them and put them in jars. Though looking back on it now, that seems kinda cruel."

"They are pretty," he says. "And you didn't know better then."

We sit in silence, drinking our beers and listening to the crickets and cicadas. A soft breeze finally picks up, rustling the leaves, and I moan in appreciation at the coolness I haven't felt all day.

When Ramiro finishes his beer, he sets it down next to him. "Sara, I want to apologize to you."

"For what?" I fold my elbows over my knees so I can rest my head on my arms and look at him.

"You know for what."

"No ..."

He lets out a long breath. "For ... looking."

"I didn't mind," I say, knowing exactly what he's talking about.

"I minded."

I'm not sure if that should offend me or not. "Okay ..." I say, unsure of how I should respond.

"I don't want to make you uncomfortable or make you feel like you don't want to be here anymore, but I want to be honest with you."

"I want us to be honest too," I agree, encouraging him.

"Before Francisca, I was very ... active, if you know what I mean." He stops to scratch the back of his head, his eyes glued to his beer. "And then with her, too. This is the longest I've gone without—without … errr … you know what I mean."

I want to laugh, but I don't because I don't want to make him even more uncomfortable, but I won't lie, this is adorable coming from a man I've known to be confident the entire time we've been friends. "It's the longest you've gone without sex?" I ask.

He nods. "Yeah. Since she died, I honestly hadn't even thought much about it, and then today … well, today I saw you in that tiny red bikini. And then you were in the pool, wet, and those beautiful blue eyes, and your blonde hair wet, well … I'm just sorry if I made you uncomfortable by, uh …"

"Looking?" I finish for him.

"Yeah. I couldn't help it. And I'm sorry."

"You don't have to be sorry, Ramiro."

He shakes his head. "I do. Because, damn it, I feel so goddamn guilty for looking at another woman like that."

I sit up. "Oh," I say, realization hitting me head-on.

"I feel like I'm cheating on her."

"You still love her," I say, not asking. It's a statement.

"It's so weird loving someone who's not here anymore. But yeah, looking at you today felt like cheating. Like I'm betraying her memory."

"Ramiro, it's normal. It's only been a few months and you're a young guy, at the prime of your sexual life. You shouldn't feel guilty. I don't think she'd want that. As for me, you didn't make me uncomfortable. It's … flattering," I say, deciding to go for honesty with him, too.

He laughs, but it sounds watery. It's too dark now to tell if he's crying or trying not to. "Anyway," he says, grabbing his beer bottle and standing up. "Can I ask you a huge favor?"

"Anything," I say.

"Cover up a little more around here?"

I laugh. "It's summer," I say. "But I'll see what I can do."

CHAPTER 7

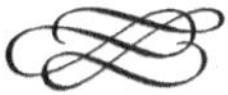

I can't cover up.

The next day, I wake up with my skin on fire. Primarily my shoulders, upper back, and upper chest. Apparently, two re-applications of sunscreen weren't enough. I tried putting on a shirt today, I really did, but the fabric against my skin was excruciatingly painful. Somewhere, in the back of my closet, I know I have a tube top from my college days. Hopefully, it still fits. Finally, I find it. The small strip of fabric will have to do, and Ramiro will just have to deal with it. I do attempt to put on a strapless bra but stretching my arms to clasp it sends searing pain through my shoulders, so I abandon the idea.

The ta-tas go free today.

Since it took me forever to get ready for my day, I find René and Oscar already at the kitchen counter eating cereal by the time I head downstairs. Thank goodness they're somewhat self-sufficient.

"Whoa," René says when he sees me. "You got roasted. Like … literally."

"Thanks, buddy," I say to him and head to the fridge for the water pitcher to pour myself a cooling glass.

I gulp it down and stare at the two brothers. Their deep brown skin is a shade darker today, but they don't look sunburned at all, and I'm glad for it because today would be disastrous if it confined all of us in our mobility.

"Where's Ramiro?" I ask.

"In the garage," Oscar says.

I grab a muffin from the counter and walk to the garage. I take a bite as I open the door and then freeze.

Ramiro has a giant headset on and doesn't hear me opening the door. I knew we couldn't park here because he uses this space as his gym, but I didn't realize the extent of his professional-quality setup.

He's holding a barbell with an impressive amount of weight behind his head, over his shoulders. Then he squats. Low and slow. As I stare at his perfect ass, I take another giant bite of my muffin, forgetting to chew and letting it rest in my cheeks. Another squat, this time he grunts, and my god, it's the sexiest sound I've heard.

I need to stop ogling him like this. It feels like I could get pregnant just from watching him. Sweet baby Jesus.

I finally swallow the dry muffin and wait for him to set the barbell on the rack before I tap his shoulder to get his attention.

He turns around, and I immediately take a step back. He's breathing hard, and his sweat lingers on my fingers from tapping his shoulder.

He's a shade darker today too, and I'd say could easily pass for the boys' biological father.

After pulling off his headset, he grabs a towel from the bench to wipe his face. Then he focuses on me. On my naked shoulders, to be more specific.

"Sara!" he says. "Oh god, you got sunburnt."

"Yeah, I just came to tell you I'm heading out for a bit—going to the pharmacy. Wanna get some ointment or something for the burns—"

"No, wait. Hold on. Head back inside. I'll be right back."

I don't get to ask him why before he's at a jog toward the driveway. A man has never run so sexy.

I really need to start dating. It's been long enough since … I stop myself before I dare think of his name.

Being around Ramiro is dangerous. Especially now that I know he finds me physically attractive, or at the very least, is horny enough to actually consider me, of all people.

I know if we hook up now, it will only be because he's sexually deprived, not because he's ever had any sort of romantic feelings for me, and the result, well, the result would be my heartbreak because I'm still in love with him, aren't I?

Don Gustavo taught me one of my favorite Spanish phrases: un clavo saca otro clavo. One nail takes out another nail. Meaning you can forget about heartbreak by finding new love. It's time to find a new nail to help me forget about Ramiro. I need to get over him one way or the other. And where does one go to find nails? The hardware store.

Speaking of Don Gustavo, I'm sitting on the couch when the front door opens, and in comes Don Gustavo, Ramiro trailing behind him.

"Hola, güerita," he says. "I heard you got some sun. Don't you know better by now?" Though he's chastising me, he's smiling, the laugh lines etched around his eyes deepening further.

I laugh. "I used sunscreen! I swear. Ramiro is my witness," I say.

When I say that, Ramiro looks everywhere but at me.

Then I notice what Don Gustavo is holding in his hands. Two long leaves of an aloe plant.

"No! Don't tell me you cut those from that beautiful plant at your house!"

"Relajate, güerita. That's what it's for."

He goes to the kitchen, and I follow, watching him grab a cutting board and knife. He expertly filets the leaves like a fish, uses a butter knife to scrape the jelly inside, and collects it in a bowl.

"I'm gonna get back to my workout. You okay for a bit, Sara?" Ramiro says.

I nod. "Thanks. I'll be fine."

Don Gustavo helps get the jelly on the parts of me I can't reach, and I thank my lucky stars he's here helping and not Ramiro. I can't imagine a repeat of yesterday's sunscreen debacle. I'm surprised when he dabs some on the apples of my cheeks.

"You got a little sun there too."

I squeeze his forearm. "Gracias, Don Gustavo."

That first year, when Carolina took me to her home for the holidays and I met Don Gustavo, we took an instant liking to each other. And even though I was a year behind Carolina, she went on to med school, so I was done with college first. She was so busy back then, and her dad was so lonely, I spent a lot of time with Don Gustavo. Mostly getting Spanish lessons and cooking lessons.

When I graduated, I panicked because I was about to be homeless unless I could find a job soon. Don Gustavo suggested I stay in Carolina's old room while I looked for a job and saved up for my own place. Carolina and her dad were the ones to give me a leg up in the world, and I really would have been homeless without them.

For the past eight years, Don Gustavo has been the closest thing to a father I've had. And what a difference from my biological father. He actually gives a shit.

He and Carolina are my only family now. A few years ago, I gave him and Carolina power of attorney as a gift since I was too old to be formally adopted, but I really wanted them to know they are my family now.

Don Gustavo's eyes misted over when I explained what the paperwork was. Sure, it was a little morbid, but I definitely don't want my biological parents to ever have to make medical decisions for me. I've seen too much at the hospital to let that happen.

Don Gustavo almost never cries either, just like Ramiro. Well, there have been a few exceptions. The most memorable of which was when I sought refuge in his home again after my last breakup. When he saw my arm in a cast and my nose bandaged up, he cried like I'd never seen before. He wouldn't let me out of his sight for months after that.

"Would you like un cafecito?" I ask him.

He nods. I know he'd never say no to a good cup of coffee.

I make it how he taught me, on the stove with cinnamon sticks and piloncillo. It's a slow process, but the result is divine.

"How are you holding up with the boys?" He asks after making sure they're both upstairs and out of earshot.

"Good. René's been picking on Oscar more than usual since school let out. I wish Ramiro would let me take them to counseling."

"Give it time, Mija. I'm sure they'll be back to normal soon. And Ramiro? How's he doing?"

"Good. Those first few weeks were rough, but he got it together, and he's been amazing with the boys."

"I like the look of you together," he says.

I laugh. It wasn't so long ago that he liked the look of Ramiro and Carolina together.

"Well, I have to get going. I have a caldo on the stove," he says, excusing himself.

I shake my head after him. Leave it to Don Gustavo to make a caldo at the peak of summer.

～

BY THE FOLLOWING WEEKEND, MY SKIN HAS HEALED. RENÉ HAD A great week of good behavior. Maybe he felt sorry for the pain I was in, or maybe making a new friend in Trevor helped. Trevor's mom, Jaleesa, stopped by Wednesday to introduce herself since the boys wanted to go to each other's houses so much.

Whatever the reason for his behaving, I couldn't be more grateful because we were fast approaching a breaking point. As a reward, Ramiro and I decide to treat them today to a trip to our local amusement park, Worlds of Fun.

"I'll get the door!" I yell up at the boys when the doorbell rings, but even as I head towards it, René clamors down the stairs and reaches it just before I do.

A smiling Trevor greets us on the other side, his mom behind him. "Hi, Jaleesa," I say.

"Hi, Sara. Thank you so much for inviting Trevor to join you."

"It's our pleasure," I say truthfully. The few times Trevor has spent time with us, he's been the model of a polite, well-behaved kid, and I'm grateful for the positive example.

"Hi, Miss Sara," Trevor says.

"Come on in, Trevor. We have to wait for the guys. Ramiro takes forever to do his hair." I roll my eyes playfully.

Trevor blinks up at me. "But he doesn't have any hair."

Jaleesa and I burst out laughing. "I know," I say.

"Let me know when I can take the boys and return the favor," Jaleesa says.

"Thanks, I might take you up on that one of these days. You doing anything fun?"

She smiles so broadly, every one of her teeth is on display. "Date with Travis," she says, referring to her husband.

"You two have fun," I call out as she turns around.

As she walks back to her car, I can't help but get excited at having made a new friend too.

When Ramiro joins us downstairs, he's holding something behind his back. Oscar trails him, his arms behind his back as well.

"What's going on?" I ask, my tone suspicious.

"We have gifts for you!" Oscar says, and Ramiro grins wide.

"We do," Ramiro says.

Oscar reveals his first, placing a bulk-size bottle of sunscreen in my hands. "It's the highest SF we could find!" Oscar says, like it's the most impressive thing in the world.

"It's SPF, buddy," I say with a laugh. I kneel to hug him. "Thank you. That was very thoughtful." Then I turn to the taller conspirator, placing my hands on my hips. "And you? What gifts do you bring?"

He swings his arms in front of him and reveals a hat that reminds me a little too much of Crocodile Dundee's.

"Uhh," I say. Without moving to grab it, Ramiro steps forward and places it on my head. "There."

I blink at him. I don't know what to say or how to turn down the horrendous hat.

Before I can think of how to turn him down nicely, René steps forward and hands me a white button-up shirt. "And you should wear this—to protect your arms."

I hold the shirt in front of me. I'd swear it's not new, and it's definitely Ramiro-size.

"And," René adds, "it'll cover you up from pervs." He covers Trevor's eyes while I put the shirt on, which swallows me whole.

So here I stand, looking at all four boys, with a ridiculous hat, a shirt that looks like a muumuu, and a gallon of sunscreen in my hands. I do my best to smile. "Uh, thanks, guys."

In this ridiculous get-up, we make our way to Worlds of Fun.

THE DAY WAS AMAZING, THOUGH EXHAUSTING, AND THE BOYS don't want to leave. Inviting Trevor was a brilliant idea, if I do say so myself. One of us had to stay back when the rides were too scary or too big for Oscar to get on, so one of us could go with René and Trevor on the rides. Mostly Ramiro went. I did all the smaller rides with Oscar.

As Oscar and I walk out from the spinning teacups, all dizzy and walking like drunks, we find Ramiro, who is waiting with the boys and cotton candy. He smiles at me as he hands me the pink one and Oscar the green one.

"Thanks," I say.

I'm so dizzy, and the ground is still tilting from the ride; I can't think straight when I see *him*.

He's facing the other direction, getting in line to another ride across from the teacups, so I only get a glimpse of the back of his head. The unmistakable patch of black hair pokes out from under his baseball cap, and he's wearing the football jersey with his favorite player's name. I haven't taken a bite of the cotton candy yet, but bile rises to my throat anyway, and I run to the nearest trash bin I can find.

I dry heave into it, dropping the cotton candy in the bin as well.

Gentle hands rub my back.

"One too many spins?" Ramiro asks, teasing.

When my stomach settles, and the world stops spinning, I search for him again. He's still there, waiting, facing the other direction.

Then Ramiro tracks my eyes to where I'm boring holes into Brian's back. As soon as I notice it, I try to shake it off.

But I can't. A flash of my kitchen counter and the sound of a bone breaking is all I can see and hear. I'm no longer at the amusement park; I'm back in my old apartment. On the ground, taking kick after kick from a sneakered foot.

I blink the memories away, but he's still there, and I'm hyperventilating.

I grab onto Ramiro's forearm tightly. This is a panic attack. I haven't had one in so long I'd forgotten how awful they are.

"Sara?" Oscar asks. "You okay?"

I shake my head. "I think," I wheeze. "I think I got dehydrated," I lie. "Hand me the water bottle?"

Oscar grabs the bottle from Ramiro's backpack and hands it to me.

"Thanks, buddy."

I gulp it down and face the other direction. Brian hasn't seen me, and he can't see me. Herding my boys in the opposite direction, I feel Ramiro's arm squeezing around my waist as he props me up while we walk. Seeming to think I'm okay, the kids walk in front of us. When they're out of earshot, Ramiro whispers in my ear, "It wasn't him."

I turn to blink at him. "What?"

"It wasn't your ex."

My mouth falls open. "Wha—how did you …"

His big, comforting hand rubs my back again. "I know more than you think, Sara. I've paid attention to you, you know. All this time. I've watched. I … see you. You're not as secretive as you like to think."

To that, I don't know what to say, so I just clamp my mouth shut.

When we get back to the warmth of Ramiro's house, I'm comforted by the fact that I am safe here. Protected by all my boys. Brian is long gone from my life, and it's time to move on from the memories too. This is my home for now.

I don't know what I'll do when I have to leave it.

CHAPTER 8

Luckily for Ramiro, today I work a rare evening shift. He forgot the lunchbox I packed for him this morning, and I have time to drop it off before I have to head to the hospital.

Don Gustavo is hanging out with Oscar and René until Ramiro gets home from work later today. I don't know what we'd do without his help sometimes.

I say goodbye to all of them, and none look up as their eyeballs are glued to the pre-recorded soccer game.

When I get to Tavo's Auto Repair, I head inside with Ramiro's lunchbox in hand. No one is at the front office, so I round the building to the garage, and my heart nearly stops.

It's like Don Gustavo only hires male models to work for him.

There Ramiro is, his coveralls unzipped and bunched around his waist, his ribbed tank tight around his torso. He's all sweaty, with black grease tracks running down his arms and cross down his left cheek. On the other side, working on a second car, is a new mechanic I haven't seen before. A couple of inches taller than Ramiro, blond, and in a similar outfit, his muscles tightening with the use of each tool under the hood of the car.

I close my mouth and call out to Ramiro. Both men look up.

Ramiro smiles wide when he sees me, then goes to the speaker system to lower the Industrial November song playing.

"What are you doing here?"

I raise the lunch box to show him.

"Oh, thanks. You didn't have to do that. I could have ordered in."

"No trouble. I'm heading to the hospital for my shift anyway. I told Don Gustavo you'd be home by six."

"Great. Thanks, Sara. Really—"

"Who's this?"

Both Ramiro and I turn to look at the blond mechanic as he walks up to us.

"Oh, Sara, this is Devyn."

"Hi, Devyn. I haven't seen you around. You new?"

"Yeah, this is my first month." He's cleaning his hands with a rag, and shrugs. "I'm sorry, I'd shake your hand, but I'm all full of grease."

I laugh. "I'm used to grease," I say, eyeing Ramiro.

Devyn looks between Ramiro and me, his eyes going wide. "Oh, are you two—"

I laugh. Maybe too loud because Ramiro narrows his eyes at me. "No. We're friends—"

"And roommates," Ramiro adds.

Okay, somehow, this just got awkward.

"Thanks again, Sara. I'll see you at home tonight."

Ramiro heads back to the car he was working on, and Devyn lingers.

"Well, it was nice to meet you," I say.

"Yeah, here. Let me walk you to your car."

"Oh, you don't have to do that—"

He flashes me a perfect pearly-white smile that I'm sure

melts the knees of many a woman. "I want to." He follows me back out. "So, how does a nice girl like you become roommates with a hothead like Ramiro?" he asks as we walk much too slowly.

"Family friends. And then, with everything that happened, I've just been helping out."

"Oh, right," he says. "I heard about his fiancée. That's sweet of you, to help with his sons."

I blink at Devyn. Does Ramiro talk about Oscar and René as his sons? For some reason, that thought makes me grin the widest grin.

"Yeah, well, that's how we became roommates."

"You work at the hospital?" He asks, eyeing me in my scrubs from head to toe in a way that makes my step falter a little.

"Yeah, I'm a nurse at Heartland Metro."

"You don't say." His smile is mischievous. I don't know why some men find my profession sexy when it's anything but. If they only knew.

When we get to my car, Devyn surprises me by opening my car door for me—like what happens in the movies. "Maybe I'll see you around sometime, Sara Moore."

"Uh, how do you know my last name?"

Devyn points to my name badge. "It's on your chest," he says with a wink before closing the door gently and walking away.

Now, when I say his ass is perfect, that's an understatement.

THREE DAYS LATER, I SEE DEVYN AGAIN, LIKE HE'S A FREAKING oracle who could see the future when he said he'd see me around.

After work, I head to the gas station to fill up, and when I'm pulling away, my car stutters and then dies. I turn the key, trying to get it to turn on again with no luck. Just great. Pressing my forehead to the wheel, I take a deep breath.

Okay think, Sara. Action plan. I start by calling a tow service, and half an hour later I hitch a ride with the tow truck to Tavo's. I ask for my car to be left in the lot, and head inside.

"Hey, Devyn," I say when I see him.

No one else is at the garage now that it's almost closing time, and I don't see Ramiro's car parked outside.

"Well, hello nurse Sara. What can we do for you?"

Oh, he's a smooth talker, this one, with the faintest twang of a southern accent. Green eyes framed by long, blond lashes light up when he talks. "Is Ramiro gone already?"

"Yeah. He left early today. Said he had to pick up the boys?"

I smack my head. "Right. I forgot Don Gustavo had to leave early today. Can I leave my car here?"

"What's wrong with it?" he asks.

"Don't know. It just kinda died after I filled up, and I was going to ask Ramiro to take a look at it. I'll leave it here for him tomorrow."

I loop my key fob out of my key chain when Devyn stops me.

"Well, hold on there, darlin,' I'm a mechanic too, you know."

"Uh, I know."

"I can take a look at it."

"Oh, it's past closing. I don't want to keep you."

"It's no trouble."

"You said it died after you got gas?" I nod. "Kay, let's take a look fuel pressure. I'll bet ya all you need is a new fuel pump."

I watch him as he works, the entire time with a half-smile on his face as I keep him company. "Ah," he says. "Just like a thought. We need a new fuel pump. Easy enough. I don't think we have the part on hand, though."

"It's all right, I'm sure Ramiro can order it."

"Nah, the local auto parts store should carry it. They're still open a few more hours."

I grab my phone to pull up my car service app. "I just ask for a fuel pump? Is there a particular brand I need?"

"Whatcha doin, sugar?"

"Getting a car to take me to the auto parts store."

He gently grabs my phone from me and closes the app. "I'll take you."

"You really don't have to do that—"

"I don't have to, Sara. But I want to. Got it?" He says it with such gentle authority, I find myself nodding.

Devyn is a beast, with finely honed muscles, well over six feet tall, but his size doesn't intimidate me because his eyes and smile are so darn endearing. Which is why I follow him to his car.

"So, you from Kansas City originally?" he asks to fill the silence as he drives.

"Born and raised. You?"

"Nah. I grew up mostly in Texas"—that explains his faint accent— "until high school. Then Dad got a job in Garden City, and I've been there till recently. I thought I'd try my hand at the big city, you know?" he says with a laugh that I enjoy more than I should.

"I love Garden City."

He turns to glance at me before flickering his eyes back on the road. "You been?"

"Yeah. Best Mexican food in the state."

"You got that right."

It's dark now, and I watch the city lights flash by Devyn's face, illuminating his Grecian features. That easy smile of his. The sheer size of him would have sent me into a panic attack only a few months back if I'd been alone with him, but somehow, I feel safe.

It's been long enough since Brian that it's time to start

thinking about dating again—and my new counselor agrees. I need to let someone in, even if just for some fun.

And maybe a little sex. It's been so long, and watching Ramiro workout can only do so much for my battery-operated fantasies.

"Devyn, can I ask you a personal question?"

"You can ask me anything you like."

"Do you have a girlfriend? Or, uh, a significant other?"

He chuckles. "No ma'am. I'm single, and that second part of your question there—I like women."

I laugh. "I wouldn't want to assume."

"I know," he says, winking at me again.

"Do you think maybe you'd like to go out for coffee sometime?"

His eyes flicker to me again. "Like on a date?"

I'd felt brave asking, but now that he seems to be questioning it, I feel the heat creep up my neck. *You're so stupid,* Sara. Asking a guy out when your car is out of commission, and you're stuck with him for at least another hour.

I clear my throat and try to sound as confident as I did when I asked. "Yeah. Would you like to go on a date with me?"

"I'd love to go on a date with you, but sugar?"

"Yeah?"

"We can do a lot better than coffee."

CHAPTER 9

I t's been years since I've had butterflies in my stomach. Maybe not since high school. Now, getting ready for my date with Devyn has the butterflies fluttering all the way up to my chest.

I style my long dirty-blond hair into loose waves and put on my little bodycon dress. It has a high, wide neckline that covers my cleavage well but highlights my hips and cuts high on my thigh. It's sexy but not too overstated. My makeup is minimal except for a bright red lip that makes my blue eyes pop.

When I get downstairs, Ramiro is at the kitchen island on his laptop, going over the garage's bookkeeping. Oscar and René are watching a movie.

Ramiro peers up at me, does a double take, then shuts the laptop gently. "You look nice," he says, an eyebrow raised, the faintest smirk tugging at the corners of his lips.

For some reason, I blush at his praise. "Thanks, Ramiro. How about you guys?" I ask the boys. "Do you like my dress?"

Oscar turns around first, nodding. "Sara! You look pretty."

"Thanks buddy. How about it, René?"

He peels eyes from the screen, then frowns. "The dress is too short. You need pants."

That's the third time he's insinuated I should hide my body. I've wondered if he was this protective of Francisca but haven't wanted to ask him if he's redirecting his 'man of the house' ideology on to me. That's what Doña Pancha told him when he was growing up, until Francisca started dating Ramiro—that René was the man of the house. I think maybe he took the role too seriously.

"It's not too short," I say, defending my mini dress. "And perfect for a date—"

"A date?" Ramiro chimes in.

I spin on my high heels to face him. "Yeah. I have a date tonight."

"You said you were going out. I thought you meant with Carolina and Sofia."

I laugh. "Those workaholics hardly have time for me," I say. "No. I have a date with Devyn."

Ramiro's eyes nearly bulge out of their sockets. "With Devyn?" he asks.

"Yeah. Remember last Wednesday I told you he helped me with the car? I asked him out—"

"You asked him out?" René asks, incredulous.

Oh my god. These boys. "Yeah, buddy. The best girls ask the guy out sometimes, too."

René frowns, not buying it, but Oscar nods. Maybe there's hope yet—at least for the little one.

Not for René, though. He crosses his arms over his chest, and he's about to say something when the doorbell rings, cutting him off. He's the first to get to the door.

We all hear Devyn ask for me.

"You have the wrong house," René says and closes the door in Devyn's face.

"René!" both Ramiro and I shout. "That was so rude," I add as I go to open the door.

Devyn is facing the other direction but hasn't made it off the porch yet. When I call his name, he turns around, and that's when I see it, the single red rose in his hand. Could he be any sweeter? I mean, they don't make them like this anymore.

"Oh, I thought this wasn't …" He trails off, looking past me, and I realize a murderous-looking René is standing behind me, arms crossed. I roll my eyes. Give me strength.

"Come on in. You can meet the boys."

"Uh … okay."

He kisses my cheek, making René groan, then hands me my rose.

"Let me put this in water, and we can head out."

"This here is René," I say, palming the top of his head. "He's grounded—"

"Sara!" he whines.

"No," Ramiro says. "You were rude. No TV the rest of the weekend."

René storms off to his room and slams the door.

"And this is Oscar." Oscar blinks up at Devyn, then at me, a little confused.

"Why doesn't my brother like you?" he asks with that transparent honesty only kids are capable of.

Ramiro and I watch as Devyn crouches down to meet Oscar's height. "Hey, buddy," he says, offering a giant fist for Oscar to bump. Oscar blinks at it, then when realization hits, bumps the tiniest fist to Devyn's mammoth one. "He's just protective of Sara. It's no big deal. I was like that with my ma when I was his age. I was always jealous and trying to protect her."

"Oh," Oscar says. "Do I need to be jealous, like him?"

"No, buddy," Devyn says. "I'll take good care of Miss Sara. You don't have to worry."

"Okay. I'll go tell René."

"Thanks, bud."

Once we're alone, Ramiro steps in between Devyn and me, and if I'm not mistaken, his frame is vibrating like he might be angry for some reason, but his words are cordial.

"Good to see you man," he says, shaking Devyn's hand.

"You too. You ready?" Devyn asks me.

I've placed the rose in a cup of water on the kitchen counter, so I take Devyn's arm and lace mine through it. As I walk past Ramiro, I could have sworn his jaw muscle is bulging just before he wishes us a good night.

"Sorry about that," I say. "I didn't mean for you to meet everyone tonight."

Devyn chuckles as he opens the car door for me. "Don't be. They should be protective of their ma."

I choke while he walks around to get in the car.

Their mom? I shake the thought. "I'm not their mom," I say as soon as he gets behind the wheel.

"No, but I'm sure they see you as a type of mother figure."

I glance out my window and stare at the boys' darkened window. Do they think of me as a mother figure? When I moved in, we had a family meeting. We explained I was just staying with them for a year, then I'd move back to my place. They'd seem so unconcerned, I never even stopped to think about how they'll handle my departure when I leave.

"I don't know that they should," I admit.

"Hey." He places a knuckle under my chin to turn my head toward him. "I meant nothing by it. What do you say to a nice dinner and some dancing?"

My eyes widen. "You can dance?"

He lets go of my face and winks before turning on the car. "Sure can. I told you I lived in Garden City, right?"

When we get to the restaurant, we both order steaks with salad appetizers.

Our conversation is light most of the dinner, getting to know each other. Devyn had a football scholarship to the University of Texas, but he wanted to work with his hands, not unlike another mechanic I know. He has a sister in college, and his mom is still in Texas. His dad passed away last year, which is why he left Garden City.

Through all of it, I do my best to carefully avoid telling him about my parents, or anything about my last relationship. I just want to have fun tonight.

"If you could live in any decade in history, when would you have liked to have been a young adult?" I ask him one of the questions in the list of date night question I looked up online earlier. Yes. I'm that nerd. This is my first first-date in years, and of course I'm nervous. Do not judge the conversational cards.

"I dunno, darlin'. I'm pretty happy in this one, with its medical advancements."

"You have a point," I say. "I still think I was supposed to grow up in the sixties and seventies."

"Why's that?"

"That's when jogging really took off, and the rise of the track suit! I don't know, guess I'm nostalgic for those places in movies, you know? Diners, drive-ins ... Then there's wide bell-bottom jeans, and oh! The Beatles! Hippies and flower power."

Devyn laughs. "I don't know that I'd make a good hippie."

I eye him carefully. He's wearing dark jeans and a dark navy button-up shirt that he has rolled up at the sleeves. With his short hair perfectly styled and angular jaw freshly shaved, he does seem too clean cut to have been a hippie. "You're probably right, but I do think it would have been cool."

"Sure," he says. "Cool if you don't count 'Nam, the Cuban missile crisis, the assassinations of JFK, Malcolm X, Robert Kennedy, MLK, what else? Oh, Nixon getting elected ... I'm not even into the seventies yet. You sure that's where you wanna be?"

My jaw drops. This man is smart. And he likes history. You wouldn't think it of his pretty boy looks, but Devyn Holland has a huge brain. I immediately wonder what else about him might be huge. Then I shake my head to snap out of my wandering thoughts. "Uh, well, yeah. There's conflict in any decade, though, including ours."

"Fair point," he says with a bite of his steak. I watch his Adam's apple bob as he swallows.

"And did I mention the track suits?"

He chuckles with a shake of his head. We finish our delicious meals over pleasant conversation and a bottle of wine. When we're done, with a waggle of his brows, he asks, "Ready to go dancing?"

"I'll believe you know how to dance when I see it."

DEVYN HOLLAND CAN DANCE. LIKE, REALLY DANCE. I WAS skeptical when we stepped inside the club to blaring cumbia music.

I told him I couldn't really dance that well, that I'm still learning from Don Gustavo, but he just flashed that smile and said, "Sugar, I'm an excellent lead."

Then he whisked me onto the dance floor, and he was right. All I had to do was follow his lead and do my best to mimic the hip swaying of the women dancing around me.

We drink through the night—well, mostly I do since he has to drive—but immediately turn around and burn off the alcohol on the dance floor.

When the song turns into a slow bachata song, I think it's

"Baila con migo" by Ephrem J., Devyn's body presses to mine and he takes me in his arms, his large palm spread across my lower back, our legs interlaced as they're intended to be during bachata, and he expertly leads us in the repetitive sideways steps of the slow and sexy dance. He ducks his head until my nose can reach the crook of his neck and I nuzzle into his warmth. He smells like man, a combination of spicy aftershave and musk mixed with the sweat from our dancing.

The perfect first date ever.

We dance and we dance, and not once do I check the time, even though I know it's probably past midnight.

When I'm skeptical my pinky toe is still attached to my foot inside my heels, I tap out first. We leave the club sweaty and laughing.

Devyn's fingers lace through mine as he leads me to his car.

I'm grinning like an idiot the entire ride home—my hand laced with Devyn's on top of his lap.

"Thank you for tonight, Devyn," I say when he parks outside the house. It's one in the morning and all the lights are out. "It's the most fun I've had on a date in a long time."

"I had a great time. Maybe we could do it again soon? You free next weekend?"

My heart somersaults at hearing him making concrete plans so soon, but my confidence falters. I need to take this at glacier pace. Gaining trust in men again will be a long process, and Devyn deserves to know what he's in for if he still wants to keep seeing me.

"Devyn," I say with a sigh.

"Oh, no. What did I do?" he asks.

I take his hand in mine and laugh. "You didn't do anything. I'd love to see you again, but you should know a few things first."

His gaze cuts behind me to the house. "You and Ramiro—"

I laugh. "No. Trust me. There's no history there." I don't add that Ramiro has always seen me as Carolina's annoying little sister because my pride can only take so much.

"It's just—it's been a while since my last relationship, and it wasn't a great one. I'd love to keep seeing you, but if you want that too, I need you to understand. I need to take this really, really slow."

His brows furrow when he looks at me. "Mind elaborating on that a bit? I mean, I'm trying to understand."

I lift my chin and take a deep breath. "My last partner … he wasn't a great guy. It ended badly—though that's an understatement. And my trust in men was shaken up a bit. I'm in counseling, working through it, and I'm ready to start dating again, but it just has to be on my terms. I understand if it sounds too complicated and you'd rather not go on a second date."

He leans forward, gently, and he cups my face in one hand, his thumb caressing my jawline. "I didn't say that, Sara. We can take things slow."

"Good. Because I like you. A lot."

He sits back again, his face suddenly hard. "Now, when you say he wasn't a great guy, what do you mean? Did he—did he hurt you?"

My eyes well, and that's all the confirmation he needs. He leans forward again, taking me in his arms, then leans back to look me so deep in my eyes, I'd swear he's looking into my soul.

"I need you to know, Sara, I'd never, ever lay a finger on you."

"Trusting that is hard, but I'm working on it," I admit.

"Good. I'd like for you to one day trust me."

I smile at him. "I'd like that too."

"Now, I'm not the kinda guy who asks permission to kiss a pretty lady, so if you don't want to be kissed, you need to get out of my car this second."

He pauses to give me the time I need to pull away, but I don't. Instead, I lean in closer, waiting for the promised kiss.

The hand that had been on my jaw glides to the back where he cradles my head gently. Then he finds my lips with his, soft and gentle. A kiss so tender it's like he's making a promise that he'd never hurt me.

And against all odds, I believe that kiss.

WHEN I TIPTOE INTO THE HOUSE, MY SHOES DANGLING FROM MY hands, I notice something in the kitchen.

Someone took the rose Devyn gave me out of the cup, and it lies on the counter, dead and wilted—like someone crushed it in their fist.

Three guesses who.

CHAPTER 10

Devyn and I date the last few weeks of summer.

He's been wonderful and so patient with me. I've never, not once, seen him lose his temper. And though I've become an expert at reading red flags, there simply aren't any.

Which only makes me wonder if that's a red flag in and of itself.

This is so complicated.

He is kind and patient. He's never pushes me to do anything I haven't been ready for.

I'm hesitant to get too excited. It's so soon, but I am hopeful my happiness might just be found by his side. With every minute I spend with Devyn, I long for Ramiro just a little bit less, and I'm hopeful my 'forget-Ramiro' plan is starting to gel.

The only downside has been René constantly shutting the door in Devyn's face. He just needs time, I remind myself. Even with him, Devyn has been extremely understanding.

Oscar is another story.

Apparently, Devyn has seen all the Marvel movies, and he and Oscar have no shortage of fan theories to chat about every time he picks me up for a date, and they wait while I finish getting ready.

The best was when Devyn suggested—spoiler alert—that Thanos knew what would happen in *The Eternals* and that's why he did the snap. Oscar almost started shaking as he tried to work out the mathematics of that problem in his head. I had to tell Devyn, with a laugh, not to break Oscar's mind. Dazed, Oscar floated up the stairs to repeat the theory to his brother. The debate that ensued between Oscar and René lasted two full days.

As for Ramiro, he's been acting a bit off, and for the life of me, I can't quite put my finger on it. Anytime I'm heading out with Devyn, Ramiro disappears into his gym and hardly crosses paths with Devyn when we head out.

I suspect Ramiro might be worried I'll end our agreement soon and move out before the year is up, but I gave him my word. He should know it means something by now, shouldn't he?

For tonight's date, I'm wearing jeans and a simple black t-shirt. Devyn said to be casual, but that tonight is to be a surprise.

When I head downstairs and he's hanging out with Oscar, Devyn's face lights up when he sees me.

"Sara, you're overdressed. I told you, casual," he says with a mischievous grin.

"I'm wearing jeans and flip-flops. How much more casual can I get?" Then I eye him warily. He's wearing an electric blue track suit with white and blue stripes at the hem.

"Here." He hands me a gift bag that had been hiding under the coffee table. "Go change."

Nervous, I take out the contents and laugh when I see a matching track suit in purple. I clamor up the stairs and hurry into the outfit, which I'm surprised to see is the right size.

I head back downstairs in my tracksuit, and he laughs. The

jerk laughs at me. He takes me off the bottom step and into his arms to spin me around. When he lets me down, he turns to Oscar. "We look great, don't we?"

Oscar shakes his head. "No." Then he keeps coloring in his new sketchbook Devyn got him.

"Where are we going?"

"Oh, a great many places. Bye, Oscar."

"Bye!" He shouts as we leave the house.

When we step outside, I'm greeted with a cherry-red Mustang convertible straight out of a sixty's movie. I squeal, and I jump into his arms. "Our date is the sixties?"

He grabs me by the waist, pulling my body flush to his. We must be a sight to the neighbors in our ridiculous matching track suits in front of the convertible rental.

"For one night only, ma'am. You get to be in the sixties."

"You made a decade for me?" I say, a little more emotional than I'd like.

He grins widely at me and let's go of me long enough to open my door.

Our next stop is a vintage diner in town I never knew existed before tonight. We have burgers and share fries and a strawberry shake.

He won't say where our next stop is after dinner, but realization hits as we pull up Merriam Lane. "We're going to the drive-in?"

"Yes." He grins again.

"I love the drive-in! I haven't been in ages."

"I figured you'd like it. I'm sorry we can't watch something more romantic. It's a horror flick tonight. You okay with that?"

"I like horror."

"Good, because the drive-in is on the straight and narrow."

"What do you mean?"

"I tried to get them to play one of them sixties chick flicks I'd thought you'd like, but they wouldn't take a bribe."

"You tried bribing them?"

"Sure did."

"What movies were you asking them to play?"

"You know. Something like *Breakfast at Tiffany's* or *West Side Story*."

"That would have been great," I admit, "but horror is awesome too. And when I get scared, because I inevitably will, I'll need someone to hold me."

He glances at me quickly. "Well, shit, sugar, then we'll always be watching horror movies."

We only make out minimally during the first movie, and Devyn has me feeling like a teenager all over again.

During the break before the second movie, he asks me if something's wrong with Ramiro.

"Why would you think that?"

He shrugs, taking a sip from his soda. "When I first got the job, I thought he was going to be a buddy. Even worked out together a few times. But lately ..."

"Lately what?"

"I don't know. He's different, but only with me." He pauses to cup the back of his neck. "Do you two have a history?"

I laugh. "What?"

"That's the only thing new. Us dating. Picking you up at his house."

I shake my head. "No. Trust me, there's no history there."

Devyn looks at me for a long moment, assessing, not saying anything. Finally, he asks, "Why'd you say it like that?"

"Like what?"

"Sarcastic. Like it's unfathomable."

"Mr. Holland, have I told you how sexy your big vocabulary is?"

I wiggle over to straddle his lap.

"Miss Moore, my vocabulary ain't the only thing big about me. But you're dodging my question and trying to distract me."

I giggle in his arms. "Is it working?"

"No. Now, behave. Why is Ramiro acting jealous of you?"

I blink at him. Jealous? Ramiro? "Are you insane?"

"I know a jealous man when I see one."

I collapse back into my seat since clearly my tactic didn't work. "There's no history with Ramiro. I promise."

"He has feelings for you, though."

"Trust me. He does not."

"There's that tone again."

"What tone?"

"You know perfectly well what tone."

The last thing I should do is tell this man that I've been in love with Ramiro most of my adult life but given that Devyn has been nothing but honest and patient with me, I feel I owe him the truth in kind.

"Fine. But this is in the past, okay?"

He nods. "Understood."

"I used to be in love with him."

"Used to be?"

I nod. "Yes. When I first met him, he was head over heels in love with Carolina."

"Your older sister."

"That's right. I met him through her. When he finally moved on from her, he almost immediately fell in love with Francisca, Oscar and René's mom. That's why when I say he has no feelings for me, I'm so certain. I've always been Caro's annoying little sister. A pest. A friend, but still a pest."

"Do you still love him?"

I sigh. "To be perfectly honest, maybe? A little? I try not to."

"Not so sure I should have asked anymore."

"I'm sorry. I'm trying to be really honest here. My feelings for him … they don't matter. I like you, Devyn. And you seem like someone I'd like in my life … maybe even someone I could love one day. The last thing I want to do is lie to you. So, there it is. The embarrassing truth."

"Don't be embarrassed. Man probably had a lobotomy to overlook you."

I laugh, then turn serious again, searching in his beautiful eyes. "Is it enough that I'm working on not loving him in that way? That I want to move on with someone else?"

"Are you asking if I'm okay with you letting yourself fall in love with me instead?"

My mouth dries up, but I guess that is what I'm asking him, at the bottom of it all. "Yes," I breathe out.

"Yes, Sara." He chuckles. "I'm okay with you trying to fall in love with me. Now, my lap is mighty cold without you on it."

CHAPTER 11

The rest of summer, whenever Devyn picks me up to go out, he doesn't come inside anymore. He'll wait on the porch, and sometimes Oscar will go hang out with him while I finish getting ready.

Ramiro hasn't said a word about it or asked at all about our relationship, which I take as a good thing.

Summer is nearly over, and next week, the boys go back to school, which will make things so much easier for Ramiro and me to work out our schedules so someone is always home.

I'm lying in bed, worried about Oscar. He begged and begged to go to his friend Bobby's house for a slumber party. I thought he was too young, and René confirmed his mom wouldn't let him go to sleepovers yet.

Ramiro, on the other hand, thought he could handle it. Gave him a pep talk and everything about being a man, being brave. I worry he's teaching them to suppress their feelings like he does, like he was taught to—or to suppress their feminine side.

It's somewhat of a restless night, worrying about my sweet, gentle Oscar, but I do finally manage to fall asleep.

At some point past midnight, a sensation of someone

running a hand through my hair wakes me up. I blink, groggy, to find Ramiro standing over me.

Then I sit up, and don't pay attention to the bedsheet rolling of my body, nor do I remember the loose, silk camisole I wore to bed. It's a bit too big for me, and the neckline falls so low, it just barely covers my nipples.

It takes Ramiro's eyes dropping and fixing on my chest to remember what I'm wearing. For a moment, I consider covering up, but I don't want to embarrass him by showing that I caught him looking. Then everything Devyn said at the drive-in so many nights ago comes rushing in. Is Ramiro interested in me after all this time?

The more important question—is he interested in me as a person or as a body to warm his bed because he is hurting, lonely, and sexually deprived at the moment?

It doesn't matter because Devyn is in the picture now.

"What is it?" I ask, my voice groggy with sleep.

"Oscar—"

I rush to my feet in a panic and stand in front of Ramiro.

"No, It's okay. Go back to bed. Bobby's mom called. He's crying and wants to come home. I'll go get him. I wanted to let you know I'm heading out, but René is still in bed."

"Oh, okay."

He shoves his hands in his pockets but doesn't leave. His jaw is one hard line, with the night's stubble already shadowing the lower half of his face. "Sara, I ..."

"What?"

In the quiet room so late at night, the sound of his hard swallow is so loud. He wants to say something but can't bring himself to. My hand drifts to his upper arm where I squeeze it, and duck to meet his gaze. "What is it?"

"I—um." He shakes his head. "Nothing. Be back in a bit. Go back to bed."

WHEN THEY GET HOME, I'M READY WITH A MUG OF HOT chocolate and marshmallows for Oscar. "Would you like some hot cocoa?" I ask him as soon as they walk in.

He nods and follows that up with a little sniffle.

"I have one for you too," I say to Ramiro, and they both sit in front of the coffee table.

Oscar is next to me, and I run a hand through his hair. "What happened, buddy?"

He takes a sip and shrugs.

"It's okay to miss home or to get a little scared. Did you know I have a night light in my room?"

"You do?" he asks, incredulous.

"I do. I don't like the dark."

"But you're a grown-up."

"Some grown-ups are afraid of the dark."

He thinks for a moment and takes a few more sips. "I wasn't scared."

"Then what happened?"

He shakes his head, not wanting to talk about it, but Ramiro chimes in for him. "I talked to Bobby's mom. They apparently watched *Coco* before they went to bed. She thought it was fine, but she found him awake when she checked on them later on."

"Oh, buddy—"

"I don't remember her that well anymore," Oscar admits.

Bobby's mom has no idea about Francisca, definitely not how recent it was. I'm sure she wouldn't have let them watch that movie if she had known. From what I remember of the film, the entire premise centers on the idea that so long as we can remember our dead loved ones, they get to come back and visit us during the Day of the Dead.

I grab his hand and cup it in mine. "Oscar, listen to me.

Ramiro remembers Francisca. And he will remember her always. Right?"

"Of course, I will," Ramiro says.

"You were so little, Oscar, when she died. But you're getting so grown up now. It's okay if you don't remember her as clearly anymore. And I remember her too."

"Do we need to have an ofrenda for her to visit us?" Oscar asks.

Shit. I know next to nothing about this. Despite all my Mexican-American education from Don Gustavo and Carolina, they never celebrated the Day of the Dead. But as with all things, I'm honest with Oscar about this too.

"I'm not too sure how it works, but I'll tell you what. Carolina's assistant, Mandy, put together an art exhibit all about the Day of the Dead. Why don't I ask her if she can let us have some things for the ofrenda and tell us how it works? And in November, we'll be sure to honor your mom."

He nods, and the look of relief on his face breaks me.

Ramiro helps me to tuck him in tonight, and we don't leave their room until Oscar is sound asleep.

He closes the door so gently behind him, I don't dare move and make a sound to wake him up again.

Then Ramiro turns to me.

"Sara, I—I don't know what I'd do without you. You're so good with them."

"I'm so happy to be here, Ramiro. I promise I'll stay till next spring. I gave you my word. I'm here for the year."

His brows furrow. "Why do you say that?"

"It's why you've been so weird, about Devyn and me, right?"

Ramiro takes a step closer, and I take a step back. He shakes his head. "No, Sara. I didn't ever think you'd shorten your stay. Not for one minute."

"Oh."

He takes another step. Then another, until I have nowhere to go, and my back is pressed against the wall. He's so close to me now, his head bowed, our noses could almost touch.

"Ramiro, I …" My breath hitches when he draws one finger over my collarbone. "What are you doing?" I ask, not making a move to step away from his touch.

How many times did I dream of this? Of Ramiro looking at me with so much hunger it's a little scary? Countless. Countless dreams of his big, rough hands all over my body. Of big palms against my flesh and thick fingers digging into my skin. Never like this, though. Never so gentle and light. I almost wonder if I'm imagining the feel of it. And yet, my brain stops working. I should be stepping away. I should be thinking about Devyn, about how Ramiro is still grieving and refusing to deal with it.

I want to let him take his sadness out on my body, but I can't be that for him. Not when the boys need me … not when I'm still in love with him despite what I tell myself every time I'm with Devyn.

If I let this happen and we take this further, I will regret being his emotional cushion. And in the light of day, Ramiro will apologize. He'll want to pretend it never happened, just as he handles everything else in his life, and I'll be left heartbroken. "Ramiro?" I ask again.

His eyes lift from my chest to meet mine, his finger still trailing my collarbone. "I thought I asked you to cover up more around the house?" he whispers.

I laugh nervously, doing my best to diffuse the electric current between us, and finally, finally, pry my body away from his hand. "Laundry day is tomorrow. These are my last pair of pajamas. And to be fair, I didn't think we'd have quite the night we had. Good night!" I nearly trip over myself to get away from him and don't give him a chance to get another word in before I shut my door and lean on it, as if I'm afraid he will barge in.

CHAPTER 12

"You rang, Mr. Friedman?" I ask my needy but cheerful patient of the day.

Mr. Friedman smiles widely when he sees me. "Oh, thank goodness it's the good one."

I laugh, stepping into his room and taking a glance at his monitors. "What can I do for you?"

"I got all tangled up in the bed and accidentally pulled my IV out." He shows me the inside of his elbow with one catheter missing.

"Oh, no, Mr. Friedman. I'll take care of that for you—"

"Thank you, Sara. I don't want another student nurse poking me a million times before she gets it right."

"How else are they supposed to learn?"

He waves away my comment with one hand. "Yeah, yeah. I know. Still, this once, could you take care of it?"

There's really no good way to say no to the sweetest patient I've had in a while. In his seventies, Mr. Friedman has been a frequent flyer in my unit, and he has made it known that I am his favorite nurse.

"You haven't been around as much as you used to be," he says while I put on my gloves and get to work.

"I've been a bit busy. Took some vacation time and have had to work more night shifts lately."

He throws me a dubious smile. "Finally got a life, I see."

"Mr. Friedman!" I say with a laugh.

"Good for you. You're too young to bury yourself in work. Live a little. Trust me."

I laugh again. "Don't tell that to Dr. Ramirez."

"I've told her that many times. I don't think they have ever admitted me when Carolina is not on shift."

I raise my brow at him. "You on a first-name basis with our doctors?"

"Listen, blondie, I'm seventy-five years old. I've earned my right to call anyone by their first name, regardless of how many letters they've strung after it. Got it?"

"Got it," I say, leaving my patient with a new IV line in place and a broad smile on his face. Hopefully, Carolina will listen to him even if she won't listen to anyone else. Though I doubt it.

I head to the nurse's station to text her—maybe pry her away from work with the lure of lunch.

Me: Sushi?

Carolina: Can't leave for lunch today, but I can grab a quick bite with you at the doctor's lounge if you want.

Me: Come on. I didn't pack any lunch today.

Carolina: I'll split what I brought.

Me: Who made it …?

Carolina: <eye-roll emoji> Dad. Meet me there in ten.

When I get there, Carolina is sitting at a table in the doctor's lounge. Before I have time to sit, both of our cells notify incoming texts. I check my phone to find a notification in our group chat.

Mandy: 911!!!! Where are you?

"Did you get Mandy's text?" I ask Carolina.

"Yeah. She's overly dramatic. She would have paged if it were a patient. This is personal."

"Okay."

Me: I'm having lunch with Caro in the Onc doctor's lounge.

I sit and bum half of Caro's sandwich, stuffing it in my face. "What is this?" I ask her, savoring the breaded steak sandwich.

"Milanesa."

"It's heavenly," I say, and wash it down with some water.

"I'm glad Mandy's coming down to say hi. I wanted to ask her about Day of the Dead stuff."

Caro's brows flow up slowly. "Oh?"

"Yeah, we had a bit of an incident."

"What happened?"

I tell her about the sleepover Oscar went to and everything that happened after that while she listens intently.

"Oh no," Carolina says, immediately understanding. "They couldn't have picked a worse movie, could they?"

I shake my head. "Anyway, I talked it over with my therapist, and she thinks learning about the tradition and honoring Francisca might be good for the boys."

"That's not a bad idea," Caro says. "I wish I could help, but it's not something we've ever celebrated. That's always been a more central-and southern-Mexican tradition."

"Yeah, I figured. But with the art exhibit she's planning, I'm sure Mandy has leftover decorations and things we could use for the altar. And you know she did tons of research for it, so she can tell us what we're supposed to do."

I barely finish my sentence when Mandy whirls into the lounge, shaking off unruly strands of hair from her face. Her high heels are purple today. The only research assistant I know who wears heels to work every day. She scans the break room from her spot, holding the door behind her back like she wants to barricade it with her entire body.

"Mandy?" Carolina asks. "What's wrong?"

Mandy lets out a long breath, leans on the door for support, and scans the doctor's lounge to make sure we are alone. "Can you be a friend for the next ten minutes? Can we be off the clock and Vegas rules?"

Carolina gets out her phone, sets a 10-minute timer on the table, and says, "Anything you say while this is going will not be held against you professionally—we'll call it your off-the clock work break." She smiles at Mandy encouragingly, and I take advantage of the distraction to steal the last two bites of Carolina's sandwich.

Then Mandy blurts out a string of words I never in a million years would have guessed would be combined together in a sentence. But I heard them. From Mandy. I have to replay them in my head to make sure I understood her correctly.

"Last night I fucked an ex-naaaaht-seee!" she says, stretching the word into multiple syllables, leaving no room to question what she has just said.

The last bite lodges in my throat, and I cough. Carolina's jaw drops, then she pats my back to help my choking.

I swallow, finally. "Mandy! You didn't!"

Mandy smiles wide, then leaves her spot at the door to come sit with us. "I so did," she says.

"How could you?" I ask, my eyes wide.

"Just hear me out, okay?" Mandy eyes the timer on Carolina's phone before she keeps talking. "I met him on a dating app, and before we met, he admitted he had done time—"

"You went on a date with a felon?" I screech.

"A felon who is also a—a—" Carolina can't even get the word out.

"Just listen. I don't have much time now. He came clean, was upfront, and told me he's rehabilitated now, and he understood if I wanted to back out."

"You should have," Carolina says.

"Well, you know me. I'm curious about the human condition

—and I'm an equal-opportunity fucker. I needed to know more. So, I asked him to elaborate before I decided. He said his stepfather indoctrinated him, and it was actually in prison where he was reformed."

"So he's not a racist anymore?" Carolina says.

Mandy shakes her head. "So, picture this, he warns me, before he takes his shirt off, that there's a tattoo of a square on his right pec."

"A square?" I ask.

"It's a cover-up tattoo. One guess what it's covering," Mandy says.

"That's when you bolted, right?" Carolina asks.

Mandy smiles back at her not-boss for the next two minutes. "So, picture this, I'm riding on top of him, looking down at what I know that square tattoo is covering up, my brown ass riding his face. It was a thing of beauty. Poetic justice. I cannot begin to tell you how much of a power trip that was. Ten out of ten. I highly recommend you both find reformed—"

Mandy's words get cut off by the sound of footfalls.

Both Carolina and my jaws are at floor level when we hear the sound. We turn in the kitchenette's direction to find Dr. Bel, a surgeon from the orthopedic department, holding a lidded cup. He clears his throat.

"I was, uh, waiting for the coffeepot to fill." His lips press together, and without a single look at Mandy, he leaves the lounge, shaking his head as the door closes behind him.

Mandy's head immediately falls to the table, where her hands grip the top of her head, burying her fingers in her waves. She groans a muffled sound under her mass of messy hair. "Why didn't you tell me Dr. Bel was here? He heard everything!"

Carolina and I bust out laughing. "We didn't know he was back there," I say. "He was probably asleep while standing waiting for the coffee."

"I quit," Mandy tells Carolina. "I can never show my face at Heartland Metro Hospital again."

"I decline your notice of resignation," Carolina says. The timer on her phone goes off, and Mandy's bronze complexion is nearly crimson at the apples of her makeup-free cheeks when she comes up for air and sits upright.

"I'm going to die," Mandy says.

"Well, before you do," I jump in, "I need to ask you for a favor. I need to know more about the Day of the Dead."

Mandy looks at me, flabbergasted. "Dude. Read the room. Not the time." With a shake of her head, she stands to leave. As soon as we're alone, Carolina and I can't stop the bout of giggles.

We laugh so hard our bellies hurt.

"A Ben Franklin says she calls in sick tomorrow," I say with determination.

"You're on."

CHAPTER 13

Carolina is swallowed by the large box and several bags in her hands when I open the door.

"Oh, let me help you."

I grab a few of the bags and guide her to the kitchen table so she can set everything down. "Mandy sent all this?"

"Yeah," Carolina says. "Here," she says, pulling a bill from her jean's back pocket and placing it in my hand.

"Ha! I knew she'd call in sick."

"Yeah, yeah. Anyway, are you picking up Doña Pancha?"

"Maybe. I don't know if the guys will want to do the ofrenda today or wait until November. Oscar was pretty shaken up, but I thought learning about all this would help him through it even if we don't set up the altar tonight."

"Good idea. Where are the boys anyway? I wanted to say hi."

I smile at my friend. Her heart so big, with the few precious hours she gives herself off work, she's here, checking in on us.

"Ramiro took them to the park. René said he needed actual goal posts to practice. They took Oscar too, I think to take his mind off things. Want a cup of coffee? Have time to chat?"

"Got anything stronger than coffee?"

I grin at her. "Sure do."

I hand her a beer, though I know she meant something stronger than that, but it's not even two in the afternoon.

We catch up. I tell her about how it's been going with Oscar and René more than what I've been able to tell her in brief glimpses at work. I also find myself telling her all about Devyn, our dates, how great I think he is. I don't miss the wary look on her face. "What?" I ask.

"I worry about you."

"He's nothing like Brian."

Carolina sighs "I didn't say he was. Promise me you'll be careful? I couldn't handle seeing you like that again. Dad couldn't handle it."

The mere thought of Don Gustavo's crestfallen face when I hid out at his home after the breakup sends shivers down my spine. There was so much pain in those dark brown eyes when he saw my bandaged nosed and arm in a cast. Until that moment, I hadn't realized I had the capacity to hurt someone so deeply.

"I know." I say, doing my best to hide the sting in my eyes.

"That's one thing about Devyn. He's so patient, Carolina. More than any man I've ever known. He knows about my past—"

"You told him?"

"Not in so much detail—no—but enough for him to know I need to take things slow. He's been so incredibly gentle, and not once has he pressured me into going faster than I'm comfortable with."

"So, you haven't …" Carolina trails off. Those incredibly thick brows waggle up and down suggestively.

I laugh. "No."

"Not once? And you've dated all summer."

"Pretty much. I mean, we make out and stuff, but he understands I'm barely opening up to the possibility of dating … and sex … will take a while."

"And he's okay with that?"

"He's incredible. You can stop worrying, I swear."

Her hands go up in surrender. "Okay. Okay. I think this time around, I'm more worried about your heart."

"My heart?"

"Yes. Living with Ramiro, so close to each other, and dating Devyn."

The sweat from the beer bottle cools my hands as I blink at her. "What does Ramiro have to do with anything?"

She lets out that silky, tequila laugh of hers. "Oh, gee, I don't know, that you've been in love with him for the better part of a decade?"

Mortified, I drop my eyes to the table between us, my face feeling a million degrees hot. "How long have you known?" I ask her.

"Since the second you laid eyes on him."

"Oh my god! Was it that obvious?"

She reaches with one hand to palm the back of mine. "You wear your emotions not just on your sleeve, but on your face. I don't think you can help it."

"Does everyone know?" I ask, wondering if my skin is turning green with how sick I'm starting to feel.

Her smile then is half amused, half sad. "Yes. Well, everyone except Ramiro. Though I'm sure he suspects. I always assumed that's why he tried to avoid you so much."

"I want to bury my head in the sand and never come up for air again."

"It's not a big deal, Sara. And for what it's worth, I always thought he was a damn fool for not seeing it—or not wanting to see it."

Carolina doesn't get a chance to say hi to the boys. By the time they get home, she's already gone to check on Don Gustavo and head back to her place for the night.

Rene comes into the house with his sweats torn at the knees, caked in more dirt than I'm prepared to fight in the laundry room. But it's his face, stony and upset, that gives me pause.

"René?"

He says nothing and runs up the stairs. "What happened?" I ask Oscar and Ramiro as they, too, walk into the house.

"Ramiro kicked his ass at soccer. It was so cool," Oscar says.

"Language," both Ramiro and I scorn the little guy. Then we smile at each other, at what a united front we have established when it comes to co-parenting these guys.

"Sorry," Oscar says, his lip trembling a little.

"I forgive you," I say, and brush his hair away from his forehead. "How did you do?"

"I don't like running," Oscar says.

"But you walked around the field a bit. It's nice to move our legs a little, isn't it?" Ramiro asks.

Oscar shrugs. "I guess. I don't have to go again, do I?"

Ramiro laughs. "No, buddy. Not if you don't like it. But we do have find something active that you like to do."

"You liked swimming, didn't you?" I ask him, and that definitely piques his interest.

He nods. "Swimming is awesome. But it's too cold now."

"We can find an indoor pool if you want to keep swimming off-season," Ramiro says.

Oscar gasps, incredulous. "Really?"

"Yeah, we'll look into it. Why don't you go wash up when your brother gets out of the shower?"

"Okay."

When Oscar is gone, Ramiro goes through some of the bags on the table. "All this is for the ofrenda?"

"Yeah, I think so. I thought I'd wait for you guys before getting all the stuff out."

"I'll go wash up too then," he says before leaving me alone.

As he walks away, I try too hard not to look at his perfect butt in those grass-stained joggers or how sweaty and dirty he looks. When I'm alone, I wonder why I have to work so hard to not think of him, and even harder to think of Devyn instead.

Time.

I just need a little time.

"It's not even November," René whines as Oscar and I empty all the contents. Calaveras, picture frames, sugar skulls, fake flower arrangements, and vases for them. He flicks a flower petal like it's a bug.

"No, but I thought we could start thinking about what we want to put on the altar. You can remember your mom, and pay respect any time of year, not just November."

René slumps in his chair, and it's Ramiro who tries to steer the conversation. "So, how does it work?"

"Can you get some pictures of Francisca printed?" I ask.

"Yeah. I have some upstairs, actually," he says and disappears for a few minutes before coming back with a small box full of pictures of Francisca and the boys. Some with Doña Pancha.

"Maybe Oscar and René can pick their favorites and put them in the frames?"

"What's the point, though?" René asks, still fighting this.

Ramiro nods at me, and I try to explain what Mandy told me at work over lunch. I hope I understood this right. "On the Day of the Dead, our loved ones go on a journey to visit us. It's a long journey for them. We'll want to make their favorite food and drinks to place on the altar to receive them with." I turn to look at Oscar. "Do you remember what your mom's favorite food was?"

He thinks for a moment, then nods. "Chocolate!"

"Great. We'll go pick up her favorites at the store—"

"This is stupid," René shouts when he stands, sending his chair falling backward. When it thuds on the floor, we all startle.

"René!"

"She's dead," he says, almost in a whisper now. His eyes glassy. "She's not coming back. It doesn't matter how many photos we have of her, or how many candles, or how many of her favorite foods. She's dead, and she can't come back." With that, René leaves us, stunned, in the kitchen.

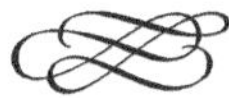

CHAPTER 14

"You know your brother gets angry because he misses your mom, don't you?" Ramiro asks the youngest boy in the house.

"Yeah," Oscar says with a little pout.

"He misses her," Ramiro says.

Oscar nods that time but says nothing.

"I miss her too," Ramiro says. "And so does everyone who loved her—Pancha, Gustavo, and Sara. We all miss her so much."

"I know," Oscar says. "I forgive him." He fiddles with the remote controller to his game but doesn't turn it on. We didn't tell him he couldn't. I think his heart isn't even in the video game, when I know his heart is always in the video game.

"Ah buddy," I say. "Different people handle bad situations— or sad situations—differently. Ramiro sleeps. I cry. René …"

"Explodes?" Ramiro offers and we both laugh, making Oscar share the tiniest of smiles.

"Yeah," I say. I run my finger through Oscar's hair, pushing it to the side as I've done so many times before. "He gets angry. Sometimes I do too. It isn't fair." I pause to give Oscar the time to think and speak, but he just shrugs. "Are you feeling better since watching that movie at your friend's house?"

"Yeah. It's just a cartoon," he says, shrugging it off.

"I think it's an important cartoon, though. It's about important traditions. I think we should try them, don't you?"

Ramiro smiles at me, telling me with that warm gaze he is grateful we're having this conversation with Oscar. His presence is reassuring to me, and I know mine is to him.

Parenting is hard.

So difficult that I can't imagine having to do this alone—without a partner to share the responsibility. It is special, and you get to watch these little humans grow in real time. The beauty is unfathomable until you experience it. But for its many gifts, how did Francisca ever do it alone? I guess she always had her mother, and the boys did have two parents, but I just know that having a man telling them their feelings are okay must mean the world to them.

I thought René would return to his outbursts, but he's grown quiet and pensive. So pensive. He seems so much older than the ten-year-old boy he is.

When Don Gustavo asks to take the boys for the weekend, I couldn't be more grateful. He claims to want to have a watch party for an important soccer game, but I know he's seen how tired Ramiro and I have been lately and wants to give us a break before fall break when we'll have them full time.

A break is well deserved, and I decide to ask Devyn out on a date, whom I've neglected lately with my busy schedule.

"I'm sorry," he says when I call him. "I'm at a poker game tonight, but I'd love to take you out tomorrow night if you're free."

"It's a date. See you Saturday." I hang up just as Ramiro gets home.

"Where are the boys?" Ramiro asks.

"Don Gustavo's. The game, remember?"

"Oh, yeah."

"You going to watch it with them?"

"Honestly, I could use a break too."

Grabbing my beer, I push off my chair. "I'll get out of your hair, then." I'm about to head to my room and pick up my book that I've hardly gotten to read lately, when Ramiro's voice stops me.

"Sara, you don't have to go—"

"I thought you said you could use a break. I don't want to be a bother."

He rubs the back of his head, those thick biceps bulging as he sighs. "You're not a bother. I'd love the company if you'd like to have that beer with me."

"You don't have to—"

"I'm not. I don't remember the last time it was just the two of us. Talking."

This gives me pause. We've never had that kind of friendship. Thinking back on the last eight years, I don't think I've ever been in the same room alone with him. At least not purposefully, and definitely not for a one-on-one chat. "Never," I say with determination—sure of my answer.

"What?"

"It's never been just the two of us talking."

He laughs, then stops when he sees the earnestness tightening my mouth. "What? Never?"

I shake my head. "Not unless Don Gustavo, Carolina, or someone else was around."

"That can't be right."

"It is. Until very recently, you hated me," I say, without an ounce of resentment. It's a fact, like the sky is blue, avocado is the best food in the world, and that I love Ramiro.

There's no way to tell this man, when he's standing in front of me, asking for something he thinks is so simple, to share a beer, when it's anything but. How do I remind him how much of an annoyance I was to him? Because there's no other name for what Ramiro has always felt about me.

I want to, though—to remind him how he only ever spent time with me if Carolina was also around. How he would spin around the minute he saw me if I was alone in a room. I don't think he ever hated me. I'd always felt like that family member you tolerate because they're family, but you sometimes wondered how amazing it would be if you could choose your family.

After a pause that seems to last forever, Ramiro lets out a long exhale. "I've never hated you, Sara," he says. "But I am sorry if I ever made you feel that way."

Before I can think better of it, the question comes flying out of my mouth. "Why?"

"Why what?" He asks.

"Why did you avoid me? I believe you if you're telling me you didn't hate me. But you did avoid me. Why? What did I ever do to make you—"

"You did nothing, Sara." He takes a series of deep breaths. "Fuck," he says, but the word is soft and gentle. "Back then, I was being stubborn about ..."

I smile, a bit sadly, but mostly with understanding. "About Carolina?"

"Yeah. I thought I loved her."

"Thought? Past tense?"

Ramiro nods, pacing the length of the living room, trying, I can tell, to find the words to express himself. "I wasn't. I didn't know what love was. That was ... childish infatuation."

Then, like everything else that has ever been important,

understanding dawns on me. "You know because you love Francisca."

Ramiro's eyes glisten the next time he looks at me, then he sniffs the tears back. "Yeah. I loved her, and when I fell in love with her, I realized that what I'd had for Carolina wasn't even a fraction of that feeling."

"She taught you how to love." I reflect his thoughts, trying to understand.

"What?"

"Francisca—she taught you how to love."

Ramiro laughs a watery sort of laugh. "Yeah. If you want to put it that way."

As much as Ramiro has revealed about himself tonight, I don't for one second forget that he never exactly answered why he's always avoided me. I want to press on, to get to the bottom of his indifference to me. I want to know why he never talked to me—really talked to me—until this year when he needed help and he so adamantly declared that I was the only person who could help him. So instead, I try to return the conversation to the last place I remember being neutral.

"But yeah," I say. "It's never been just us."

"Well, let's change that, then. Unless, uh, you need a break from me?"

I retake my chair and he looks at my near-empty bottle. "Need another one of those?" He asks.

"Sure."

Ramiro heads to the kitchen, and I hear the refrigerator open and close before he joins me in the living room again.

"So how come you're not out with Devyn tonight?"

I smile at him, thankful for the change in conversation. "He's at a poker game."

A small sound escapes him, something that sounds like a snort, before he sips his drink.

"What?" I nudge his thigh with my socked foot.

"Idiot. He's an idiot."

"I didn't call him till he was already out."

"I would have left that game so fast."

It's my turn to snort, but Ramiro has the decency not to comment. He knows he'd never give me the time of day, so I'm not really sure where this line of thinking is coming from.

Instead, I decide to steer the conversation into safer territory.

"Can I ask you something?"

"Anything," he says.

"Both your parents are hotshot lawyers. You never thought of going to law school like them?"

"Ah," he says like he's been expecting the question. "That. I did think about it. That was the future they outlined for me. And I got on that conveyer belt for them, out of gratitude, out of obedience, or obligation, I don't know, but I did."

"What do you mean?"

"I went to law school. I finished the first year, and that summer, I decided I wasn't going back."

"I'm sure that was hard."

"Harder on them than it was on me, I think."

"Do you regret it? Not going back?"

"I have, before. Not sure I do anymore."

"Any particular reason you're being so vague? You know, you can always just say"—I lower my voice and twist my expression into a disapproving one— "'Sara, it's none of your business.'"

He laughs, cupping the back of his neck. "Was that supposed to be me?"

"What? That was such a good, and accurate, imitation of you," I tease. "Now, why are you being so evasive tonight?"

"It's just … I'm not used to this. Honest conversation like this." He stops to motion between us. "My parents are great in many ways, but never … open like you are."

"You can always be honest with me. I'd never judge you."

He smiles at me briefly before fixing his eyes back on the bottle in his hands as he picks at the label. "I always knew I wanted to work with my hands. It wasn't really about liking cars, necessarily. I could have been a carpenter, a plumber, a potter. It didn't matter, I just know my hands have to be busy for me to feel … at ease."

"I see."

"College was hard, but that year in law school, when I had no time except to push pen over paper, sucked the soul right out of me."

"Doesn't sound like you regret it at all," I say, with an encouraging smile he won't see because he still can't look at me.

"I don't regret what I do, Sara. I love being a mechanic. I love the people I work with. I make a decent living, and my hands stay busy so I can stay happy."

"Then why does it sound like you're apologizing for being you?"

"It's … feeling like a disappointment all the damn time."

"You're not—"

"I know. But I saw it in the way my parents would look at me when I got home all greasy after a long day of work. In how Carolina never saw me. Not really. She only ever saw the dirty mechanic who worked for her father."

"You know that's not true."

"Isn't it? She went on to fall in love with one of the world's most renowned doctors. I wondered often, before Francisca, if I were a hotshot lawyer like my parents, would she have seen me any differently?"

"You know that's not Carolina," I say defending my sister because I know in my heart that's not what she was thinking.

"Maybe it's easier for me to think that than to think she could just never love me for no reason at all." He stops to smile, then looks up at me. "That's why I fell so hard for Francisca. For the first time in my life, someone actually looked at me and really saw me. I finally … mattered."

"You've always mattered, Ramiro." I don't add that he's always mattered to me. That I've always looked at him like that. That I've always seen him for the wonderful man that he is.

I also don't tell him he never noticed because he was always too busying looking at Carolina.

"I know. Maybe I just have this complex of never feeling good enough. Not good enough for my high-achieving parents, or my high-achieving crush." He pauses, rubbing his chin for a few seconds. "Is being ordinary really all that bad? I don't feel like it is. I'm happy—or I feel like I should be happy—with the life I've made for myself."

"No. Being ordinary isn't bad at all," I say, and I mean it. "Small dreams are just as valid as big ones. I should know."

Safety. Wanting a quiet life means safety to me. The closest I've come to that is when I'm with Carolina and Don Gustavo. Once I would have envisioned that quiet life with Ramiro. Could I push myself to envision it with Devyn now?

When I was that little girl in the hospital bed, I didn't gravitate to the doctors who spent precious small minutes with me. I clung to the nurses who held my hand. So, I never desired to be a doctor. I didn't have big dreams, not in the way that Carolina did. And it's not that I'm any less ambitious than she is. It's that my ambition is for a happy, safe life with a loving family of my very own instead of one that took me in out of pity.

As much as I adore Don Gustavo and Carolina, I want a family of my very own. One I can claim and build from scratch myself.

"You'd be happy?" he asks out of nowhere. "With a quiet life? Just comfort and love?"

Our eyes lock and for a moment he seems to be asking so much more. Some secret meaning only he knows, dissipated in his words, stretched so far, I can't decipher it. "Ramiro, that's the goal."

Several drinks later, we're both in tipsy territory. Our conversation turns less serious, and I'm surprised—relieved—that Ramiro seems to be a happy drunk. He blasts salsa music, pushes the coffee table to the side, and stands in front of me holding out his hand.

I shake my head. "Don Gustavo has been teaching me, but I'm terrible, and the alcohol won't help."

"All you need is a good lead. Come on. I can keep up your lessons." An echo of Devyn's words on our first date flashes through my tipsy, hazy brain. Why does this feel so different? It's more intimate, somehow.

Without hearing another word of protest from me, Ramiro pulls me up to him. With clumsy balance, I crash, not so softly, to his chest. His rock-hard chest that he works on daily. He doesn't make it weird when I linger there too long, with my cheek nestled over his sternum, taking in the manly smell of leather and musk. Why can't I force my skin to sing like this when I'm in Devyn's arms?

After a long moment, I pull away, and he expertly spins me. His body commands mine. With his hands, he pushes, pulls, and turns me in such a way that my body is never confused as to where to go next. Confident jerks and tugs guide me with confidence.

I should be losing my balance in this tipsy state of mine, but instead, I feel graceful. Led by his expert handling of my body to the rhythm of an upbeat song, I envision us from an outside perspective. Looking from the outside in, I'd guess this woman, who is me, to be an expert salsa dancer.

The song changes, and it's a bachata. Evil bachata that is too sensual for its own good. I gulp because I know the sensual way bachata is intended to be danced. How close bodies get together to sway side to side.

He takes me into his arms, so close our bodies are flush. It's hard pushing away memories of how I danced with Devyn like this on our first date. It didn't feel like this. It's not butterflies in my stomach like what I read about, or like what songs croon about. It's a thumping in my chest that feels almost painful from the longing.

I need this with Devyn. I need to find a way to feel this for him and stop reacting this way to Ramiro. I can't go on loving him.

I'm done.

I step away from him, head to the Bluetooth speaker, and shut off the music, my face suddenly serious.

"What's wrong?" Ramiro asks when I turn to face him again.

I blink at him and trace my gaze down his body. His signature ribbed black tank, those jeans low on his hips. I settle on his bare feet, unable to look him in the eye.

"Ramiro—" I take a deep breath for bravery. Just like he once asked me to cover up more around him, to stop tempting his body with mine, I need to ask him the same, only I need to ask him to stop tempting my heart.

We need boundaries.

Now.

I don't know that you get to choose who to love, but I know that I need to try.

"What is it?" He reaches, trying to take my hand, but I pull back, shaking my head.

"We need some … uh, boundaries."

"It's just dancing, Sara—"

I shake my head and force myself to look him in the eye. "No. I mean it is, just dancing, but I had feelings for you—"

"Had?"

I nod. This is it. Eight years coming to a head. "For a long time. And I tried to stop. I tried harder when you got engaged. It's not working out so great," I say with a nervous smile.

"You don't have to stop, Sara." He takes a step forward, and I another one back, keeping the distance between us, keeping out of his reach.

"I do. I need to stop. I like Devyn. So much. I think we could be great together, but I need to stop ..."

"Having feelings for me?"

I lift my chin and make myself taller to deliver to the undeniable truth. I can no longer lie to myself—to him. "I need to stop loving you."

"You think you can?" Ramiro asks, not a trace of anger—or smugness—to his voice. "You've loved me for so long."

My fake strength giving way, I stumble a step back when I nearly lose my balance. "You knew?"

He scratches the back of his neck. "I ... suspected. I mean, I thought you had a crush. I didn't think you loved me, though. Maybe that's why I kept my distance back then. Didn't want to give you false hope. But, Sara, now—"

"Good," I say, "That's good. Keep doing that. Don't give me false hope. Keep your distance. We need boundaries. I need a chance with Devyn. A real one. Please."

Ramiro looks like he's about to say something, but then he stops himself, his mouth setting into an unforgiving taut line.

That's enough bravery for one night. Before he can open his mouth to say anything else, I hightail it to my room.

CHAPTER 15

When I get to work on Monday morning, the nurse manager of my unit, Leah, asks me for a meeting and leads me to the conference room, the closest thing she has to an office. Great way to start my week.

I think through all my patients from last week. For the most part, everything went smoothly. Nothing that happened recently would warrant a trip to her office, I decide.

Our unit is lucky to have Leah as a manager. She's strict but pairs it with the empathy of someone who started her career at the very bottom as a nursing assistant.

So, getting called into her office is particularly worrisome because it happens so rarely. It means something.

A soon as I take a seat across from her, she smiles at me, but it's a bit tight.

"Sara, what's going on with you?"

"What do you mean?"

"When you went into your master's program, you had goals to be promoted. Isn't that what we talked about when you decided to go back to school?"

I remember the conversation we had about my career goals. At the time, Leah had been extremely supportive.

"That's still true," I admit.

Leah nods. "I guess I just assumed once you graduated, you'd take on more. Volunteer for more opportunities to lead. To take on more shifts, tougher cases. If anything, you seem to be cutting down to the bare minimum of time and shifts."

"I'm sorry. It's been rough since spring. I promise I'll get it together—"

"You don't have to tell me if it's personal, but I'd like to help if I can. What can I do to help you succeed at Heartland Metro?"

Bosses like this are so rare. I know this. And it warms my heart how invested she is in my success. "I don't mind telling you. I guess I've always wanted to separate work life and home life, be professional, but ..."

"But?"

"I'm spread a little thin."

"You know you can tell me anything, right?" Leah says, an encouraging smile on her mouth.

"I promise it's temporary," I say. "We had a death in the family last spring, and since then I've been co-parenting two little boys with their stepdad. It's been ... a little rough."

"I'm so sorry, Sara. But why didn't you tell me? You could have had bereavement time. We could have—"

"I guess I didn't want you to think I was cutting back when I was supposed to be stepping up."

"Oh, Sara. I wish you'd told me. I'd never hold life events against your career goals. And you're a mom now?"

I laugh, and then something bitter tightens my throat. I clear my throat before I speak again. "No. I promised their stepdad I'd help for a year, help them stay afloat, but it's temporary."

"I see. That's why you took time off in the spring."

"Yes. And I'm sorry I'm not stepping up—"

"No, it's not a judgment. You should have told me. We could have found a way to get you maternity leave."

"They're not my kids," I start to argue, and that uncomfortable tightness in my throat spreads to my stomach. What's going on here?

"If you're co-parenting, even temporarily, you're a parent. Foster parents are parents."

I smile at that. I'm so lucky to have Leah as my mentor. Then I tell her everything—or mostly everything. I tell Leah about Ramiro and Francisca, and how much of a hard time René and Oscar, but especially René, are having. She listens, at one point she takes my hand in hers to pat it for a moment. I also confess how I wish Ramiro would let me take the boys to therapy, and how I've been going myself to cope with it all.

Leah listens. Really listens, with the empathy of a phenomenal nurse.

"Good. I'm glad you're getting counseling. If you need to use sick time for appointments, please prioritize that. Give me enough notice to get in some floaters, and we'll have your back." She pauses, and when I say nothing, she continues. "Listen, I was a little worried. I think I'll be retiring soon—"

"No, Leah—"

"It's not for a little while yet. But I'm glad I know now. I'd been hoping to nominate you to be manager when I retire, but before I knew your situation, I was doubting my choice."

I gulp. She changed her mind. Of course, she changed her mind. She's right. I've been taking more and more vacation days. I leave early often when I need to pick up the boys from school. I used to volunteer all the time to pick up shifts for others, and I no longer have the luxury of time to do that. I've neglected my career.

My patients still get my undivided attention, and I'm still doing a good job, but it's not enough, is it? I'm not going above and beyond like someone who is aiming for a promotion.

"If I'm no longer in the running, Leah, I understand—"

"That's not what I'm saying. I was a young mom once too. I wish I'd had a boss who understood. Keep on as you're going. Stick to the day shift on weekdays, use as many of your vacation days as you need. It's what they're there for."

"We're so short-staffed though—"

Leah chortles with a laugh. "This profession has always been, and will continue to be, one of the most short-staffed fields. Why should that mean we can't have lives? We'll manage. Work will always be here, especially for good nurses. When does your arrangement end? You said next spring?"

"Yeah. April, or thereabouts. I have a better idea, though," I say, a bit embarrassed I haven't thought of it before now.

"What is it?" Leah asks.

"Put me on the night shift."

Her lips purse. "I'm not so sure. You'll be invisible to upper management, which will make it harder for me to sell you as my replacement."

"Just temporarily, until I move out of my current situation. Until April."

I should have really thought of this before. I used to love the night shift and only moved to the day when Leah and I started planning for my future career more deliberately.

Nights are quieter, and as much as I hate to say this, we don't have to deal with the doctors a lot. Rounds start after we leave in the morning and the day nurses show up. But what I love most about the night shift is that's when I feel that I make the most difference.

At night, after visiting hours are over and patients are at their most lonely, vulnerable, and scared, it's when they need nurses the most. Sitting by the bed of a convalescing patient, holding their hand in the quiet of the hospital at night, was the most rewarding part of my career to date. I only let it go when I decided to work more closely with Leah and have her mentor me. As much as I've enjoyed being her protégé, I've missed that feeling of doing something that matters even more.

"Can't say I won't miss you, but that plan actually makes a lot of sense," Leah says.

"It does. And it's temporary."

"Okay, we can have another check-in when it's time to transition you back onto days. There're still a few years left in these old bones."

My eyes brim with tears. Leah trained me. This was my first job straight out of college, and Leah has mentored me the entire time. I can't imagine the oncology unit without her. "Leah," I breathe out.

"No. It's okay, love. I'm looking forward to spending some time with my grandbabies. And when I leave, you are going to be promoted. You're the best nurse I've ever trained."

My tears do spill then. I've always been professional with Leah, but thinking about this unit without her, I can't help but take her into my arms. "I can't imagine this hospital without you."

"You'll be here. I trained you, and now you will lead the hospital into its next phase. It's how it works. You'll train other nurses, and one day, you'll pass the baton too. But for now, you prioritize your family and your boys. And stop trying to be so needlessly strong. Tell me when you need an extra hand."

I step away from her, dabbing the corners of my eyes with my fingers. As if the universe has some twisted sense of humor, my cell goes off in my pocket at exactly that moment. When I glimpse at the screen, it's the boys' school. I'm mortified, but also, somehow relieved we just had this conversation. "I'm so sorry," I say. "It's the school. I might have to pick one of them up."

Leah laughs. "Go. Go. We'll cover you."

"I'm sorry."

"Don't be. If those little boys are grieving, they need you more than ever."

We stand, and for the second time in my professional life, I reach over and hug Leah, taking her by surprise. She wraps an arm around me and rubs my back. I have a flashback to that little girl with burnt legs, to the nurse who held her hand at her bedside.

Nurses are the best.

CHAPTER 16

FALL

After picking up René, I text Ramiro to let him know he has been suspended for the week. I'm horrified I need to take up Leah on her offer of using more vacation days so quickly. Maybe I can split the time with Ramiro and Don Gustavo. Somehow, we'll make it work.

The principal told me René and another boy got into a fight during a basketball game in gym class.

On our ride home, I try to get answers out of René about the fight, but he stays quiet, staring out the window, his face still twisted in anger.

In the afternoon, I meet Oscar at the bus stop, and when we get back to the house, René is still in his room, where he's been all day. He won't say a word. He didn't come out even for lunch, and I'm getting more and more worried about what happened during that gym class.

I'm doing the dishes when Ramiro gets home, slams the door, and shouts René's name. The shouting startles me so much, the plate in my soapy hands slips out of my fingers.

It shatters on the floor, and Oscar comes running to check on me.

"Stay back," I tell him, as I stand between him and the broken glass. "Don't come into the kitchen until I clean this up."

"René!" Ramiro shouts again, and both Oscar and I wince.

"Ramiro, calm down." I try to soothe him, even if my voice is shaking to match my shaking hands.

"René!" he roars again, completely ignoring me. René comes downstairs, his lids puffy like he's been crying. "You got suspended?" His shouting makes all three of us wince now.

"Ramiro," I say soothingly again. "Please stop shouting."

He turns that murderous glare at me. "I'm grateful, Sara, for your help. But you are not their mother. Just this once, you need to stop overstepping." That last part, he yelled again.

Not their mother. Yeah—I know that. It doesn't sting any less having it thrown at my face.

Oscar's chin trembles, and he's clinging to my shirt until René walks over to him so that Oscar can grab his hand instead.

"You got suspended?" Ramiro shouts, and now even René seems like he's about to cry, though his eyes remain murderous as he glares daggers at Ramiro.

I turn to them and do my best to smile. "Guys, can you please go next door to Don Gustavo's?"

"No!" Ramiro snaps. "We're going to talk about this!"

"You're not talking, Ramiro. You're shouting." I turn to the boys, and mouth, 'go' at them. They don't hesitate before they dash out of the house.

Ramiro stares at the door René just slammed shut, then turns to look at me. "Did I not just tell you to stop overstepping? Didn't we agree to be a united front? You just went against me!"

"Ramiro," I say calmly, "I need you to stop shouting." I do my best to take deep breaths and count to ten, calming myself in hopes of de-escalating the situation.

"Damn it, Sara! This is none of your business." He slams his hands on the counter, making me jump.

My hands are still soapy and shaky as I try to dry them with the tea towel hanging from the oven's handle. I've just finished cleaning the kitchen, and I can't see anything on any surface that I could use to defend myself. A rolling pin would be nice right about now.

Feeling unprotected, with nothing between Ramiro and me, I hyperventilate, and my heart feels like it's going to burst straight out of my chest. I grip the granite countertop in front of me. My fingers are shaky as I try to open a drawer, searching for anything I can use if he attacks me. It's not just my fingers shaking—my entire body shakes like a brittle, fragile thing. And I hate it. I hate my body for betraying me. Shouldn't there be a fight-or-flight switch in these situations? Instead, my body freezes in fear, and for the second time in my life, I'm afraid of the man I've placed all my trust in.

"Sara?" his voice is calmer now as he takes in my shortened breaths. "What's wrong?" The deep lines from his forehead smooth out as his eyes soften.

I hurry to duck and open the cabinet where I'd just put away a large frying pan and grab it. Clutching the handle to my chest, I try to make myself tall, but it's hard with my lungs constricting so much they're hardly letting any air in.

It's hard to breathe. So freaking hard.

"Ramiro," I say his name between wheezes, "please stop shouting."

"Sara," he whispers, then steps forward, reaching for me. His eyes fall to my hands where they're tightening their grip on the pan handle while I try to take a step back, but I can't because the counter is right behind me.

The scene is so familiar, bile rises in my throat, and I push it down. If I'm in danger, the last thing I need to do right now is vomit. The panic attack at the amusement park was nothing compared to this one. Everything in this room reminds me of that day.

It happened in a kitchen, with so many hard and painful surfaces that caught the full weight of my body.

The sound of bone cracking and the blinding pain that seared through my forearm. I'm not here at Ramiro's house anymore. I'm at my old apartment, and it's not Ramiro's eyes I'm looking into, but Brian's dark ones, molten with rage. An uncomfortable spicy smell attacks my nostrils from the cinnamon whiskey he drank all the time.

"Sara, I think you're having a panic attack."

I peer up at him, the pan clutched to my chest. His face has gone completely relaxed. The crease between his brows is gone, and his jaw is nice and round, with no rigidness to it. He brings up his hands in front of him, palms spread wide, and takes a step back and away from me. He ducks, making himself physically small when he searches my eyes.

"Sara, I'm not going to hurt you. I'd never ..."

His eyes are glassy again. I've only seen that once before. At the funeral—and now. Two times when Ramiro Jimenez has been on the brink of tears.

For me?

"Sara, I'm going to step closer to you. Is that okay?"

I nod, still clutching the pan, still unable to breathe or let go of my grip on the handle.

"Can I touch you please?" he asks. I nod. With a soft touch, Ramiro caresses my arm, then leads his hand to mine, where he gently unfurls my fingers and nudges the pan from my hands. He sets it on the counter next to us.

His hand goes to my back, where he rubs small circles. "Try to take deep breaths, Sara. It's me. Ramiro. I'd never hurt you."

His words return me to the here and now, and I grip the greasy coveralls he's still wearing. I pinch the hard fabric between my fingers, hoping it grounds me. It's Ramiro. It's Ramiro. It's Ramiro.

Not Brian.

Brian always smelled like sharp cinnamon whiskey, uncomfortably spicy. I get close to Ramiro's chest to get a whiff of that comforting garage grease smell he always brings home. What Don Gustavo smells like so often. A smell I've associated with safety for the entirety of my adult life.

My heart rate slows, and the desire to vomit vanishes, leaving only my tears to stream freely. When my diaphragm relaxes, and my lungs can fully expand so I can finally gulp precious air, I get lightheaded.

I bring my hand to my head, pressing firmly against my temples.

"What's wrong?" Ramiro asks, his voice still buttery soft.

"I'm getting lightheaded."

"Oh," he says. "I'm going to touch you again, okay?" He asks.

I nod, and Ramiro ducks to place one arm under my knees, the other behind my upper back, and like a child, carries me to the couch.

He sits, leaving me on his lap, and I nuzzle into his body. Ramiro rubs my back, pets my hair, kisses the top of my head. He whispers over and over, "You're okay. You're okay." I grip to his shirt tightly, and his arms tighten around me like a comforting weighted blanket. I feel so safe, so different from how I felt only seconds ago.

"I'm sorry I shouted, Sara. I'm so fucking sorry," he says in a gentle whisper. "But please believe me, I'd never hurt you, or René, or Oscar. I know I'm a big guy, but I'd never throw my weight around my family to feel like a man. I am not that man. I'm not Brian—"

When he invokes his name out loud, I push away from him so I can look into Ramiro's eyes. They're so close to letting those tears loose, so red and puffy. "I know you're not Brian," I say in a voice so breathy I'm embarrassed at my own weakness. I clear my throat. "I just had a panic attack, that's all. I know you wouldn't hurt me," I say, because it's the truth.

How could I, for one second, have thought Ramiro would lay a finger on me or the boys? This is Ramiro, the most caring and compassionate man I've ever known. The man who pulled Oscar back at the funeral when he had his own panic attack. The man who promised to always be there.

Tonight was the first time Ramiro Jimenez raised his voice in my presence.

And for the rest of our lives, it would be the last.

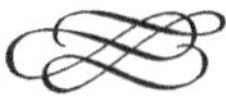

CHAPTER 17

We never get the full story out of René about what happened in that gym class that set him off so much he got physical with his classmate. What he does tell us, though, is that another kid on his team was upset he missed a shot during the basketball game and made a comment about René. What that comment was, I think will stay with René. He will carry it and let it fester and grow and not talk about it.

Exactly as he was taught.

Again, I'm tempted to beg Ramiro to get all three of them into grief counseling, but I don't. This time, for a different reason. Even if every nucleus in every cell in my body knows he would never hurt me, there's the tiniest hint of fear left in me. So maybe I'm a little afraid my request for therapy will lead to a fight. It's unfair to him. He doesn't deserve for me to be afraid of him. Maybe it's fear of another panic attack more than it is fear of him, or his large, imposing size, but fear, nonetheless.

Instead of forcing Ramiro into something he clearly does not want to do, I keep working on myself. Because in the end,

I'm not the best equipped person to help others if I don't help myself first.

After explaining all the big changes in our lives, my counselor agrees that a Day of the Dead ofrenda would be an excellent step in dealing with the boys' grief. Even for Ramiro. So, when Día de Muertos comes around, Oscar and I spend quite a bit of time making the ofrenda.

He seems to enjoy the crafting part of it. Gluing together a collage of pictures of his mom and painting the wooden frames. It's therapeutic for him, I think, to create something out of nothing, or maybe to create something out of his pain that he believes his mom would like very much.

René is surly as he watches us but doesn't have another outburst. I think he understands his little brother needs this—this connection to a memory he's already admitted he's afraid of losing.

Oscar and I pick our favorite photos to frame, and we set a tablecloth over a small table in the living room. He picked out dark red carnations at the flower shop because he said his mom's favorite color was red.

Her favorite food? Chocolate and arroz con leche. I'm glad it's something I actually know how to make, and I make a big pot of the rice pudding with Don Gustavo's secret ingredients—lemon peel, cardamom, coconut milk, and star anise. Don Gustavo brings over tamales. He told us he could swear Francisca could smell his tamales from down the street like a hound and would show up at his house with a beggar's plate. He knew to always make extra for her. René remembers because he always ate some of the yummy tamales.

I pick up Doña Pancha to join us for this memorial to her daughter. It's a little strange doing this when Francisca hasn't been gone a year yet, but Oscar is desperate not to forget her. Doña Pancha is the ever-flowing fountain of Francisca-starring stories, so her role tonight is critical.

I don't invite Devyn to the celebration. René won't warm up to him no matter what I do, and Ramiro, though cordial, still gives him a cold shoulder.

And at the heart of it all, he's not part of this family. I'm hopeful one day he could be, but his role is not here with us tonight.

"Did I ever tell you," Doña Pancha says as she sets down a bottle of tequila on the altar, "the story of the day Oscar was born?"

Ramiro, Oscar, René, and I all say "no" at the same time and stare at her until her eyes turn to gaze at her youngest grandchild. A bit of a mischievous smile upturns the corners of her mouth.

"René was little, so I dropped him off with Gustavo," Doña Pancha starts. She taps Oscar's little nose. "You weren't due for a week yet."

"He came early?" I ask.

She nods. "He sure did. And we know why."

"Why?" Oscar asks, completely enthralled with his very own origin story.

In a conspiratorial whisper, she says, "It was a full moon. I got your mom to the hospital just in time. ¿Y sabes qué?" She asks.

"¿Qué?" Oscar asks in a stage whisper to match his grandma's.

"When you were born, you were born with an eyelash down to here." She stops to touch the apple of her cheek. "We had to cut it to match your other lashes. You were so hairy, Oscar. Completely covered in thick, black hair. It was all over. Your back. Your belly. The top of your head. Even on your toes. And you know what else?"

"What?" Oscar asks again, his eyes growing to saucers as the story goes on.

"You know babies are born with no teeth, right?"

Oscar and René both nod.

"Well," Doña Pancha continues, "you were born with a fang!"

At the same time René yells, "No way!" Oscar asks, "Like a wolf?" And his index finger flies to his mouth where he feels the edges of his teeth.

Doña Pancha's right brow lifts as she looks down at her youngest grandchild. She grabs the bottle of tequila, opens it, and pours two shots, one for her daughter, which she sets on the altar, and one for herself. She slams the shot, then she says dryly, "Or like an hombre-lobo."

Oscar laughs. "I'm not a werewolf, buelita," he says in a tone so condescending; he never saw his grandmother's response coming.

With a face that says she's being completely serious, she teases, "That you know of."

Little Oscar's mouth gapes open, and when he has a moment to think about it, he seems absolutely over the moon about this new revelation. "Whoa," he says.

René shakes his head and catches me doing the same, so he doesn't burst his little brother's bubble.

"Do you feel funny around the full moon?" Doña Pancha asks Oscar.

The little boy shakes his head. "I don't know, buelita," he says. "I don't remember." His palm goes to his forehead like he's checking his own temperature. I have to bite both my lips not to laugh, and I glance over at Ramiro, who is doing the same, his fists balled in his jean's pockets with the strain not to laugh.

Doña Pancha pours herself a second shot, downs it, and sets the glass on her daughter's altar. She shrugs. "Well, it probably won't set in until you're a teenager." Then she goes back to the couch where she takes a seat like she's just told the boys about watering her plants.

"What's going to happen when I'm a teenager?" Oscar asks with his little face and big bright eyes full of hope.

"Big changes, buddy," Ramiro says, then changes the subject. "Now, who wants to light the candles?"

We all work to make plates with all of Francisca's favorite foods and place them on the altar. Next, we light the candles, and I hug the boys.

By the time we're done decorating the altar and adding all the food, Oscar is crying freely, looking at pictures of his smiling mom. I'm so proud of him for not having internalized what so many men and boys in this community do. What Ramiro and René have internalized—that they can't cry. So, Ramiro and René stand rigid, with stony faces, pushing down the pain. Oscar holds my hand on one side and Pancha's on the other as she says a prayer for her daughter.

We follow Pancha's prayer with a moment of silence. The candles flicker, and my skin immediately pebbles for some reason I can't understand. Then it hits me.

She's here.

Francisca's presence is all around us. I feel it thick in the air, making the hairs on the back of my neck raise. It's more than the images of her on the table or the smells of her favorite foods. There's a cozy warmth in the room—an intangible, gravitational force that pulls all of us together in an embrace. Ramiro, Oscar, René, Pancha, and me. Like she's sending us a message. *Stay together.* I hear the words in my mind's eye.

But are they Francisca's words? Or is my imagination getting ahead of itself and they are my words? What my heart desires?

Either way, the message is clear: Stay together.

CHAPTER 18

When the ofrenda comes down at the end of the month, all the pictures of Francisca get moved to the boys' room. I've caught René smiling once or twice when he's looking at them. Whether he'd admit to it, the Day of the Dead was healing for René, too. He doesn't seem as angry as he did only days before.

He cracks a smile now and then. An honest-to-god smile, so rare, it lights up the room when it does happen, and my heart soars. This family is healing, slowly, but surely. The idea of leaving them in April makes me so desolate, I avoid thinking about it, and my only comfort is knowing that they will be a little bit better by then.

For the rest of the fall season, I spend as much time as I can with Devyn. Forcing myself to have a life outside of that small family unit in Ramiro's home. Designing a path that I must take when spring comes. I need to start my own life, make my own family, start my own traditions. It's a good time to prioritize myself.

René doesn't ask me to attend his last soccer game, not in so many words. But when he mentions it, trying to play it off as no big deal, just mentioned in passing, I don't miss the glint of hope in his eye.

"Why don't we make it a family thing? Bring Oscar, Don Gustavo, and Doña Pancha?" I ask him.

René shrugs. "Whatever," he says, but there's a hint of a smile there, telling me that the idea makes him extremely happy despite the unaffected tone he insists on using.

"And," Ramiro says, "win or lose, we're going out to eat after. Anywhere René wants."

"Really?" René asks.

"Really."

During the game, René is only a little embarrassed by his family. We're loud. So loud. So much louder than any of the other families. He can count his lucky stars I decided not to invite Mandy. She'd blow the lid right out of this place with her unbelievably loud whistling.

Now that I'm really watching him play, I wish I'd gone to more of his games because René is good. Really good. Even to my inexpert eye, I can sense he has a gift in this sport. I won't say he's the best because of course I'd be biased ... okay, biased or not, he is the best on either team playing.

So good, I think he could do this professionally one day.

Doña Pancha has some lungs on her, and she whistles and hollers every time René scores a goal. As for Don Gustavo? Have you ever heard a Mexican sports announcer on television? How they stretch the 'o' into at least one hundred vowels instead of one? That's what Don Gustavo sounds like anytime the ball connects to the net in favor of our team. And honestly, Ramiro, Oscar and I also add to the madness. We can't help it, even as other parents on the sidelines throw odd looks our way. It only makes me shout even louder.

And Ramiro, Ramiro has gone so far as to have special

jerseys made to match René's. The green and gold jersey displaying the number seventeen reads 'Garcia.'

During halftime, one dad near us walks over to our loud little group to introduce himself. He shakes hands with Ramiro first.

"I'm Tobi," he says. "Number six"—he points to a little redheaded kid— "Patrick. He's my son."

"Nice to meet you, I'm Ramiro. I haven't seen you around."

"I know. Work makes it hard, but my wife, Jacky, never misses a game." Tobi waves at his wife with a smile. A tall woman, with dark brown hair and a cautious smile, waves back from her spot on a lawn chair a few feet away.

Tobi shakes all our hands, then goes to stand next to Ramiro. I watch as René takes a lazy jog to us. "Is number seventeen your son? He's really fantastic. Could do it professionally," Tobi says.

That compliment has me beaming at René as he approaches us. Even more so because René is within earshot and I'm sure he heard it. He also hears Ramiro's response. "Yeah, René. That's my son." Ramiro says it with so much pride, with such a wide smile, it almost brings a tear to my eye.

And maybe it's because Ramiro said it so easily, without a second thought, but I watch as René stops moving. He freezes where he stands, looking between Tobi and Ramiro. I can almost see the gears turning in his head when he blinks. He shakes his head, not like he's angry, but more like he's trying to shake a thought away and saunters up to us.

I hold my breath as I observe him, fully expecting an outburst. For him to yell at Ramiro that he is not his dad. Something.

Anything.

Instead, René surprises us all by not addressing it. As if he didn't hear the exchange, he just comes up to me and asks me for the Gatorade I'm keeping for him in my purse. I hand it to him, and he chugs it before returning to his team and their huddle without so much as a glance at Ramiro.

From the corner of my eye, I watch Doña Pancha place a hand over Ramiro's shoulder. Her hand is wrinkled, liver-spotted, and fragile. Gently, Ramiro pats it with a smile.

Our team won. Of course, we won, with René on our side. He requested pizza and Ramiro even invited Patrick and his parents to join us.

I volunteer to drop off Doña Pancha while the boys head home since René is feeling utterly exhausted and I know he'll get grumpy soon.

We all stayed out far too late celebrating the win. After I get back home, I'm dead on my feet when I'm heading to my room, but soft voices from the boys' room reach me before I pass their door.

"You did a great job today," I hear Ramiro whisper.

"Thanks. I almost felt bad for the other team," René whispers back in that stage whisper of his.

They both snicker, and they must be trying not to wake Oscar.

"Good night, buddy—"

"Ramiro? Wait …"

"What's up?"

There's silence, and I tighten my sweater around my middle with anticipation. I feel guilty for eavesdropping, but if I go by their room now, they'll hear me, and their exchange will be interrupted.

"I, uh …" René trails off, and whatever he wants to say is difficult for him. "I've never had a dad," he says finally.

"I know."

"It was just Mom and Abuela, but our dad … he was never around."

"That's awful, René. He's missing out. Big time. He has no idea."

"Do you think maybe …"

"You know you can tell me anything, right?"

There's a pause, and Ramiro stays quiet, giving René space to formulate his thoughts. After several seconds, René whispers again. "I heard what you told Patrick's dad today."

"Oh yeah? What part?"

"That I'm your son."

"I did tell him that."

"But I'm not your son."

"No. But your mom and I were going to be married. I was going to be her husband, and you and Oscar were going to be my stepsons. I can't be her husband anymore, but I'd still like to be your stepdad. Would that be okay with you?"

"I guess." René pauses for another thoughtful moment. "Is it okay if I call you 'Dad' then?"

"Aww, buddy. Nothing would make me prouder."

"It sounds weird. *Dad*."

Ramiro laughs, but it's a sweet, soft laugh. An encouraging laugh. "It does to me too. I guess we'll just have to get used to it, then, won't we?"

"I guess."

"Night, buddy."

"Night—uh—Dad."

CHAPTER 19

The house is quiet. Too quiet. Even though Ramiro has been great about keeping the boys mostly on the first floor during the day when I've had a night shift on the weekend so I can sleep, it's never *this* quiet. One thing I've learned about children this year, is that if it's too quiet and calm, they're up to something. I jump out of bed, hurry to put on my sneakers, and search for them in their room but they're not there. The first floor is just as eerily calm, and when I hear music from the garage trailing in, I follow it to find Ramiro under the hood of my car.

"What are you doing?" I ask loudly over the music. Ramiro straightens to look at me. He leans to turn the volume down on the Metal Red Day song playing on the Bluetooth speaker.

"Good morning," he says.

"Where are the boys?" I ask.

"Oscar and René have been invited to spend the day at Trevor's," he explains.

"And you're working on my car because …?"

"Maintenance. Getting you ready for winter. Oil change,

antifreeze. I'll need to get you new windshield wipers and some winter tires, but I'll get to that next week."

My chest squeezes a little. Don Gustavo always took care of that for Carolina and me. "Ramiro, you don't have to do that."

"It's nothing," he says, getting back to his work as he keeps chatting. He tosses me a small black remote.

I barely manage to catch it, my brain still foggy from sleep. "What's this?"

"Garage remote. Park here from now on."

"What?" I shake my head. "No, Ramiro. Your gym."

"Just for the winter. I don't want you dealing with the snow, especially now that you're working the night shift, leaving and getting back in the dark. I'd feel better if you park here. I can always move things around if I need to for a workout and put them back."

I want to argue more. To tell him he doesn't need to do this. He does enough with taking care of all the expenses around here. Then I remember it's his day off, and I feel guilty he's working on a car when he should be having time away from cars altogether. But he's smiling and bobbing his head to the sound of his music like this is what he wants to do with his time off anyway, so instead of arguing further, I say "Thank you. It means a lot."

He smiles wide at me. "You're welcome. Check your glove compartment."

"Why?" I ask suspiciously.

"Just check."

I round the car, squeezing past Ramiro and get inside to open the glove compartment. There are two strings of wire with spikes of some sort, and a Velcro strap on each. "Uhh ..." I say, unable to identify the medieval-looking object. "Thanks?"

Ramiro barks out in laughter. "Here." He offers me his hand, and I hand him the object. "Turn to face me," he instructs. I stay seated in the car with my door open, and

Ramiro gets down on one knee. I'd never admit my heart skipped a bit just then. He grabs my ankle gently, lifting it to rest on his other knee for support. He stretches the spiked wire over my shoe and secures it with the Velcro. "See?" he asks.

I shake my head, unable to answer with him so close to me.

"It's for you to wear when there's ice. I hate that you have to walk so far from the parking lot to the hospital. And that uphill must be vicious when we get snow."

I nod, barely remembering when I complained to him that the doctors got all the best parking spots and the nurses always had to trek in or take the shuttle.

"See the spikes here?" he says, "They'll help give your shoes a grip on snow or ice, so you don't fall."

He takes the wire off my shoes, leans forward between me and the wheel to tuck the spiky shoe covers back in the glove compartment. As he retreats, he stops for a second in front of me, focusing on my lips. His veiny forearm rests on the steering wheel, and for a moment, I think he might kiss me, but he doesn't. Instead, he gets out of the car and offers me his hand to help me up.

He clears his throat. "You off today too? Any plans?"

"I am. And no. No plans."

"It's been a long time since we've had a day to ourselves," Ramiro says.

"I do not know what to do with myself," I admit. "What did I ever do for fun before all this?"

"I think you worked your butt off and then decided to get a second degree on top of it."

"You make me sound so boring."

He chuckles. "No. Not boring. Driven."

"Should we get Christmas shopping over with?" I ask, trying to find a task for the day.

"Or ..." Ramiro says as he wipes his hands with a towel. "We could do nothing? Relax. Have the day to ourselves with no responsibilities, just this once."

I mull it over in my head, then I smile at him. I guess we can always take care of the holiday shopping online. It'll be quicker and more incognito if we have the packages delivered next door to Don Gustavo. I can wrap them at his house and the boys will never be the wiser.

"I don't remember the last time I had a day of nothing," I admit.

The house is clean. The boys are gone. It's my rest day, so I really shouldn't run today. I have no homework. Now that I'm scheduled on the night shift and I'm off tonight, I don't even have work at the hospital to occupy my time. With no plan, I head back inside, Ramiro following, and I flop on the couch. With a grin, Ramiro does the same.

To be honest, since I've known him, I've never known Ramiro to take a day like this for absolute, decadent nothingness—at least never in my presence.

"I'm not sure how long I'm going to last sitting," he says, his knee already bouncing.

I laugh. "This was your idea," I say accusingly.

"I've had better ones."

"We can do this. Focus, Jimenez."

"Now what?" He asks after not so much as a minute.

"Conversation?"

"Should we go grab a bite?" He asks.

"That would be doing something, now, wouldn't it?"

"Well, we gotta eat," the overly-hyper man reasons.

I roll my eyes.

"We can order in. Chinese?" he asks.

"I love Chinese food."

"I know, Sara."

Forty minutes later, with our moo shu pork and dumplings

in front of us, we sit cross-legged on the floor on either side of the coffee table.

In complete and utter awkward silence.

"We'll get better at this with practice," I offer, breaking apart my chopsticks to have something to do with my hands.

"Okay. You said conversation. What would you like to know?"

I think about that for a moment. There are a million questions I've come up with over the years that I'd love to ask him, but I decide to start him off with the one I think will be the easiest for him to answer.

"So, I know you went to law school, but I guess I never knew what you majored in for undergrad."

"Criminal justice," he says. "I thought afterward I could be a cop, or maybe go into the Army—"

"With Leo?"

Ramiro smiles through his bite of pork. "Yes. With Leo."

"Then you fell in love with cars?"

"I already had, but I knew I wanted a degree. Figured I'd work for Don Gustavo a few years, save some money, then go from there, but once I got going ... Sara, I love it there. I decided instead to save to one day open up my own place. I've been taking online business classes in my free time. My own garage— that was the plan before ..."

"Before all this?" I offer.

"Yeah. Still is ... just a bit delayed."

Through a half-chewed bite, I tell him, "I doubt Don Gustavo will let you go without a fight. You pretty much already run the place."

"Actually ..." Ramiro says.

"What?"

"Well ... you see ..."

"Spit it out, Jimenez."

"Don't make a big deal out of it because it's not a sure thing, but he's mentioned selling once or twice. And Caro can't know. Not yet."

I sit up straight, more alert now.

"What? Don Gustavo retiring? I never thought I'd see the day."

"It's a ways off still, but if he were interested in selling, I'd love to keep it going."

I stare into space dreamily, and gesture with my hands in the air like I'm reading a sign, "Ramiro's Auto Repair." The mere thought of Ramiro achieving his goal fills me with pride because I know he will. One day, I know he'll be the business owner he wants to be.

He shakes his head. "No. I'd keep the name."

"What? You'd keep it Tavo's?"

"Yeah. His shop has served this community for over thirty years. He built it with his very hands, and I'd want to honor that dedication."

"Well, maybe you can call it Tavo and Son," I suggest without thinking.

"My dad would have a heart attack," Ramiro says before stuffing a dumpling in his mouth.

When I lived in Don Gustavo's for that first year out of college, he'd always come home in his greasy coveralls. He'd ditch his work shoes in the mudroom and head straight for a shower. I'd help with laundry, and getting those greasy clothes clean took some effort. And yet, that was the most peaceful and cheerful time of my life. Carolina would visit us on her breaks from med school, and sometimes we'd take him lunch at the garage.

I can't imagine what he'll do when he retires. And I'm surprised he's considering it. He seems like someone who would want to work while he's able.

"I know what you're thinking," Ramiro says with a soft smile.

"Oh, yeah?"

"Don Gustavo is as much of a workaholic, if not more, than Carolina. He wants to stay on, but only to work on cars part-time. He's done with all the administrative parts of running a business."

"Wow," I say. "So many changes are coming our way at the same time, aren't they?"

"Yeah," he agrees. "More than I'd ever imagine possible. It's a bit daunting." He pauses to chew his bite, then swallows. "But I have a great support system. That helps."

He grows quiet, and I know he's thinking about Francisca and the boys. How much his life changed this past year. A full one-eighty in ten seconds flat.

"Do you have an interest in the business side of things?" I ask.

Ramiro shrugs. "Not particularly, but Don Gustavo has taught me everything. I pretty much run the place as it is."

"So not much would change, then," I say, more cheerful now.

"Well, I'd be my own boss." The way he says it, with so much pride, a taller posture, and beaming smile is so full of hope for the future, I realize my work here is almost done.

Ramiro is making plans for his future. The future of his career. His future with the boys. Their future. I don't factor into those plans because I'll be moving on.

"But that's enough about me," he says. "What are your big plans?"

"Well, my boss—"

"Leah?" He asks.

I blink at him. I think I've mentioned her name maybe once in passing when I was asked about my day at work at the dinner table. And he remembered. But he would, wouldn't he?

This is the man who somehow knew my ex's name, and that I was afraid of him without me having to tell him. The man who knows to make me two omelets in the morning because one isn't enough.

The same man who knows I love Chinese food—somehow.

Then it's hard to reconcile this version of Ramiro with the version of last year—the man who'd leave any room I was in if we were alone. The man who hardly said a word to me unless others were around.

Now it seems like … he's been listening. Paying attention. Brian couldn't even remember Carolina's name half the time, and he knew she's my older sister.

"Yeah," I say. "Leah. She told me she's retiring in a year or two."

"You like her, right? I bet you'll miss her."

I stuff a rice pancake roll of moo shu in my face to give me time to answer. Ramiro didn't ask immediately if I was going after her job like Mandy and Carolina did. He didn't suggest it or encourage me to go after it. He knew that first and foremost, I'd be emotional about seeing my mentor go.

We think a lot alike, I realize, and for some reason, that thought frightens me a little. The similarities I was never aware of in my superficial crush from afar. I feel that crush crystalizing into something more permanent, and not even Devyn's presence in my life is slowing down that process.

My only hope now is that when I leave, some of those feelings will subside with time and distance into a focus on a different man.

"Yeah," I say sadly. "I'm going to miss her so much. She trained me."

"So, you know how I feel about Don Gustavo."

"Except you know you won't be able to keep him away."

"That's true. But it must still be scary, knowing you have big shoes to fill."

I laugh. "Are you just assuming I'm getting her job?"

Ramiro wipes his mouth with a napkin, neatly folds it, and places it back on the coffee table next to his plate. "Well, yeah. That's why you went for your master's. It's the natural next step.

I know from Caro that you are an amazing nurse, so I know you deserve the promotion."

"Thanks, Ramiro."

He goes back to planning his future with his own business. He details the upgrades in equipment he will make, how he plans to buy out the bakery next door to expand. How he wants to teach Oscar and René the basics of cars when they're old enough.

As I listen, I start to lose my appetite.

The lack of mention of my name in all his planning stings a little, even if it shouldn't.

Even so, it's hard to be anything but happy for him. I know he should plan and look to what's ahead.

It's time I do the same.

CHAPTER 20

WINTER

After grabbing the bag of low-sodium potato chips from the pantry, opening them up and munching on them, I head to the garage where I hear Ramiro's table saw running.

When I get there, Oscar is watching from a safe distance, looking adorable in the oversized safety goggles I'm sure Ramiro made him wear if he was going to hang out with him in the garage.

"What are you boys doing?" I ask as I go to stand over by Oscar.

Oscar gets to his tippy toes to peer inside the bag, and I lower it so he can sneak in his hand and grab a few chips.

"Ramiro is making a shelf for my room."

Huh, I think. Either Oscar hasn't yet heard René call Ramiro 'Dad,' or he's not buying into it. I'd always imagined that when they made that transition, Oscar would be the one to go first. That'll teach me.

Now I realize there's a hidden softness in René that is far too easy to overlook, because he does his best to come across as indifferent as he can.

The saw stops, and Ramiro looks up at me. "Thought Oscar would like to have his superhero figurines on a shelf instead of in the toy box, where he can never see them."

"Well, that's very nice, isn't it, Oscar?"

Oscar nods, stealing another chip.

"Ramiro said when I'm fifteen, he's going to teach me to use the saw," Oscar says proudly. "I'm too little still."

"That's a good age to learn that. Are you helping with anything else, though? For now?"

Oscar nods. "Yeah. I can help paint the shelves when they're done."

"That's very helpful," I tell the little guy. "What color are you going to paint them?"

"Red," he says.

"That is your favorite color, isn't it?"

Oscar nods, then keeps watching as Ramiro works to measure the next plank and mark his next cut. "Sara?" Oscar looks up at me, still munching on his potato chips. "How come you're always hungry?"

I stop chewing and blink down at my little instigator, then hear a snort come out of Ramiro as he does his best to swallow a giggle.

"I'm not always hungry," I say.

"But you're always eating," Oscar explains helpfully.

"Okay, that's my cue to go back inside," I say, trying to ignore the question. Before I get to the door, we hear a car pulling up in Don Gustavo's driveway.

"Oh, Carolina is here," Ramiro says.

"Can I go say hi to tía Caro?" Oscar asks excitedly.

Ramiro shakes his head, taking off his own safety glasses. "Not today, buddy. I actually have to talk to her about something." Then he looks up at me. "Mind taking Oscar inside? I'll put all the equipment away when I get back."

"Uh, sure."

I send Oscar to go upstairs to take a shower, and I know René is already working on his homework. Finding myself alone in the living room, I head to the window for no particular reason at all.

Carolina gets out of her car, still in her navy-blue scrubs, and I watch as Ramiro bends to kiss her cheek then takes her into his arms for a hug.

I grab a handful of chips and stuff them in my mouth as I watch on. Caro leans on her car, her back to me so I can't see her facial expressions, but I can clearly see Ramiro.

The ribbed sweatshirt he's wearing shouldn't be enough to keep him warm out there, but he seems perfectly comfortable and at ease as he stuffs his hands in his jean's pockets.

He fidgets a bit, shifting his weight from one leg to the other, his eyes downcast, then he shrugs.

Jealousy.

It's jealousy. I won't lie to myself and pretend I'm not. It still stings to know that even after everything, after Francisca, after her death and all the time since, Ramiro still has feelings for Carolina. I don't know why I'd thought even for one second he was over that.

He claimed to be, when he got engaged, but watching him now, bashful in the presence of my sister, there's really no other way to interpret his reaction to whatever it is she's saying to him.

When he heads back in the direction of the house, I'm about to step away from the window, but I'm too late. Ramiro sees me, and his brows crease for a second. I jump, accidentally crushing the bag of chips in my hands. Damn it.

I rush to the pantry, place the clip on the bag and am closing the pantry door when Ramiro comes into the house.

"Sara?"

"In the kitchen," I call out, heading to the fridge for the water pitcher to busy myself. "Hey, how's Caro?" I ask him.

"Didn't you see her at work this morning before you left?"

I shrug. "More like the blur of her."

Ramiro smiles. "I know what you mean. That's why I wanted to talk to her now while I had the chance."

I will not ask him. I will not. I don't want to know what he needed to talk to her about. The way he's smiling, and waiting, tells me that's exactly what he wants me to do, and I'm not going to give him the satisfaction.

"So," I say, waiting to change the subject, "you're teaching Oscar woodworking?"

Ramiro, thankfully, takes the bait. "Not necessarily. I'm trying to help him find his thing. René has soccer."

"I think Oscar's thing is superheroes."

"Yeah, but René is also into superheroes. I'd like Oscar to find something that he really enjoys doing—a hobby that might lead to something else when he's older."

"He's asked me about constellations," I tell him.

"He has?" Ramiro asks.

"Yeah. I think he'd be into astronomy. Maybe we should think about getting him a telescope?"

"You might be on to something there."

And because I'm the dumbest woman on this earth, I find myself asking him the one thing I said I wouldn't ask him. As soon as the question leaves my mouth, all blood rushes to my cheeks, burning hot there. "So, what did Caro say?"

For his part, Ramiro savors the victorious moment. The grin that splits his face in half is so cocky, I do not know how I stop myself from rolling my eyes, but it takes herculean effort.

"I thought I saw you watching from the window," Ramiro says.

He thought he saw me watching? What? I know for a fact he definitely saw me. We locked eyes for a full three seconds before I hightailed it away from the window. Instead of voicing my thoughts out loud, I shrug in a way I'm hoping says I'm cool as a cucumber and asked out of benign curiosity only.

When we both stay quiet for too long, Ramiro blows out a long breath. "I wanted to talk to her about my plans for Tavo's."

"Oh," I say. Then I smile. I smile wide because he was talking business, maybe not flirting like I originally thought.

"Yeah. I wanted to make sure she'd be okay with me buying Tavo's and keeping her dad on part-time during his retirement." He stops talking, and he deigns to smirk. He's smirking at the relief I couldn't hide for even one second.

"Anyway," I say to change the subject, "I'm going next door to wrap some presents."

As I reach the door, Ramiro calls after me. "Guess you can talk to Caro yourself, huh?"

I turn around to look at him, finding a self-satisfied grin molded into his perfect lips.

Great. Just great.

CHAPTER 21

The best holiday celebrations of my life have been with Carolina and Don Gustavo. Either at our home, or at one of our neighbor's.

I've had Christmas with Ramiro before, but we've never hosted it together. This year, we do our best to keep it small, inviting only Don Gustavo, Carolina, Devyn, and, of course, Doña Pancha.

When I tell Ramiro I want to invite Devyn, I hold my breath, but he just smiles and says, "Of course he's welcome to join us."

I allow my lungs to deflate. "Thanks, Ramiro."

"I'm going to call Devyn and ask him."

The phone rings twice before he picks up the call.

"Was just thinking about you, sugar. You read my mind."

"I wanted to know if you're planning on heading to Texas for the holidays?"

"Uh, to be honest, I wasn't sure. Didn't know if it was too soon for a holiday together or not. Didn't want to push. But I'd like to spend Christmas with you, if you'll have me. Got you a present and everything."

"Really? What is it?"

"You'll get it on Christmas morning."

"Eve."

"What?"

"At my house, we open presents on Christmas Eve at midnight. It's a Mexican thing—"

All the playfulness is gone from Devyn's voice when he speaks again. "Your house?"

"What?"

"You said 'at your house,' like Ramiro's house is your house."

"You know what I mean. Anyway, ever since I've spent the holidays with Carolina and her family, it's always Christmas Eve dinner, then midnight presents, followed by lighting sparklers outside. And in the morning, the recalentado! We have leftover breakfast."

"Right."

"So? You in, Holland?"

"I don't know, Sara. I'm not sure Ramiro would want me there."

"He's all for it. He actually asked me to invite you." It's not a total lie. He did ask once I brought it up.

"No, he didn't."

"Yes, he did. And besides, I want to spend it with you, but you know I can't leave the boys. It's their first Christmas without their mom."

Devyn groans on the line. "I'm an asshole, aren't I?"

"No, you're not."

"René will not like it."

I laugh. "René doesn't like much of anything these days. It'll be great. I promise." After a pause while he thinks, I bring out the big guns. "Don Gustavo is helping me cook dinner."

"You shoulda led with that, sugar."

～

Ramiro is still in pajamas when he finds me in the living room, setting decorations on every available surface.

"You really into Christmas, huh?" he asks, still groggy from sleep.

"Meh. I could take it or leave it, but Doña Pancha said Oscar and René have always loved Christmas. I've been worried about how they'll handle it this year, so I want to make it as special as possible."

"Maybe I should put up some lights outside the house."

I blink at him. I'd thought about asking, but for some reason had a hard time making the request. "They'd like that."

"I'll look in the basement. I think my dad left a box of outdoor lights."

"Great."

When the boys are having breakfast, Ramiro announces no one is to go into the garage, but won't say why. Assuming it's present-related, I don't argue and watch the boys like a hawk. We hear a table saw, a noise that doesn't let us watch tv, so instead we go next door to visit Don Gustavo, where it's nice and quiet and there's food. Don Gustavo sets a plate of pan ranchero and hot chocolate in front of us, and we don't go back home until late that evening.

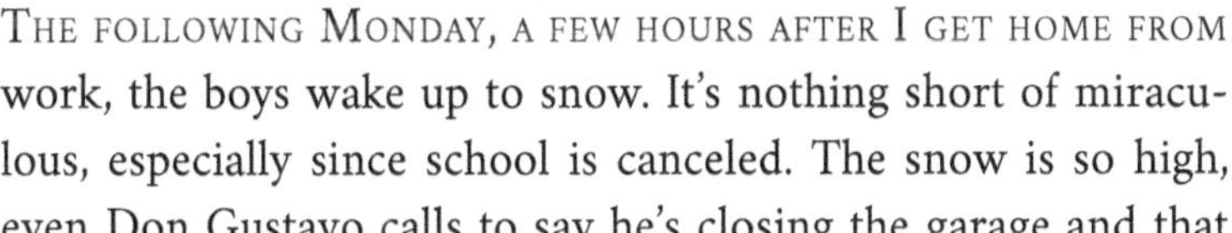

The following Monday, a few hours after I get home from work, the boys wake up to snow. It's nothing short of miraculous, especially since school is canceled. The snow is so high, even Don Gustavo calls to say he's closing the garage and that no one should drive today.

After breakfast, Ramiro heads outside to set up the lights he'd promised. He couldn't have picked a worse time since he'll have to get rid of the snow before he can get any work done.

Worried he might fall off the ladder, I head outside to check on him.

To my surprise, he's almost done. When I take in his work. I laugh.

Laugh so hard I bend over, clutching my belly.

And now I know what all that noise in the garage was. Ramiro cut a piece of wood into a life-size grinch that I just know he drew and painted himself. He wrapped a string of lights around the Grinch's hand that leads to the top corner of the roof. The effect is very obviously the Grinch stealing Christmas.

"You cheated!" I say between guffaws. Somehow, this man outsmarted the system and managed to have the best-decorated house on the block and only decorating a measly little corner of the roof. I don't know if it's brilliant or sneaky.

"What?" Ramiro says. "Work smart, not hard."

"Oh, yeah? And how long, exactly, did it take you to make the Grinch? Are you sure it wouldn't have been easier to decorate the house?"

He smiles, his face beaming with pride. He's wearing a gray beanie hat and his work gloves, rolling something in his palms. "But from now on, every year will be easy. Work smart, not hard, Moore," he says again. Then something crashes to my chest.

"Ow!" I say, more playfully than anything. It wasn't that painful, more … surprising. "Ramiro! Did you just throw a snowball at my boob?"

He's rolling a second one in his hands, and I duck behind the tree in the front yard. "No!" I say, but I'm laughing. I grab a handful of snow and pack it in my palms.

"Come out," he says. "Let me make you even." He's laughing so hard; I know I'll catch him off guard if I go on the offensive now. I dart out from behind the tree and throw my snowball at his face. My aim is off, and it lands on his neck instead.

Shocked, he brushes the snow from his neck. "Oh, you're gonna get it now."

"Bring it on, Jimenez. I have reinforcements."

"What?"

"Turn around."

He does. And the moment he does, he meets with two little boys, both holding packed snow in their fists, evil grins spread wide on their faces.

"Get him, guys!"

The snowball fight is epic—once we make it a rule that faces are off limits. Ramiro didn't mind so much that it is three against one, even if he does make a big stink of it for show.

Oscar, and especially René, maintain themselves as a barrier between Ramiro and me, my two knights protecting me, and it's more than a little heart-warming how protective they are.

We play in the snow until we are utterly exhausted, and the snow has started to melt on the fabric of our jeans.

When they have a chance to catch their breaths, the boys take in the Grinch. They both love it and sing Ramiro his due praises. And I agree with Oscar one hundred percent. We have the coolest house on the block now, ravaged as the lawn is now from our little snow battle.

"You look like you're having fun," Don Gustavo says, finding us all on the porch shaking off snow from our shoes so we can head inside.

"Hi, Don Gustavo."

"Hola, Mija," he says and kisses my cheek. "I wanted to ask you about Christmas dinner. How's your boyfriend with hot food?"

"He doesn't eat anything spicy."

To his credit, Don Gustavo doesn't roll his eyes. "All right, nothing spicy for the main course. I guess I'll make some salsa on the side for the rest of us."

"Thanks, Don Gustavo."

"Yeah, yeah." He looks at Oscar and René. "Guys, I just made a stack of flour tortillas. You want one rolled up with butter?"

"Yes, please!" René says and hurries to follow Don Gustavo as he goes back to his house.

Ramiro and I head inside and go upstairs to get out of the wet clothes. I decide to take a shower to warm up, and when I get out of the shower, I'm walking to my room when Ramiro's door opens. He steps into the hallway and takes me in. I'm still in my towel. I freeze mid-stride.

His eyes darken to a thick molasses color, filled with heat. That gaze of his is almost dangerous, but dangerous in the best way. There's no fear, even if my heart is racing for entirely different reasons.

He doesn't hide the fact that he's looking at me, eyes exploring every inch of my figure, my grip tight around my towel over my chest. My door is behind him, and I have to pass him to get into my room.

I clear my throat. "All dry?"

A sound that almost sounds like "Mhmm," leaves his throat.

"Good, um, excuse me." I take a step forward, angling my body sideways so I can sneak past him, but he doesn't move. His eyes are now glued to my hand, holding up my towel, and he steps closer to me instead of out of my way. With one finger, he dusts the knuckles gripping my towel, slowly, back and forth, setting the skin there on fire. I feel as the goosebumps sprout on my chest and arms. He's so close to me, I know he noticed too. The visible reaction from my body is more embarrassing than anything, but I can't move, and I can't hide it from him.

Ramiro angles his body sideways to let me through if I want to go, but my legs have forgotten how to work. I remain there, letting his fingers run over mine for a long moment.

Until his eyes meet mine, hungry and wanting, with every feeling of desire to have ever existed written in his pupils. I'm speechless and immovable, caught in a current of desire he has unleashed with a single look.

I wet my lips nervously as I roam his face: the clean-shaven, chiseled jaw, those full lips, strong chin, and even stronger brow. He's beautiful. Up close, he's everything I ever dreamed of in all my years of fantasizing about him.

As big as Ramiro is physically, it's the strength in his gaze that makes me want to crumble at his touch. "Ramiro, I—" my throat clamps shut, not letting words through, so I can only shake my head.

His hand immediately drops from mine, and he swallows audibly. "I know," he whispers before I watch him disappear down the stairs.

CHAPTER 22

Though I'm little help with the actual cooking part of things, I can set a table like a boss, if I do say so myself. And I'm not too shabby with plating beautiful dishes.

My heart is almost as full as this table this Christmas Eve, surrounded by all the people I hold dearest in my life.

René, Oscar, Carolina, Devyn, and Doña Pancha all wait patiently while Don Gustavo, Ramiro, and I bring the food out to the table. They are polite enough not to comment when Don Gustavo scolds me as I try to help and only get in the way.

I may have gone a little overboard with the Christmas decorations, because there's hardly room at the table for the plates with the oversized centerpiece of poinsettias and candles.

As Ramiro sets the cranberry sauce down and pivots to turn around again, everyone yells "Watch out—!"

But it's too late. I am right behind him, holding a pitcher of ponche. He runs into me, and not wanting to let go of the pitcher in my hands, I lose my balance. Ramiro stills me with me with firm hands around my shoulders. The pitcher sloshes between us, and some of it spritzes on Ramiro's face.

Oscar and René burst into laughter, and Don Gustavo runs out of the kitchen, waving his spatula in the air, worried about what I may have dropped.

"Nothing. It's fine, Don Gustavo," Ramiro says through the laughter.

"Oh my god, I got punch all over your face. Hold on. Let me get that before it splashes on your shirt and ruins it." I know Ramiro owns precious few dress shirts, and I don't want to ruin his best one—a crimson button-up he has rolled up to his thick forearms. I'm still laughing when I grab a napkin from the table and wipe his cheek and jaw. Freshly shaved, his skin is perfectly smooth as I hold his jaw in place with one hand to clean him up. "You should still wash up or you'll feel sticky."

"Yeah, all right," he says, shaking his head and laughing as he heads to the restroom.

"Well, that was a close call," I say, and look at everyone around the table. All of them coming down from the laughter and smiling.

All but two.

Carolina and Devyn.

Carolina is looking at me like a cat that just got a big bowl of cream.

And Devyn looks … stunned. Both his hands rest over the table, fingers spread wide, doing his best not to bunch his fists. I can tell.

I throw him a questioning look, trying to ask telepathically what's wrong, but then Doña Pancha asks him something, refocusing his attention, and the moment passes, so I head back to the kitchen for more dishes—like the chicken that I am.

Don Gustavo smoked a turkey as the main dish. He also spent the morning making handmade flour tortillas. I'm grateful for the diverse menu of side dishes he has planned, all things Devyn can enjoy: stuffed mushrooms, buttered corn, and roasted vegetables. He even made the chicken pozole verde mild with spicier green salsa on the side for those of us braver souls.

The first half of the dinner is amazing, and any animosity that transpired with the punch incident is all forgotten.

"Don Gustavo," I say, "Ramiro tried to make huevos con winnie for breakfast today."

"It was so bad!" Oscar jumps in.

"It was not," Ramiro defends himself.

Don Gustavo asks, "What was wrong with it?"

René, Oscar, and me all answer at the same time. "The whites weren't cooked all the way."

Ramiro rolls his eyes. "I told you, just pretend it was French."

I snort. "Yeah, when I told you I hate when they undercook eggs, what was it you said? Oh, it was so funny—"

"That maybe they just gave up," Ramiro finishes for me.

"That's right!"

"I don't know who manages to mess up huevos con winnie so bad, but …" Don Gustavo trails off, shaking his head.

Everyone is laughing, including Devyn, and I'm so glad. The conversation for the rest of the meal is lighthearted, and everyone is getting along like a dream.

Which, of course, is when things go sideways.

Midway through the meal, Devyn grabs a stuffed mushroom and pops it in his mouth. Immediately, he starts coughing. He grabs for a glass of water. Assuming he's choking, I pat his back.

Then his face turns red. Beet-red, and he starts fanning himself. "Are you okay?"

"There was something—" he coughs. "Excuse me." He gets up and heads to the bathroom, and Don Gustavo dashes to the kitchen, then follows Devyn with a glass of milk.

My eyes return to the table, where I find two little boys trying very hard not to giggle and failing miserably.

"What did you two do?"

"Nothing," René says. "I swear."

"Don't swear. Especially if you're lying."

"Oscar?"

Oscar's smile vanishes, and he pushes around the turkey on his plate with his fork.

"You know Santa doesn't come when kids lie. Are you sure there isn't anything you want to tell us?"

His fork drops to his plate, and he blinks at me, then looks over to Ramiro, then back at me. His chin trembles, and I know this is René's idea.

"That's too bad. I had a feeling presents were going to be good this year."

"René put a piece of jalapeño toreado inside Devyn's food," Oscar blurts.

I remember earlier in the night, how René chose his seat next to Devyn's. And I know they heard me tell Don Gustavo that Devyn can't eat anything spicy.

I cross my arms as I stare René down. "René?"

"You're such a dedo," René tells his little brother, annoyed.

Then I notice Ramiro is also trying extremely hard not to laugh. "You were in on it too?"

Ramiro's hands go up in surrender. "I had no idea they planned on doing this."

Devyn must be so embarrassed. And I can't have them thinking what they did was okay just because Ramiro is obviously amused. I make my voice stern when I speak to the three of them.

"That was incredibly dangerous, René. What if Devyn has a food allergy? You never, ever, hide anything in anyone's food. They can get really, really sick. Do you understand?"

René's glare is murderous as he defiantly holds eye contact with me. "Christmas is supposed to be for family. He shouldn't be here."

"René!" Ramiro and I snap at the same time.

"That's not very nice," I say. "And, I think with time, Devyn might be part of our family. When he comes back, you're going to apologize, or no Christmas presents—"

"That's not fair—"

"Sara is right," Ramiro says, finally on my side. "You apologize or no presents. Not that Santa would bring them, but if he does, we'll donate them."

"Fine," René mutters under his breath.

"You too, Oscar. You knew and didn't say anything."

"Okay," he says with a sigh.

They both make good on their promise. Several minutes later, Devyn comes back to the table feeling better, if a bit sweaty above his brow, and both boys apologize to him. He's incredibly gracious given what they put him through.

I can't blame him. Even I don't mess with the charred jalapeños, but Don Gustavo loves them, so he's always making them. I grab Devyn's hand when we're done eating and squeeze it. "I'm sorry," I say.

"They already apologized, and I'm fine. It's fine, Sara."

"Guys," Carolina says after dinner, "I'm watching a puppy for a friend. She's at Dad's next door. You wanna come say hi?"

"Really? A puppy?" Oscar asks, eyes wide as saucers.

Ramiro groans. "We're not getting a puppy, so don't get any ideas."

Carolina laughs. "We're just going to wish him a merry Christmas, right, Oscar?"

"Right," Oscar says, already jumping to his feet and diving to put on his snow boots. "You coming with us, René?"

René shrugs and says "whatever" but he's already getting his own shoes on, so Carolina and Oscar wait for him.

When the door closes behind the trio, Don Gustavo peeks out of the kitchen. "They gone?"

"Yes!" I say, and he, Ramiro, and I all run to the garage.

"What's going on?" Devyn asks.

"The presents!" I yell behind me. "Sit tight, we just gotta hurry to get them under the tree."

I sit by the tree as Don Gustavo and Ramiro hand me present after present to arrange. As I work, I explain to Devyn the puppy was the decoy this year.

"You need a decoy? For what?"

"For Santa to come. There has to be a distraction so that we can pretend that's when Santa came."

"You know this is easier if you do it in the morning, right? If they sleep while you do this?"

"No way," Ramiro says, handing me another gift. "Then we have to worry about being quiet and risk them waking up and finding out Santa isn't real."

"I'm sure René doesn't still believe—"

"Maybe. But Oscar does, so we're keeping the dream alive," I say.

Devyn shakes his head, a little amused, and I'm glad his good humor seems to be back.

THE PRESENTS ARE A HIT. MOSTLY. RENÉ GETS HIS FAVORITE soccer player's signed jersey from Ramiro, and when Oscar opens the gaming system we both got him, he is the happiest kid on this earth. He shrieks when he lays eyes on it and jogs in place with excitement, little fists tight against his sides.

We all laugh. All of us except René, who is looking at the gaming system like we just gave Oscar a box of snakes.

"What is it, René?" I ask. Oscar immediately quiets down, and we all turn to look at the murderous older brother.

It's almost a whisper when he speaks. "Mom wouldn't let us have video games."

"Well, I think it's okay—" Ramiro says, but stops when René is shaking his head. The precious jersey is now crumpled on his lap, fisted in his hands.

"It's okay, buddy," I say. "You're allowed to have video games—"

"You're not our mom!" he yells—those big, brown, water-logged eyes staring me down in what he tries to make anger, but I know is so much pain.

"René—" I say and watch him dash to his room before I can get another word out.

Ramiro says, "I'll go talk to him—"

"No," I say. "I think this one should be me."

Ramiro nods, and I head to the boys' room. He doesn't answer when I knock, so I crack the door open and let him know I'm coming in. He's in bed, his body huddled into a small ball, staring at the wall. I sit next to him and place a hand on his back.

"René. I know I'm not your mom. Your mom will always be your mom, even though she's not here anymore. Ramiro and I, we didn't know you weren't allowed video games, and we … we saw you two at the store once, looking at them. We just thought you wanted one. That's all."

He moves, his hands wiping his face clean before he turns around.

"Mom used to say video games are dangerous, and we should play outside instead."

"You know I loved your mom, right? She was a friend of mine."

"Yeah."

"But even friends disagree sometimes, and that's okay. I actually disagree with her about them being dangerous. But I do agree with her that it's better to play outside. So, what if we make it a rule that you're only allowed thirty minutes on school nights, and one hour on weekends of play time? I think your mom would've compromised with Ramiro that much, don't you? I mean, Ramiro loves video games."

He looks up at me at that. "Ramiro doesn't play video games."

"Oh yes, he does." I duck to whisper conspiratorially in his ear. "He hides them in his room because he doesn't want any of the grown-ups—including your mom—to think he's a little kid. But I've seen them."

"No way."

"Yes way. Next time he goes to the grocery store or something, we can sneak into his room, and I'll show you. Deal?"

René turns to smile at me. "Deal." His lips purse and he grows thoughtful before he adds, "And Sara? I'm sorry for yelling at you."

"I forgive you." With both arms under his armpits, I lift him up to a sitting position and tuck him into my body for a hug. I let my cheek fall to the top of his head and squeeze him tight. And René—he squeezes me right back.

Apart from the René meltdown—that let's face it, we were all expecting—Christmas went rather smoothly. The boys go to bed shortly after opening presents, and Ramiro follows. Devyn and I walk Doña Pancha, Carolina, and Don Gustavo outside and then linger on the porch.

"It was nice of Carolina to offer to take Doña Pancha home so we could have some time. You've been busy tonight," he says, scratching the back of his neck.

"You were really quiet tonight after dinner," I say to Devyn, grabbing his hand to hold.

"It was a hectic night for you."

I laugh. "Yeah. Tell me about it. It'll get easier, I promise. We knew the holidays would be tough."

"Sara, I—" He pulls his hand away from mine and sticks it in his coat pocket. "That was really hard for me to watch."

"I know. Me too. René is hurting so much, and so is Oscar—"

"That's not what I mean. I mean, yeah, that was rough, but that's not what I'm talking about."

I take a step closer to him so I can look at those beautiful bright eyes, and he does his best to smile at me, but I know it's half-hearted at best.

"Sara, I watched you and Ramiro tonight. In all the chaos. How you laugh together, how you finish each other's sentences. How he can't take his eyes off you—"

I laugh. "You must mean Carolina."

Devyn shakes his head. "No, Sara. It was like no one else existed at dinner but you."

"You're seeing something that's not there, I promise—"

"You can't promise me what he feels. Damn it, Sara. I watched you co-parent tonight. Those little boys, it's like they're your sons. Yours and Ramiro's. How am I supposed to compete with that?"

"I promise nothing has happened—or will ever happen— between Ramiro and me."

Devyn shakes his head and runs his hand over his face. "You already told me you had feelings for him, remember? Well, it sure as hell looks like they're reciprocated. It did tonight."

"What are you talking about?"

"How do you not see it? How he looks at you? How he takes care of you? Dotes on you? Ramiro has feelings for you, too. You both do. And I can't fucking compete with that." He points to the front door of the house as he finishes talking.

"Devyn, listen to me. Assuming you're right, which I don't think you are, but let's pretend for a second that you are. I would never, ever, get together with Ramiro."

"Not even if he loved you back?"

I snort, then stop myself because of how serious Devyn's

face looks. "No. I won't be his third choice. Because that's what I would be. Carolina first, Francisca second, and me third. I want to be someone's first choice."

"Don't you think I want that too? To be your first choice? I don't want to be second to Ramiro—"

"You're not!" I hurry to say. "I didn't know you when my feelings for him started, but since the second I saw you, I've liked you. I have feelings for you, Devyn. I really, truly do. And you've been so patient with me, more than I could ever have dreamed of asking—"

"Sara—"

I press my index finger to his lips. "Let me finish. Ramiro knows I'm trying to get over him. And he's admitted there's an attraction to me ... but it's only physical for him. What you saw tonight was not love. It was a man who hasn't been touched by a woman in nearly ten months. We've talked about it, and we've placed boundaries until my time here is up. You have nothing to worry about."

"I'm not sure if that makes me feel better or worse about your arrangement."

"It doesn't feel better that I'm brutally honest with you?"

He smiles, and finally the stiffness in his muscles crumbles as he reaches for my face. He cradles my cheek in one hand. "You are incredibly honest, aren't you?"

I nod. "For better or for worse. I am."

He kisses me softly, only one second, and presses his forehead to mine.

"I have a confession," I say.

He laughs. "I'm not a priest."

"Will you hear it, anyway?"

"Go on."

"My heart is so full. With both of you. What I told you at the start is still true. I'm doing my darndest to get over Ramiro. But ... uh, I never imagined I'd be capable of loving two men."

"What?" Devyn pulls back an inch so he can look at my eyes. "What did you say?"

"I'm falling in love with you, Devyn. And it's selfish because I'm still not over Ramiro, but I can't help how I feel when I'm with you. Devyn, I—" He cuts me off with his mouth.

This kiss is so much more than the earlier peck. His big body shelters me from the cold while his tongue pushes past my lips. A kiss that starts off gentle and grows into a wanting, pulsing, throbbing thing. His hand snakes behind my neck, where he cradles my head tenderly, pulling me closer so he can nip at my lips.

And I lean into it.

I kiss him with an open mouth, giving into everything he wants from my body. And for once, I'm not thinking about Ramiro when I'm kissing Devyn. For once, it's all about the man in front of me. Tall, protective, warm, and safe. Then I feel that thick pipe hardening between us, reminding me that safe haven though he may be, he's also a man. A wanting one. A hungry one. A patient one deserving of everything my heart and body can give him.

Breathy, we pull away from the kiss. "Sorry," he says. "I got carried away."

"Me too," I say, and press my abdomen against his erection.

"Sara ..." he groans. "Don't tease me."

I ease up on the pressure. "Sorry."

He searches my eyes. "Sara, I'm not falling in love with you." My face falls, and he lifts it again with one knuckle. "I've been in love with you for some time now. I haven't said it because ... I didn't think you were ready to hear it. But I do love you."

My eyes brim with tears. I think I've been right all along. My happiness is with this man.

"What are your New Year's plans?" he asks.

"Don't have any yet. Been waiting for the right offer." I smile at him, teasing him this time.

He laughs. "Well, sugar, I got us tickets to a great party. Get yourself into a pretty little dress, and let's paint the town, yeah?"

The idea of a celebration with just the two of us thrills me, even if something gnaws in my stomach at leaving my boys alone for this holiday. All my boys.

"I'd love that," I say, determined to fully invest in my future with this man.

CHAPTER 23

I'm pacing my room, biting my thumbnail. I shouldn't be nervous.

Ramiro may have shut down my idea before, but he was also still processing.

René and Oscar need to get into counseling, especially now. We need help navigating my move, and they'll need help to process their feelings during a second wave of changes in their lives. Even though they both know I'll be leaving in soon, I'm sure it will be hard for them.

For me too. I'll miss them. Fiercely.

I take a deep breath and force my feet to lead me to Ramiro's room—one step at a time. Since the kitchen incident, Ramiro has taken it upon himself to be more aware, calmer, gentler in how he handles difficult situations. Surely, my suggestion to take the boys to counseling will be better received now than it was back when I first mentioned it.

With one last deep breath for courage, I knock on his door.

"Come in," he says.

I do, then I freeze when I take him in. He must have just showered. He's standing in front of his dresser in jeans, low, low on his hips and … nothing else. No shirt. No shoes. No socks. And what do I do? Well, my brain stops functioning for one, as I follow the dark happy trail below his belly button, leading to … I clear my throat. *Focus, Sara—you have a job to do.* "Do you have a minute?"

When I find his eyes again, the jerk is smirking. I'm so busted, but damn it, I can own it. Ramiro is no stranger to the fact that he is handsome and extremely sexy. He's never been obnoxious or hyper-aware of his looks, but they've served him well in his playboy days of his early twenties. I roll my eyes, and more annoyed, ask again, "Can we talk?"

"Sure, let me put a shirt on. Wouldn't want you to be tongue-tied," he says, a crooked smile growing on his face.

I snort. "Thanks," I say in a tone that makes it clear I'm being sarcastic. If I'm truthful to myself, I'd much rather he keep the shirt off instead.

He throws on a gray Henley and sits on the edge of the bed, then pats the spot next to him. I grip the doorknob in my hand tightly. I can't think of a worse idea than to sit next to Ramiro—on his bed—at this moment.

He senses my apprehension and leans forward, resting his elbows on his knees. "It's okay, Sara. I'm not going to bite you."

Bite me, I think. What the hell, Sara? Calm down.

Reluctantly, I float to his bed, and I'm watching from outside my body as I sit down next to him.

I have a task, though, and I must focus.

"What do we need to talk about?" he asks, opening the conversation.

I clear my throat. "A few things. For one, I'll be spending New Year's Eve with Devyn."

He blows out a breath, then rubs the top of his head. "Right. Makes sense." His smile is lopsided, but he's trying so hard to be supportive. "Get that midnight kiss and all that—"

"Ramiro—"

"No, it's okay, mi ciel—" he cuts himself off with a nervous clearing of his throat before I can fully make out the half-word he was about to complete. It was a Spanish word, but not one I'm familiar with, at least not with the syllables cut in half.

"What?" I ask, hoping he'll finish the thought.

"Nothing. Just … it's fine. The boys and me, we'll be fine. You go have fun. You've more than earned it with how hard you work."

"Will you have the twelve grapes with them at midnight? Doña Pancha said Francisca always did that."

Ramiro smiles and nods. "We'll even go pick up Doña Pancha. I know she likes to make the twelve wishes with the grapes too."

"Good," I say approvingly.

"That it?"

It's my turn to empty my lungs. "No. There's more, but …"

"Yeah?"

"I'm a little afraid of bringing it up."

He takes my hand in his, sharp callouses firm against my skin. "I've told you. You never have to be afraid of me."

"Right. Well, you see … the thing is … we're going to need help, Ramiro. With what happened at Christmas with René— I'm concerned about him. And Francisca's death anniversary is coming up, and then I'll be moving out shortly after that."

He releases my hand, and even though he's nodding in understanding, his jaw is one hard line.

"Please don't be mad, but I really would like for you to reconsider getting the boys into counseling, at least them if you don't want to attend as well."

"Why are you so insistent about this?" he asks, but the question is mild, inquisitive, void of all the anger I was expecting from this conversation.

"May I be honest, and possibly too direct?"

"Of course." He smiles, his expression gentle. "I'm sorry if I've ever made you feel like you couldn't."

I know he's thinking about the yelling and my panic attack. "Ramiro, you've apologized for that, profusely. I've forgiven you. And you've stayed true to your word, managing your temper better. You don't have to keep apologizing."

He smiles at me, a grateful smile on his lips. "Good. Now tell me, why is this so important to you? We're all doing a little better, aren't we? I think we're making progress. Going in the right direction."

"We are. But I'm concerned it's not enough. Kids are smarter than we give them credit for. And you know they idolize you. I'm afraid you're unintentionally teaching them to bottle up their feelings—it's not a judgement, no. I know that's how you were raised. But you've seen René's outbursts. He'll continue to have them if he thinks he needs to bottle everything up like you do."

"Like I do?"

"Yes. He worships the ground you walk on. Haven't you noticed? You're the first father figure they've ever had. Of course, he'll take his behavior cues from you, and Oscar will follow."

"Will this make you happy? If we go to grief counseling?"

"Incredibly happy," I throw him my bubbliest of bubbly grins. "I'd love it if you continued, all of you, but I'll take even a few months, until after I leave so they have a healthy way to deal with all the changes. You know I started seeing a counselor myself, right?"

"Yeah. You told me."

"And have I had a panic attack since?"

Ramiro shakes his head thoughtfully.

"I can't tell you enough how much seeing a therapist has helped me lately. I honestly think I'll continue to go the rest of my life. My commitment to my mental health will be lifelong."

I watch him as he rolls it all over in his mind, and it's hard not to hold my breath. At least he's handling it better than the last time I brought this up. Calmer, less hot-headed. As much as the boys have tried Ramiro's last shred of patience, these last few months he's also learned so much.

Oscar and René bring out a different side of Ramiro—a calmer, more nurturing side—that I think might just be his true personality if he allows himself to stop being ashamed of it. He shouldn't be afraid of it, because it's kind and beautiful, and he has no idea what a wonderful man it's made him. What a wonderful man he's becoming through fatherhood. There was a great canvas to work with already, he's always been a good man, but now—now he's the best.

"All right," he says with a tight smile. "Set it up."

"Already have." I grin at him, and he nudges my knee with his.

"That sure of yourself, huh?"

I shake my head. "No. Just hopeful. I knew you'd do the right thing."

"Oh yeah? Why's that?"

I stand to leave his bedroom. Doorknob in my hand, I turn to face him one last time and smile brightly. "Because you always do."

CHAPTER 24

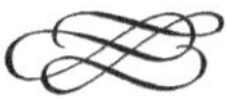

The outfit I chose for tonight may be a tad on the scandalous side, but I'm in love with how I look. I'm wearing a gold shimmery minidress with spaghetti straps and a plunging neckline. The shoes were nearly half my paycheck, but the gold stiletto sling-backs are so worth it.

I take a selfie in the mirror and send it to the group chat.

Me: Is this too slutty for a New Year's Eve party?

Carolina: Are you going out with Devyn?

Me: Yes. Is this too much? I loved it at the store … but I'm not sure anymore.

Mandy: Get it, girl! You look amazing!

Mandy: What are you doing tonight, Caro?

I roll my eyes, and both Sofia and I answer for Carolina at the same time.

Me: Working.

Sofia: Working <eye-roll emoji>

Mandy: Booooo!

A picture comes in from Mandy. She's wearing a loud red-sequined dress and lacquered red stilettos. She's also wearing a white faux-fur coat over her shoulders, making her look like a sexy Christmas card.

Sofia: Hot damn. You are both teases. Take me off this damn group chat if you're all going to send me half-naked pictures. I'm going through a serious dry spell. Mommy New Year's aren't quite as sexy.

I frown and tap my chin. Not one of them said it was too much, but no one really said it wasn't scandalous either.

For courage, I start to pregame with a with a glass of wine while I finish getting ready, so my libido is flying sky-high by the time Devyn gets here to pick me up.

"Just need five more minutes," I yell down the stairs, and hear as Devyn settles in with René to play video games. It's been a revelation, that this is what would bring them together finally. They don't have to talk to each other or pretend to like each other but can amicably share space via the controllers in their hands.

I run a last coat of hairspray over my loose waves so my hair stays put through any dancing, as I'm sure there will be, and one last layer of lipstick.

Devyn has been so patient with me, and I think I'm finally ready to let our intimacy grow. My counselor agrees it would be a good time to start forming positive associations with romantic intimacy if I'm feeling ready.

I'm ready.

At least, I want to be ready.

I'm done with the fear of a physical connection with men that Brian left in my battered heart. He will not define me or my future, and definitely not my relationship with a man who couldn't be any more different.

It needs to be Devyn; I decide. With his kindness, understanding, and gentle touch. I feel safe with him, and I'm hoping he wants me as much as I want him.

Tonight's the night.

MY DRESS HAS THE DESIRED EFFECT. DEVYN HASN'T BEEN ABLE TO keep his hands—or mouth—off me as we dance the night away. It's about twenty minutes to midnight when he yells in my ear over the music, "Would you mind if I took you to my rooftop terrace? I have a surprise for you."

"You live around here?"

I've never been to his place, and he's never asked. Knowing I wanted to take things slow, Devyn has let me lead the pace.

He nods, and I swallow. He's on the same page. All right. I can do this. I want to do this. I told Devyn I wanted to limit myself to one glass of celebratory champagne to celebrate at midnight, and he followed suit with the biggest smile. He wants to be sober as much as I do.

We walk the two blocks to his apartment building, and we ride the elevator to the top floor.

When we get there, it's a winter wonderland. Snow-peaked ledges, twinkle lights and lanterns casting off moody lighting and dancing shadows. There's a bench with a couple of blankets, like he planned this, and he leads me to the center of the terrace near an outdoor heater. I notice a small table with an opened bottle of champagne and two flutes next to it.

"How did you manage this? We've been out all night."

Devyn shrugs with a smile. "I'm nice to my neighbors, sugar. They owed me one." He wraps one blanket around my shoulders and kisses the tip of my nose.

Next, he takes out his phone and shows me. I squint at the screen that reads 11:57 pm.

I'm giddy with anticipation of the kiss, even if I have been kissing him all night.

We've made out all night on the dance floor, and yet, this midnight kiss seems important. Monumental. Life-changing. And I have no idea why.

He pushes a few buttons and plays a live countdown to midnight.

On the dot, his big hands wrap around my blanket and pull me to him, and he presses his lips to mine.

It's a much more tender kiss than the heated ones we shared at the club, but it's also somehow more wanting, more expectant, more needy.

I want this.

When we break away, all air is sucked out of the terrace as if it were a small closet instead of a wide-open space, as he gets down on one knee and opens a velvety black box nestled like something precious in his hands.

The glint of the understated diamond twinkles to match the surrounding lighting, and I'm smiling. Everything in me wants this. Before he speaks, I want to cut him off and say yes. Even if there was a second, just one second, when the image of Ramiro's face flickered through my dizzy brain. It was a moment, then it passed—I pushed it out of my mind—and now it's just Devyn and me.

"Sara, I will wait for you forever, if that's what you need. But when you're ready, will you please marry me?"

My water-logged lashes drip down my cheeks as I nod. Instead of letting him stand, I kneel to meet him on the ground and wrap my blanket around him too. Nestled under our warmth, I take his free hand. "Yes. Of course, I'll marry you."

He kisses me again, stopping only to place the ring on my finger. "It fits perfectly." I beam at him. "Thank you."

"Thank you for saying yes."

He breaks away from my hold to pour us both a glass of bubbly. We toast to the new year, to our engagement, and to the start of a wonderful life together.

A few sips later, I set the glass back down on the side table, and I kiss him again. This time, I let myself go for the first time since Brian. I let my fingers thread his hair, and my other hand explores his chest, his abdomen. I hook two fingers in his waist-band and pull him to me, forcing a groan out of him that I eat and swallow and let settle in my belly where it radiates heat through my core.

It's a breathless kiss, with no time to pause and gulp precious air. And it's a long kiss, so when we do break away, our lips swollen, red, and bruised, we're both breathless, like we just ran a marathon. "I'm ready," I whisper as his eyes lock on mine.

"Ready?" He asks, not understanding my meaning.

I nod. "Make love to me."

WE OVERSLEEP IN THE MORNING, AND WHEN I WAKE UP AND SEE five missed calls from Ramiro and three texts, I feel terrible. We didn't over-drink, so it's not a hangover, but I'm sure they're worried since I never came home.

I immediately text back.

Me: I'm at Devyn's. I'm fine. We overslept. I'm sorry I didn't text you.

Ramiro: Good to know you're alive.

I set the phone on the nightstand and roll over. Devyn's still asleep, and I run my fingers over the constellation of freckles on his naked back, then up his neck, and through his hair. He stirs, moaning, and turns around to face me.

"Good morning Mrs. Holland," he says with a sleepy smile.

I giggle softly. "Mrs. Holland? You'd like me to change my last name, would you?"

"Not if you don't want to. Are you attached to Moore?"

"Not really," I admit truthfully.

"Then, yeah, it would be an honor for you to share my name. The Hollands are a good family, and my pa was a good man. I'm proud to have his name, and it'd be the biggest honor for you to share it with me." He kisses me gently, and we spend the rest of the morning, naked in bed, making plans for our future together.

A future that looks incredibly bright from my current vantage point under the morning sun.

THE EXCITEMENT, THE ELATION, THE UTTER HAPPINESS ABOUT MY engagement, dies the minute I walk through the front door.

Oscar and René are playing video games. They glance at me once, then pretend I'm not even there. Even my lovely little Oscar is throwing me a murderous glare before he returns to his game without a word.

"Good morning," I say to them.

They mumble something under their breaths, but I can't understand any of the words. Ramiro is in the kitchen pouring himself a cup of coffee when he turns around to see me. I smile at him. "Good morning," I say.

His eyes narrow, and he takes a sip of his coffee, never once taking his eyes off me.

Awkward.

I toe off my heels and bend to pick them up, letting them dangle from my fingertips. When they're in my hands, Ramiro's eyes drop to my hands, freezing there. He sets his mug down and his mouth gapes, eyes never leaving ... I follow his stare to my hand. Oh.

The ring.

"Ramiro—"

Ramiro holds up a finger to quiet me and pulls out his phone, then takes it to his ear. After a moment, he says, "Are you home?" A pause. "Do you think you could take the boys for twenty minutes? Yeah. Thanks, Don Gustavo." Ramiro ends the call and asks the boys to go next door.

I feel like a teenager sneaking into the house about to get grounded.

I'm a grown woman, damn it. I shouldn't be ashamed of anything. I'm just living my life. Finally, after so much time of only working and going to school. I deserve good things in life. I deserve a good man, a good home, a good future. A fun time. I will not let Ramiro Jimenez shame me for wanting those things.

When Oscar and René leave, I set my shoes down again and square off with Ramiro, jutting my chin high.

"Fun night?" he asks through gritted teeth.

"The funnest," I say, syrupy sweet, though I narrow my eyes to slits. Bring it on, Ramiro. I dare you to try and ruin this. I won't let you.

"I see congratulations are in order," he says, nodding at my hand.

"Was that supposed to be it?" I ask sarcastically.

Every muscle in his body is shaking, and if I didn't know better, I'd say he's furious. The Ramiro of last year would have slammed his fists on the counter, or he would have stormed off, slamming doors behind him. But this is not the same Ramiro. His tone is measured when he speaks. "When were you going to tell me?"

"It just happened last night. It was a surprise to me too—"

"Did you sleep with him?" he asks, but this time, he looks resigned to the answer he's already expecting when he closes his eyes, waiting for my response.

I take a step back, not in fear, but more surprised. "Ramiro, that's incredibly personal—"

"Just, please, Sara. Tell me." His voice is pleading now, his tone soft and encouraging. His head ducking to search my eyes at my height. "Did you?"

"Not that it's any of your business," I say finally. "But he's my fiancé, and I spent New Year's Eve with him all night. What do you think?"

He nods at my non-answer. "Right." There's a long pause, and I don't know what else to say. What can I say? I don't want to have to comfort anyone when I'm supposed to be joyous over the best moment of my life. "I guess you'll be moving out—"

"Is that why you're upset? Because you think I'll leave sooner? Ramiro, I wouldn't do that. I intend to keep my promise and stay here for the year. I wouldn't do that to the boys."

"You don't have to, Sara—"

"I want to," I admit. "I love Oscar and René, and I want to transition them to me leaving slowly. And besides, we don't have a wedding date yet. I'm guessing April or May after I leave will be ideal."

Ramiro nods, then stays quiet for a long moment. "We're going to miss you."

I snort. "I'll be around. It's not like I'm moving away, and Devyn will still work with you. We're family, Ramiro. You're stuck with us—unless ..."

"Unless what?" He asks.

"Unless you're planning to fire Devyn when you take over the business."

His eyes narrow. "You really think that little of me? That I would do something like that?"

"I don't know, Ramiro. You don't have the best track record when it comes to thinking things through."

"I do with the important stuff," he says.

That, I have to concede. He's never, not once, let me down, nor have I ever seen him let anyone else down. Not in the ways that matter.

"I'm sorry. You're right. I guess I'm tired and not thinking straight at the moment. But if you don't plan to fire him, then we'll always be around."

He smiles and nods. "Won't be quite the same, but I'll be glad to have you any way I can."

"Ramiro ..."

"You know I want you to be happy, right?"

I smile at him. "Thank you. I do know that."

"Congratulations, Sara. Or is it best wishes?"

I smile at him, the sincerity in his words reaching my heart. "Best wishes for the bride. Congratulations for the groom."

"Well, then …" He steps closer and takes my free hand—the one not holding my shoes and not sporting a diamond—then takes it to his mouth for a chaste kiss. "Best wishes, Sara." He drops my hand, then adds, "I'll congratulate Devyn tomorrow at work."

CHAPTER 25

Wanting to put some distance between us, and likely also wanting to bond with the boys alone, Ramiro decides to take them camping. I argue that it's too cold, but he reassures me he's acquired sufficient cold weather camping gear and clothing for all three.

Oscar seems excited, while René, as usual, seems to go with the flow, feigning disinterest. That will change when they get there and Ramiro surprises him with a portable telescope so they can look at the stars when they're out there in nature. I know René will have an amazing time once they get there.

Ramiro seems to have accepted my engagement to Devyn, but Oscar and René have been angry with me since Ramiro and I sat down to have that conversation with them during our first family counseling session together.

I agreed to attend the first session with them so we could break the news. I know one day, when they're old enough to understand, they will be okay with the idea of Devyn and me.

And I also know that one day, they will fall in love with Devyn as much as I have.

"What are you going to do with us gone the whole weekend?" Ramiro asks as he packs the last of his camping gear.

"Not sure. Maybe I'll see if Carolina is free tonight to have a drink with me. I highly doubt that though, so maybe I'll text Mandy. We've been meaning to have drinks together since forever, but we've both been so busy."

"Thanks for understanding. I think the boys and I need some bonding time alone. Start getting used to doing some things without you."

"I know, Ramiro. I'm so glad you're doing this. Where are you going again?"

"Just to Clinton Lake outside of Lawrence. There's a primitive campsite there."

"I'm still afraid you will freeze to death."

Ramiro laughs. "The coldest it'll get tonight is in the thirties. We'll be fine. But just in case, I got hand warmer packets to stick in the boys' sleeping bags."

"Good. I'd like them to come back with all their toes and noses intact, please."

Ramiro chuckles. "Of course."

AFTER THEY LEAVE, I MESSAGE THE GIRLS. I WANT TO TELL THEM my big news in person.

Me: Girl's night at my place tonight? I'll make us some cocktails.

Carolina: Where's Ramiro?

Me: He took the boys camping.

Sofia: Wish I could. Don't have a sitter for tonight. Have fun.

Mandy: Drinks on you? I'm in. What time?

Me: Come any time after seven.

Carolina: Yeah, I should be done here by then. See ya later.

Me: Can you stop by your dad's first?

Carolina: Yeah, yeah, I'll go steal leftovers.

BY THE TIME MY TWO FRIENDS ARRIVE, I HAVE A PITCHER OF sangria ready on the table and cheesy Brazilian bread in the oven to snack on.

It's so rare to see Carolina outside of work these days. I'm happy to see her. "You look good," I tell her.

"Thank you. I tried to slow down this week. I'm afraid of burning out."

I never thought I'd see the day when Carolina would say that, and those words are a relief. I pat Carolina's hand with a smile, glad she's starting to take better care of herself.

Mandy barges in without knocking or ringing the doorbell, in true Mandy fashion. "The party has arrived!" she says and dramatically rips off her jacket and hooks it on the rack by the door.

"Well, please come in," I say. "Make yourself at home."

"So, where are the boys again?" Mandy asks.

"Camping."

"In this cold?" she asks.

"Ramiro assured me they'd be fine. I'm sure they have a fire going and are roasting marshmallows right about now."

I place a bowl of cheesy bread on the coffee table and settle into the couch next to Mandy.

We're several drinks in when inevitably, Carolina asks what she's been dying to. "So, how's it going with Devyn?"

"Oh yeah," Mandy says. "I have yet to meet him. Does he finally have the 'boyfriend' label? How long are you going to make us wait to meet him?"

"Actually," I say. "He's not my boyfriend anymore."

Carolina leans forward and sets her drink down. "You broke

up? Oh, thank God. I knew you and Ramiro were perfect for each other—"

"What? No!" I say, more than a little frustrated with her now. So, I hold my hand up and display the ring on my finger that somehow both Mandy and Carolina have failed to notice from the moment they each walked in.

Mandy gasps, then turns to look at Caro as a look passes between them.

Carolina's lips disappear into the thin line as she bites back words. "Just say whatever it is you want to say," I tell her.

"You're not moving too fast? You only met him, what, in June?"

"He makes me happy, Caro. Don't I deserve that? To be happy with a good man?"

"Well!" Mandy shouts and stands up, motioning for me to follow suit. Then she takes me into her arms. "Congratulations, Sara!"

"Thank you," I say, returning the hug.

Carolina follows her example, saying congratulatory words and taking me into her warm arms, but it comes from a place of decorum, and is not truly meaningful. I can tell because those expressive amber eyes of hers, framed by those even more expressive thick brows, give her away every single time.

We all retake our seats again, and Carolina asks, "Do you love him?"

"Of course, I love him," I say without so much as a second to think about the question.

"And Ramiro?" Mandy dares to ask without a care in the world about it being an inappropriate question. "Do you love him?"

Leave it to Mandy. "I won't lie. I have been in love with Ramiro for a long time, and maybe I still love him a little. That doesn't mean I don't also love Devyn. And unlike Ramiro, Devyn loves me back and has been into me since we met."

"I don't doubt you love Devyn," Carolina says. "But I think you belong with Ramiro."

I take a big gulp of my drink, chugging it in frustration now. "Can you just be happy for me?"

Carolina smiles at me, one of those heart-soothing, warm smiles of hers. "I am happy for you, Sara."

"Well, now we have to meet him," Mandy says.

I laugh. "You will, I promise."

"And," Mandy adds, "we are so planning a bachelorette party!"

I stare at Carolina with wide eyes, asking for help.

"You know," Carolina says, a mischievous tone in her voice, "I think Sofia and Mandy would be the perfect people to plan your bachelorette party."

I narrow my eyes at my traitorous sister. "We're keeping the wedding small. Wasn't planning on having maids or anything, so you don't have to plan anything."

"Oh, we're planning a bachelorette party," Mandy says, rubbing her hands together like a caricature of evil.

Great. Just great.

We chitchat for a few hours, catching up, until Mandy gets a notification on her phone. She grabs it from its spot on the couch next to her, and her grin widens exponentially as she reads on. "Well, ladies, I have to go. One of my fishing lines has a bite."

In Mandy-speak, that's one of her booty-calls inviting her over.

"But it's only eight," I argue. "Isn't it early for this?"

Mandy nods. "It is, but I have to get up early tomorrow. I'm babysitting for one of the doctors at the hospital."

My eyes bulge. "A third job, Mandy? Don't you think it's too much?"

Mandy rolls her eyes as she puts her jacket on and zips it snug. "I'm going to ignore the fact that the kettle just called the pot black. And it's not a third job. I only do this occasionally."

"What doctor?" Carolina asks what we're both thinking.

"Sorry. I have to go. We'll talk later."

Before she's out the door, Mandy sends me a text with an address for a safety check.

"Check in tomorrow morning or I'm calling the police," I call after her.

She rolls her eyes. "Yes, Mom," she says as she closes the door behind her.

I smile after her, because even though she pretends to be annoyed, she's always good about having a safety check person when she goes on her sexcapades.

A few drinks in, Carolina is nice and smiley and a little bit tipsy, so I decide it's the best time to ask her a favor I've been nervous about asking her all night.

I want to ask her to let me borrow Don Gustavo to walk me down the aisle. I'd been nervous because I know she wants to get married one day and that she thought she'd one day get married to the man who broke her heart.

"Caro, I wanted to ask you …"

She sets her wineglass in front of her, sensing the shift to seriousness in the conversation. "Yes?"

"Would you be okay if I asked your dad to walk me down the aisle?"

I know in her mind, Don Gustavo was going to be walking her down the aisle to marry Hector Medina. I see all of it flash behind those amber eyes as she smiles at me a bit sadly. She takes my hand in hers and says, "You are not *like* a sister to me, Sara. You *are* my sister, and you know Dad thinks of you as his daughter. I think it will make him very happy, very proud, to walk you down the aisle."

"You think?"

Carolina nods. "I know."

"And you? Are you okay with that? I won't ask him, Caro, not if you want him to walk you first—"

She laughs, but it's watery. "I'm never getting married, Sara." She drains her glass. "Unless you count getting married to my work."

"Who knows, maybe one day you'll fall in love with Ramiro like you were destined to from the beginning."

"What is it with you two lately?"

"What do you mean?"

"Everyone is treating me with kid gloves. Ramiro thought he had to ask for my blessing to take over the garage when my dad retires, and you think you need my blessing to have Dad walk you down the aisle? I'm not made of glass, you know. And," she adds, a little out of breath, "just because our parents wanted us to get married since we were little kids, doesn't mean we have to fulfill their wishes."

She rolls her eyes, taking a long gulp from her glass. It was a pact, in the form of a bad joke, that seemed to predestine Ramiro and Carolina since she was born. Ramiro's parents and Carolina's fated them to end up together. When Carolina's mom died when she was only a teenager, she'd thought she had to make her mom's wishes come true and end up with Ramiro.

That was not to be.

When Dr. Hector Medina, her real-life hero from her teenage years, entered her life when she started her residency at Heartland Metro, she fell head over heels, leaving Ramiro to career into drinking and fucking anyone who would have him.

Until he found Francisca.

And even now, with Francisca dead and the elusive Dr. Medina inaccessible and entirely out of her life, Carolina doesn't see Ramiro the way she saw Hector. She loves Ramiro, of that I have no doubt, but it's a sisterly, chaste type of love no different from what she feels for me, and even if Don Gustavo and I try to will them together, I know she'll never betray her own heart.

Instead, I let the subject drop, knowing full well she's heard her predestined plan a thousand times since she was a little girl. If her dying mother couldn't convince her to end up with Ramiro, no one could, least of all me. And why was I trying to push them together, anyway? In love as I may be with Devyn, the thought of Carolina and Ramiro together still unsettles me.

No one ever said you could only be in love with one person at a time.

My gracious friend changes the subject. With sincere words and a full heart, she reassures me that her dad walking me down the aisle will not in any way hurt her feelings.

CHAPTER 26

After a long week of picking up double shifts at work and having had Trevor and one of Oscar's friends over for a sleepover the weekend prior, I'm dead on my feet and need a break.

I don't have to voice this because Devyn senses it, and missing me, asks if he can cook dinner for me at his place and have a quiet night in. And I mean, who in their right mind would say no to that?

I get to his place after my shift Friday night with an overnight bag that Ramiro only slightly sneered at before I left the house.

When I get to his place, Devyn leads me to his bathroom, where he has a bubble bath ready for me with the lights off and candles lit. Soft ambient music is playing from a small speaker next to the sink, and I could cry at the thoughtfulness.

My aching muscles sigh with anticipation of a little R&R.

Devyn lands a small peck on my lips. "Settle in." He leads me to the tub and helps me undress. Once I'm cocooned in the warm water, he steps out for a moment and comes back with a glass of white wine. "You've worked so hard," he says, handing me the glass.

"Thank you," I say, my toes curling with the first sip.

"I'm going to finish up dinner. When you're ready, join me in the dining room."

I smile at him, still thinking of his tender but chaste touch as he undressed me. I could tell he wanted me, and there was no way to hide the enormous erection straining against his jeans as I got in the tub, but he minded it no attention, and instead doted and me, brought me wine, and let me relax.

He left a robe on a hook, and when the water cools, I get out of the tub and decide I'll have dinner in his robe, smelling him on me.

"Why are you working so hard?" Devyn asks when we settle into our meal.

"I just took a few extra shifts."

"But why? Is it money? I can help. We're going to be a team now, you know?"

I laugh. "No. I actually don't have expenses other than my student loans. Ramiro takes care of everything else."

Devyn's beefy hand tightens around his fork as he cuts off a corner of the homemade lasagna. "Right. So, what is it, then?"

"We're getting married," I say. I'm surprised he hasn't guessed the real reason. "My parents aren't part of my life. I won't have their support, so I need to save up for the wedding."

When he lets out a long sigh of relief, he's smiling. "I was hoping you'd bring up the wedding. The last thing I want is to rush you, but I'd love to set a date so we can start planning together."

I smile around a forkful of lasagna. "I'd like that too."

Devyn beams at me for a second, then a crease forms between his brows as his scowl grows. "But no more of this overworking nonsense."

"Devyn, I—"

"I mean it, Sara."

Over the best homemade lasagna of my life and a full bottle of wine, we decide on a plan. It will be in early May if our local church has a date open. The reception will be small, just our closest family and friends. Don Gustavo will have a fit if he can't invite every person he has ever known, but I'll convince him. He'll want to invite the entire neighborhood, and we'll have to keep him in check.

May also gives me some breathing room to transition out of Ramiro's house slowly before the wedding.

We don't decide on much else. We could move into his place, but I think picking out a home together would be a great fresh start. I don't bring this up because setting a date seems so monumental; I don't dare break our good mood.

After dinner, Devyn leads me to his bedroom where he proceeds to give me the best massage of my life, infused with the seductive aroma of almond oil.

THE FOLLOWING WEEK, WHEN WE FIND OUT OUR LOCAL CATHOLIC church does have an opening in May—anything for Don Gustavo's daughter—that's when the planning really goes into overdrive.

Having decided on a small reception simplifies both the planning and the budget, and I've stopped taking on the extra shifts, choosing instead to spend more time with the boys and my friends.

I'm not under any illusions that I'll find my wedding gown today, but I've decided to start looking and even invited Carolina and Sofia for this first round of trying on dresses. This should be my mom with me, I realize, but my sisters are a great choice under the circumstances.

"Come out, already," an impatient Sofia calls out.

"One sec. The zipper's stuck."

"I'll help." Carolina slides open the curtain to get a look at me. "Oh, Sara. You look beautiful."

For some reason, my face grows hot at the compliment. "Thank you. I don't think this one's it." I'm not the biggest fan of the halter neckline, but I love the dreamy tulle skirt.

She helps me with the zipper, and I step out of the dressing room, where Sofia is sitting sipping on a glass of champagne the saleswoman offered us. She whistles when she sees me, and both Carolina and I laugh, even if we're all ignoring Carolina's red nose.

I wouldn't have believed it possible, but the third dress I try on is the one. It has the dreamy organza skirt that I wanted, with a beaded corset bodice and spaghetti straps. It's understated and perfect for the small wedding we have in mind.

"So," Sofia says. "When are we meeting Devyn?"

I smile at both of them. "When are you both free?"

"Do you have plans Friday night?" I ask Ramiro when I get home from the dress shop.

I found him in the garage, working out excessively on his bench. "No. Why?" he asks, looking up at me and grabbing a small towel to wipe the sweat from his brow.

"Sofia and Caro want to meet Devyn officially. We thought we'd go to Sofia's bar since she can't get away. Mind staying with the boys?"

"I have a better idea," Ramiro says, standing up in front of me. "Why don't I come too?"

My eyes bulge. "What? You already know him," I argue. "You work with him."

Ramiro takes a big gulp from his water bottle, tipping it all the way back. I watch as the tendons of his neck contract with every swallow. "Yeah," he says, "but he's going to be part of the family now. If you plan on staying in the boys' life, then he will too. Would be good for us to get friendly."

Eyeing him warily, I have to concede because Ramiro is making a lot of sense, and I want to positively reinforce this calm and reasonable behavior that I'm sure has a lot to do with the counseling he agreed to.

"What do we do about the boys?" I ask him.

"We've had Trevor over enough. I'm sure Jaleesa could take the boys for an evening. If not, Don Gustavo would be happy to have them, I'm sure."

When I call Jaleesa to ask for the favor, I'm fully hoping she'll say no. Instead, she says, "Of course they can come over. You take Trevor often enough."

I swallow hard. Damn it. Why does she have to be so nice? "Are you sure?" I ask, offering her one last out.

Jaleesa laughs. "I'm sure. If you want, I can pick them up after school and bring them straight over here."

"We're going to a bar," I explain. "We might be late."

"They could sleep over. We'll make a night of it."

I think about that for a few beats. "I don't know ..." I say, still wanting to find an obstacle to keep Ramiro from going with us. Then there's the problem Oscar had last time, so I decide to go with that instead. "René would love to sleep over, but I don't know about Oscar. His first try sleeping over at a friend's house didn't go so great."

"Didn't you tell me that was because of some movie that triggered him?"

"Yeah. It was."

"Then we'll be careful not to watch *Finding Dory*, or *The Lion King*, or *Coco*, or any other movies that have dead or missing parents."

"*Bambi*," I add, still trying to think of excuses.

"That's right," Jaleesa says. "No *Bambi*."

Out of any reasons to avoid this, I sigh into the phone. "Thanks, Jaleesa. Truly."

"You're welcome. Let me know how the introductions go."

"I will. I promise."

~

As is true every time we all hang out together, Carolina is early and already waiting for me when I get to La Oficina, and Mandy is late, showing up ten minutes after me.

It's happy hour and not crowded yet. Since I came from work, Devyn decided to meet us here after he gets done at the garage.

"Ramiro is coming tonight," I tell all my friends.

Mandy picks up her beer instead of making a comment, and Carolina asks, "What?"

"I couldn't help it. He invited himself." I rest my elbows on the table and bring both hands to my forehead. "This is going to be a disaster, isn't it?"

Carolina squeezes my forearm tenderly. "Not if we don't let it."

I look up at my friend, and so does Mandy. "What do you mean?" I ask.

"Mandy and I are here. I'm sure Sofia will join us for a bit when Devyn gets here. We'll act as buffers and guide the conversation away from anything uncomfortable if it comes up."

Mandy snorts, then gulps her beer, pretending like it didn't happen.

"What?" I ask her, my eyes narrowing.

"If Ramiro invited himself, he's here to mark his territory."

I groan. God. What if Mandy is right? I don't want anything to sour the good place Devyn and I have been in lately.

I look past Mandy when I see Devyn enter the bar from the

corner of my eye. I jump out of my seat and meet him there, lacing my arm in his when we walk back to the table together.

"Devyn, this is Caro."

Carolina stands to shake his hand.

"Your sister?" Devyn says, their hands still linked. "Nice to meet you, doctor."

Carolina laughs. "Please call me Carolina."

"Carolina," he says, with a soft roll of his 'r' that has one of Carolina's brows floating up with approval.

"This is Mandy. She works with Caro and is an amazing artist. I'll take you to her next solo show."

"That'd be great," Devyn says as he shakes Mandy's hand.

Pleasantries all done, we take a seat and let the grilling begin.

Carolina asks the practical questions, while Mandy asks the intrusive ones.

"Where are you going to live after the wedding?" Caro asks.

"We're going to look for a house not too far from either of our jobs."

That has Carolina smiling. I didn't realize until now that she might be worried I'd move to Texas where the rest of Devyn's family is.

"How many kids are you planning on having?" Mandy asks.

"Whoa, Mandy!" I scold.

Mandy just shrugs but doesn't take her eyes off Devyn's face.

"We haven't really talked about that—"

"You're planning on getting married and you don't even know if you both want kids?" Mandy asks with disapproval.

Before either Devyn or I have a chance to answer, Sofia cuts us all off. "Sara wants to have two to four," she says. Then she borrows a chair from a nearby table and squeezes in between Devyn and me. "Hi," she says. "I'm Sofia, Sara's other best friend."

"Nice to meet you, Sofia."

The Spanish inquisition continues for about fifteen minutes, and my back starts to break into a sweat. Poor Devyn. I'm sure his shirt is drenched by now too.

I suppose my friends are right, at the end of the day. We've talked a lot about what our relationship will be like as a married couple. Devyn shared what makes him tick, and I did the same. But all of those conversations were theoretical; if we get into an argument, Devyn needs alone time to cool off and think, and I need to go on a run.

We discussed absolutely nothing practical. I'm not even sure if he wants to have joint bank accounts, and I'm starting to dread asking him. I absolutely need separate finances but do not know if that will be a deal breaker for him. What if two kids are too much for him? Does he even want to have kids? What if he wants to have six or eight? I think I'm about to be sick with all the worrying as Devyn continues to answer question after question, letting them roll off his back with his easy, carefree demeanor.

It's only when Ramiro steps into view, standing right in front of me, that any sense of calm enters my body. His presence—steady and true—soothes me more than anything these days.

"I see you got the party started already?" he asks from his position behind Caro.

"Hey," Sofia says, a bit confused, not having heard earlier when I told Carolina and Mandy that Ramiro would be stopping by. "Take my seat. I'll go grab you a drink."

Ramiro tips his chin, tells her his beer preference, then sits in her vacated chair. Between Devyn and me.

Mandy's words from earlier flicker through my brain. He's here to claim his territory. I chug my beer and catch Sofia's attention behind the bar, signaling with my fingers to make it two. Since moving in with Ramiro, I've become quite fond of the beer he likes.

When Sofia sets both bottles in front of us, it would be impossible to miss the way Devyn's eyes fixate on them.

Reaching for anything to break the tension that has fallen over the group, I scan the bar. "Hey, Mandy, isn't that Dr. Bel?"

Mandy twists in her chair to take a look behind her.

"Isn't that the guy from work you've had a crush on for a while now?" Sofia asks from her spot, still standing.

Mandy whirls back around to throw daggers with her eyes at Sofia for her comment. "No," she says. "I do not have a crush on him. But I am going to go say hi."

"What?" Carolina asks, no trace of her surprise hidden. "Since when do you talk to Dr. Bel? I thought you were avoiding him since the break room—"

"No. I'm not avoiding him." Mandy rolls her eyes. "I'm babysitting for him, remember?"

At the same time Carolina and I both asks, "He's the doctor you've been babysitting for?"

Mandy groans. "Ugh. I'll be back. You two keep him in the hot seat," she says, standing and taking her drink with her—a sure sign she has no plans of coming back to our table.

"Oh, we will," Ramiro says, a mischievous grin on his lips.

Devyn laughs, and Ramiro follows, but it's forced and awkward. I keep chugging beers to cope with this pressure-cooker moment.

Since Sofia had to get back behind the bar, that's two friends down and two to go before I can unclench every muscle in my body.

"I'm just messing with you, man," Ramiro says. "I'm here to be supportive. Anything I can do to help with the wedding? Want a bachelor party with the guys from work?"

"It's nice of you to offer," Devyn says in a friendly tone that feels odd in contrast to his calculating gaze. "But no thank you. My baby sister will be my best man, and I don't think she'll be too keen on going to a strip club."

"All right," Ramiro says. "No bachelor party, but if I can do anything, let me know."

Devyn stands and rounds the seats, taking Mandy's seat on the other side of me. He laces his fingers with mine, but it's Ramiro he's looking at. "We will," he says coolly. "If we think of anything."

Ramiro nods, a forced smile pressed to his beer bottle as he takes a sip.

"Who wants to play darts?" I ask to diffuse the moment.

"No," Carolina groans. "I hate darts."

Ramiro is about to agree—I know he likes to play darts—but Sofia leans in between us, setting another beer in front of Ramiro.

"I didn't order another one," Ramiro says.

"From the lady at the bar," Sofia says. The rest of us, including Ramiro, follow her gaze to the bar.

"The redhead?" Ramiro asks.

Sofia shakes her head. "No, the brunette."

"Even better," he says, picking up his beer and leaving the table.

I'm relieved for all of one second someone finally managed to pull him away from this table and distract from the fight that I'm not entirely sure was inevitable. Then I think about what just happened. A woman just picked up Ramiro, and he—he went!

From that moment onward, I have an incredibly hard time not glancing up from my drink to peek up at Ramiro and the woman. He says something that must be the funniest joke in the world by the way the woman laughs.

I roll my eyes. How obvious can she be? Then I wonder if this happens to him everywhere he goes, but of course it must. The man is walking sex-on-a-stick hot. In fact, no one dared ask him out when he first sat next to me, but the minute Devyn took my hand in his and didn't let go, that's when the first drink arrived.

My stomach sours the more they keep on flirting, and I'm so distracted I'm no longer listening to Carolina and Devyn's conversation.

"Right, sugar?"

Devyn asks. Sugar is what he calls me. He's talking to me. Oh.

"What's that?" I ask innocently.

"We're keeping the wedding small. Just friends and close family," he says, not once faltering in his smile.

"Yeah. Simple. You know I'm not one for big parties."

The rest of the evening, I do my best to ignore the flirting going on at the bar. What Ramiro does is none of my business. Especially now that I'm wearing Devyn's diamond on my finger.

Carolina calls it a night first, and Devyn and I settle our tab before we head out.

"Would you drive me home?" I ask him. "I'll get a ride share tomorrow to get my car."

Devyn nods. "I can bring you back in the morning, maybe make a date of it—go to brunch or something?"

I stop on the sidewalk and get on my tippy toes to kiss him. "That sounds nice," I say.

When I'm ready to keep walking, I feel Devyn stiffen, holding his ground, and I turn to face him. "What is it? Did you forget something?"

"I was thinking better of it. The boys are with Jaleesa for the night, right?"

"Yeah. They are."

"Why don't you come home with me, then? We'll get brunch together, then come pick up your car."

For some reason I can't explain, the first thing I think about is Ramiro and the brunette. Will he take her home? Will he go to her place? What time will he get back?

It's none of my business, I remind myself.

It shouldn't matter … and yet … it does. It matters in a big way I don't want to analyze too closely in my beer-foggy brain.

"I didn't plan on it," I explain. "Don't have my overnight bag."

"I've got everything you need," Devyn says with a flirty grin.

I laugh and pull on his arm, so he'll start walking again. "I don't have any clothes."

"Aww, sugar, clothes weren't exactly part of my plans."

"Not tonight," I say more firmly, though I'm starting to question myself. Why do I need to be home so badly, when I could in theory have a night completely off?

"All right," Devyn says, "I won't push." And despite his soft words, for the entire ride to Ramiro's, there's a heavy scowl painted on Devyn's face—a scowl that not even a fervent kiss in his car can wipe off his face before he drives away back to his place—alone.

CHAPTER 27

SPRING

Wednesday afternoon I get a text from Carolina that she got us lunch, so I head to the doctor's lounge where she awaits with a caprese sandwich.

"Thank you," I say. We're understaffed today and I'm exhausted from this morning alone.

"You're welcome. I also wanted to ask how the boys are doing. We're coming up on a year, aren't we?"

I swallow my bite. "Yeah. I'm not sure how to handle this, but I'm sure Ramiro will talk with their grief counselor. I'm hoping they'll want to go to her gravesite. Tidy it up, freshen up flowers."

"You have to do what's right for them," Carolina reminds me.

"I know."

We eat our lunches in relative silence, and when I'm done, before I have a chance to leave, she drops the bomb that I'm sure was her plan when she lured me here with food to begin with.

"I want to talk to you about the wedding," she says.

"Okay, shoot."

"Are you sure you're ready to walk away from Ramiro?"

"Carolina, we've been over this," I say, annoyed.

"I know. I just don't think you know how much potential there is with him. And I'm not saying Devyn isn't wonderful, I'm sure he is. He's seemed nice the few times I've been around you two together. He definitely passed muster during our initial meet, and Dad approves. But I really think Ramiro—"

"Why can't you let this go?"

Carolina's lips thin between her teeth. I know my sister too well to not recognize when she's keeping something from me. Sometimes, I wonder if we share a brain because I'm so in-tune with her feelings and emotions, and at this very moment, she is hiding something.

"What aren't you saying, Caro?"

She lets out a breath. "Okay. You're not supposed to know any of this. So help me god, Sara, if you tell a soul what I'm about to tell you—"

"Spit it out, Ramirez."

"Remember after Brian," she says, and I flinch at hearing his name. I'd love nothing more than to scrub the memory of him or his name from my brain, but it seems I'm destined to live with the reminder of my mistakes forever. Carolina keeps talking, pushing past the flinch I know she saw. "I took you home and Ramiro helped me get you out of the car and settled at Dad's?"

"Vaguely. I was still slightly medicated when you took me home."

"Well, Ramiro kinda forced me to tell him what happened."

"Carolina! You didn't!"

"I didn't have a choice. If I hadn't, he was going to go interrogate you, and you had been through enough. All I told him was his name, and that you had dated him. And roughly where I thought he was working at the time."

"Okay, that was a long time ago. What does this have to do with now?"

"You never knew, and I think you should know. Ramiro

wanted to keep this from you—he wanted to keep this from me too, but I forced it out of him. After I told him Brian's name, Ramiro disappeared for a few days. He came back with a busted brow and lip, and he never said what happened. He never confirmed he found Brian. He didn't want me to know in case Brian pressed charges, but when I asked if he got you justice, Ramiro … well, Ramiro smiled."

"He did what?" I screech.

"Did you ever hear from Brian again? I'm pretty sure Ramiro scared him off."

My eyes sting thinking of Ramiro doing that for me. But why? And why keep it a secret? There's no doubt in my mind that back then, Ramiro would have exploded without considering the possible consequences of his actions. But that was such a long time ago. "Why are you telling me this now, Caro?"

Carolina rubs her hand over her face, exasperated, because apparently there is something she is thinking that I can't catch on to. "Because both of you are too stupid to realize Ramiro is in love with you. How do neither of you see it? He maybe won't admit it to himself, and you're distracted with Devyn, but everyone knows he's in love with you."

"Carolina—" I whine.

"Just think about it for two seconds, okay? You should have seen him, Sara. After I took you to my room and he forced Brian's name out of me. He was wild. I'd never seen Ramiro like that, and that's saying something because he's always been so damned reactive. And it wasn't because he loved me and you're my little sister. Ramiro was out for blood because someone hurt you, because he loved you even then—even if he wouldn't let himself admit it."

"You're insane—"

Carolina snorts, then throws her hands in the air, signaling resignation. "Fine. I tried. All I want is for you not to go into your marriage without having all the information. Do yourself a favor, though, will you? Before you go any further with wedding planning, talk to Ramiro. Be sure you've picked the right guy, because I think the one you've always loved has been right there all along. And he still is."

TALK TO RAMIRO.

Should be easy enough, right? We're both adults, and we've had many a difficult conversation this past year. For two people who hardly said hello before becoming roommates, we've come a long way.

The harder part will be deciding if I continue with Devyn, if Carolina's suspicions are true.

If, and there's a really big 'if,' Ramiro does love me, and has loved me, I can't deny I also love Devyn. It would have been one thing if Devyn had never come into the picture, but he did, and I do love him. I love them both.

It is possible to be in love with two people at the same time. The question is, who am I willing to devote loyalty and a future to?

After I pick up René and Oscar from school, I'm practicing the conversation in my head. While I cook dinner for them, I practice asking him if he loves me—and if he does, for how long.

I'm determined to talk to him tonight after the guys go to bed, but right as dinner is ready, I get a text from him asking if I can stay with the boys tonight. Leonardo, his best friend who's been in the army, is on leave and in town for a few days, so they are going out to a bar.

I remember Leonardo vaguely from before he enlisted. I remember Leo and his younger brother Marco raising hell along with Ramiro, but I mostly heard about it through stories

Carolina or Don Gustavo shared over the years. Shortly after I moved to this neighborhood, both Marco and Leo enlisted.

While Ramiro is friendly with many of the other mechanics he works with, I know he misses his best friends like hell. I know that much for a fact, so I can't very well deny him the precious few days he might have with Leo.

It looks like our conversation will have to wait until tomorrow.

It's two in the morning when I hear the door open and whispered voices filter into the living room.

After grabbing my slippers and wrapping myself in a robe, I head downstairs to find Leo propping up Ramiro, who is holding on to him with one arm around his neck.

"Sara!" Ramiro shouts in a stage whisper with the biggest smile.

"Shhh, you'll wake the boys up," I say.

"Shhh," he repeats, bringing his finger to his mouth, smiling around it. "Okay. You are so pretty tonight."

I shake my head. "Please tell me you didn't drive like that."

"No, ma'am," Leo says, followed by a hiccup. "Took a ride share. Where do you want him?" Leo asks.

"The couch is fine. Thanks, Leo."

The minute his head hits the pillow, Ramiro lets out a soft snore.

Realizing he's heading out the door, I stop Leo with a hand on his massive bicep. "Why don't you stay a few minutes? Have a cup of coffee? Sober up a little before you go?"

He spins around to find me again, and with a huge grin he nods, then follows me to the kitchen where he sits at the kitchen island.

Leo sips on the coffee gingerly after I pour it, and I have to fight not to snicker at the sight of this behemoth sipping coffee from what looks like a tiny cup of espresso in his massive hand. I can almost picture him poking out his little finger, though he doesn't. Instead of laughing, I make myself a tea and join him.

"Can I ask you something?" Leo asks.

"Of course."

"What the hell did you do to Ramiro?"

I rear back. "What? I didn't do anything."

"You got him all fucked up."

"I don't think—it's Francisca ... not ..." I trip over my words. "Oh dear. I don't know what you're talking about."

"All night," Leo says, then hiccups again. "All night, it was Sara this, and Sara that. Sara says. After the bar, I took him to a strip club to get his mind off you. Got him a lap dance with this beauty who I know for a fact is his type, and he shoved her right off his lap. He said something about Sara."

"Really?" I asked, not at all pleased.

Leo nods. "Yeah. The poor woman landed on her ass on the floor, and we got kicked out."

I grab my mug of tea to hide my smile.

Leo barks out a laugh that has me shushing him again. "It's not funny, Sara. They kicked us out! I'm now banned from the only strip club worth any salt around here."

"Too bad," I say with a shrug, still amused as all hell at what happened.

"Well, I didn't do anything to Ramiro. I'm just temporarily here to help him out with the boys and look—" I bring up my hand to flash him my ring.

Leo's jaw drops as he sways slightly in his seat from trying to focus on my hand. "Oh," he says a bit forlornly in a way that is almost comical. "So that's why he's all fucked up. You're getting married."

"I sure am."

"Do I know him?"

I shake my head. "Don't think so. He's a mechanic at Tavo's with Ramiro—moved up here this last year."

"So, not only do you not give my boy the time of day, but you also then get engaged to his coworker?" He shakes his head solemnly. "Damn, Sara. I didn't know you were so cold-hearted."

"Hey," I whine. "I'm not cold-hearted. I'm here helping him, aren't I?"

"I'm just teasing you," Leo says.

Heading to the living room, Leo trails me. I kneel next to the couch to take Ramiro's shoes off and lift his head gently to prop a pillow under his head. Ramiro murmurs something I can't understand followed by a barely there whisper that I think is, "Sara, please."

Leo snorts, and I sense him walking to the door, so I stand to follow him.

We continue to chat in the living room as we head out together. He beams when I tell him I got my master's in nursing, and I beam equally brightly at him when he admits this might be his last year in the military. Unsure if he wants to re-enlist, he might be back home next year.

"You're not driving, are you?" I ask him.

He shakes his head and points next door with his thumb. "Don Gustavo is letting me crash at his place for a few days."

"It's great seeing you, Leo. Really. I'm glad you've stayed safe," I tell him and mean it.

"Thanks. You look good, too. Thanks for taking care of my boy. Take care," Leo whispers by the door.

"You too," I say with a smile and reach for a hug. I meet with the hard wall of muscle the army has transformed him into. Leo is tall and handsome, with beautiful swarthy skin and inky-black hair like Ramiro's, if he ever lets it grow out. I remember most of the single women on this block were head over heels in love with Leo before he left. I can't imagine what they're like now that he's nearly doubled his size in pure muscle.

Despite having said goodbyes already, Leo lingers. Feeling awkward as I tend to do, I fill the silence. "How's your baby brother?"

"Ah, Marco is somewhere on the Pacific."

That's right, Ramiro's other best friend left for the Navy straight out of college. Can't believe he's still there.

"Can I ask you something?" Leo asks, his eyes downcast and suddenly looking a little sheepish.

"I haven't seen Camila," I say, anticipating that he was going to ask about a young woman from down the street he was once in love with. "Last I heard, she went to the east coast for med school. She should be done this year, if my calculations are right."

"I wasn't going to ask about Camila," Leo says, unable to meet my eye. It's too dark, but I'd bet my favorite running shoes his cheeks have turned red at the mention of her name.

"Oh, you weren't?"

He shakes his head. "No. I was going to ask that you fix whatever you did to Ramiro."

"What? I already told you. I did nothing."

"You sure? Cuz tonight he was …"

"What?"

Leonardo scratches the back of his head. "Fucked up, Sara. He got drunk, and he was fucked up in the head over you."

"What did he say?" I ask, running his words from earlier through my mind. He never really gave any specifics about why he thinks Ramiro is messed up about me.

"It's not my place to say, but do me a favor? Don't hurt him?"

Thanking him for his service and asking him to stay safe one last time, I walk him out into the dark night. I watch the broad back of the lovesick soldier retreat into the darkness, hoping he and Camila will find a way back to each other one day.

When I place a blanket over Ramiro to settle him in for the night, he stirs. "Sara," he whines.

"I'll go get you a glass of water," I say, but Ramiro grabs my hand, holding me in place.

"Sara, don't do it," he says.

"You don't want water?"

"Don't marry Devyn. You can't," he slurs.

"Ramiro, you're drunk. This isn't the time for this conversation."

"I'm not that drunk, Sara, I lo—"

"Don't, Ramiro. Don't say what you were about to say. Not today."

"Why not today?"

"You really don't remember?"

Ramiro sits up and swings his legs so his feet reach the floor. He studies me, and he doesn't seem quite as drunk as I thought he did when he walked in. I pry my hand from his to head to the kitchen and bring him a glass of water.

So many years imagining he'd love me back, when he's finally about to say it, he couldn't have picked a worse moment. Any other time, any other day, it would have been a welcome declaration. Understanding he is drunk, I do my best to keep my temper in check, but inside I'm seething at his timing. I can't believe I'm asking him to stay quiet, but I have no other choice.

When he gulps down the water, I grab the glass. "It's her one-year anniversary, Ramiro. Francisca died a year ago today."

"It is?"

"I thought that's why you got hammered."

"No. I didn't realize … I … oh, how are Oscar and René?"

"They're fine. We talked about playing hooky from school and work. Instead, we're planning on heading to her gravesite to freshen up her flowers. Maybe ice cream for breakfast after. They were both on board for skipping school, at least."

Ramiro smiles. "You think of everything."

"Will you come with us?" I ask him, knowing he will.

"Yeah, Sara. I'll come with you."

AFTER I'M DONE GETTING READY IN THE MORNING, I HEAD TO THE boys' room to wake them up. I'm startled to find René already dressed. The shower in their bathroom is running, so I know Oscar is in there.

René is freshly showered himself, wearing his church clothes, and has styled his hair with gel and a side part I remember seeing all the time on him when Francisca took them to church.

"You dressed for your mom?" I ask.

He nods at me from the reflection in his mirror. "She said we had to dress our best for church. I know it's not church ... but it feels like it."

"It does, doesn't it?" I say, validating his feelings.

"You got Oscar to wake up and start getting ready?"

"Yeah."

"That's so helpful, René. Thank you."

"I think Mom would like that."

"She sure would. Would you like me to do Oscar's hair like yours, or you think you got it?"

"I got it," says the little boy who has had to grow up so fast.

OSCAR PICKS OUT A BOUQUET OF BLUE IRISES, RENÉ ONE OF WHITE calla lilies, and Ramiro a dozen red roses. The colorful blooms brighten the face of Francisca's tombstone, where they're carefully and lovingly placed.

"Miss Jenna says we can talk to her, especially when we

come here to see her," Oscar says helpfully over a stretch of silence.

"I think your counselor is right, buddy," I say. "Would you like to say a few words now, or do you each want alone time?"

"Alone time," René says. "Oscar and me. If that's okay."

Ramiro offers me his elbow and I lace my arm through it so we can go on a short walk to be out of earshot but not out of sight.

"When they're done talking to her, I can go on a walk with the boys if you want alone time with her too," I say.

Ramiro smiles sadly at me. "No. I talk to her all the time. I don't need to be here to do it."

For some reason, that thought makes me smile. Maybe Miss Jenna is doing more to help this man through his grief than either of us could have imagined.

CHAPTER 28

After a long weekend and longer week at work, I rush home after a rare day shift Friday evening, and don't so much as wince when the door accidentally slams behind me. I run to my bedroom, find a change of clothes, text Devyn, and hop into the shower.

After I'm done dressing, I get a disappointing text from Devyn. I forgot he has poker with his buddies tonight, so I can't share my good news. I check on the boys next, and they're not in their rooms.

The house is quiet until the front door opens and Ramiro walks in, still in his work clothes. "Ramiro!" I squeal and nearly jump on him when I throw my arms around him.

"What is this?" he asks, wrapping an arm around my waist.

"I have good news! Where are the boys?"

"Trevor's. Jaleesa picked them up after school for a play date since we had them over last weekend."

"Oh," I say with disappointment. I'm buzzing with excitement about telling everyone what happened at work today.

"Well?" Ramiro asks.

"What?"

"What's the good news?"

Right. I smile at him, my excitement coming back in a second wave. "I got the promotion I wanted!"

"You did?" Ramiro asks, his entire face glowing with the brightest smile I've seen on him all year.

"I did! You are now looking at Heartland Metro Hospital's oncology department day nurse manager." I prop my hands on my hips and make myself tall. "And I got a huge pay raise."

"This is amazing," Ramiro says, throwing his hands in the air, then bringing them down around me for a hug.

I hug him back. While he congratulates me, he twirls me in his arms one too many times. When I complain I'm getting dizzy, he sets me down and pulls away from me—both of us a mess of giggles and painfully wide smiles.

"I knew you'd get it," he says. "Never doubted you."

"Thanks, Ramiro," I say at hearing his genuine words.

He brushes a loose strand of hair to tug behind my ear. "I'm so proud of you," he breathes out, looking me straight in the eye like he wants to dare me to doubt just how proud of me he is.

I press my hand to my heart. "You don't know how much that means to me."

What happens next stuns us both. I don't know if it's gratitude for his words, sheer elation at reaching one of my biggest career goals since I became a nurse, or simply the beautiful man standing in front of me, but I close the distance between us again.

I wrap my arms around his neck and pull him down for a kiss. A breathy kiss while we both continue to recover from all the excitement. I nip his lip and he kisses me back harder, his hand cupping the back of my head to keep me in place and so close to him.

For long seconds we kiss and kiss, and I'm not thinking about what this means, or why it's happening. I don't so much as stop to analyze why he's kissing me back, or what this means for Devyn and me.

Instead, I focus on the silky feel of his tongue, on the softness of his lips. I rub my mouth against his to feel the scruff of his five o'clock shadow scraping my skin so I can feel the pain within the tenderness. His bicep flexes in my palm when he moves to tighten me to his body. We're both desperate to stay like this, to have our bodies connected and never let go.

He grows bolder with his kiss and shoves his tongue down my throat in a kiss that feels a lot like … like we're having sex.

The mere thought of a naked Ramiro Jimenez heats my very core, and my toes curl inside my favorite sneakers.

I drag my weight to fall to the couch, and he follows, pulling on top of my body. That's when my legs get a mind of their own, wrapping around his waist, pulling his groin painfully against me.

My eyes almost fly open when I feel every inch of a massive hardness between us. In the million and one times I pictured Ramiro naked, I always imagined he'd be big, but my meager imagination didn't imagine this big.

Even with the surprise of it, I don't let my eyes open, not right away. I let myself pretend for all of one moment that this is right. That we are doing nothing wrong by kissing like this— by wanting like this.

But we are. We are doing something incredibly wrong, and my conscience won't let me live with it for long.

When I do finally open my eyes, and I see him in front of me, his eyes closed while he kisses, and it's not Devyn I'm kissing …

I stop moving. I slacken my legs' death grip on his middle, and break our kiss, turning my head to the side, so he continues kissing my neck instead.

With every drop of shame I have ever felt, I whisper, "Stop, please."

The words aren't even fully out of my mouth when Ramiro

freezes. When his lips pull away from my neck, my stupid, stupid tears brim to the surface at the loss of his mouth.

He immediately gets to his feet, respecting my wishes, and takes a step back. I sit up, straighten my top, then stand. "I'm sorry," I say. "I don't know what happened, what that was."

"Sara, look at me." He lifts my face with one knuckle under my chin, but my eyes only move from the floor to his chest. "Look at me, mi ciel—" he clears his throat. "Look at me, Sara."

I drag my gaze to his, and I meet with soft and tender eyes, not at all angry.

Ramiro moves to grab my arm, and he lifts my hand until my forearm is in front of his face so he can kiss my scar there. A small little peck, and when he's done and gingerly lets my arm down, he massages the scar with his thumb in small circles, not letting go. My brain freezes. I was fully expecting for him to be angry or frustrated that I stopped the heated kiss before we went too far—beyond a point of no return. But there isn't a trace of anger or frustration anywhere on his face, just tenderness.

"As long as I have breath in me," he says, "you'll never have to do anything you don't want to again. I won't let anyone hurt you. You hear me? Not even me."

MY LEG IS SHAKING UNCONTROLLABLY AS MY FOOT TAPS THE pavement. I'm sitting on a bench outside Devyn's apartment building. I thought about calling him, confessing just what kind of fiancée he has, but I couldn't do that to him over the phone, and I know his poker game is over soon and he'll be home.

I stand to pace in front of the building, then I sit.

Stand and pace.

Sit.

Fidget with my phone.

Thirty maddening minutes later, I hear his voice as he reaches the front door.

"Sara? Baby? This is a pleasant surprise."

The second I stand, he wraps his arms around me.

"You don't know how happy I am to see you," he says.

"Devyn, we need to—"

He cuts me off with a silencing kiss. That's when I break out into a sob and start shaking with the shame of it all. Devyn pulls away and studies me, one hand cupping the side of my face. "Well, what's this, sugar? Am I that bad a kisser?"

"No, it's just—"

"Just what?"

"We need to talk. Can we sit?"

I break away from his hug to sit on the bench again and pat the seat next to me.

"Wouldn't you want to come inside? Talk there? More private?"

I glance at the busy street, with beautiful dressed-up people heading to bars and other nightlife activities. All of them in their own little happy worlds. The thought of him kicking me out of his apartment sickens me, so I opt to stay here. I shake my head. "No. Here. It's important, please."

Devyn sticks his hands in his hoody pocket and takes the spot where I patted with my hand.

There's no dancing around this, no rationalizing what I've done, no explanation that I could provide that would spare him this hurt, so I just say it. "I cheated on you tonight."

Devyn freezes for a second, then he hunches over in his seat, crumpling like a deflating mylar balloon until his hands catch his head. His fingers tighten in his hair, and he takes several deep breaths before sitting up straight again.

His eyes are clear when he looks at me again, but his set jaw and the bulging veins on the side of his neck give away the anger he's bottling in. Instead, he smiles. It's not a sweet or encouraging smile. It's a defeated one. "Come on. Let's go upstairs and talk."

I glance around us at the safety of people, and he follows my line of sight. His face falls when realization must hit him. "You think I'd hurt you?" he asks, incredulously.

I shake my head, tightening my sweater around my middle. "No, I—"

He scoots closer and squeezes my arm, then kisses my temple. "I wouldn't hurt you." Ramiro's words echo from Devyn's mouth.

And I believe them. Both of them. Neither would ever physically hurt me. My lack of trust in men has nothing to do with Ramiro or Devyn, and I can feel as that trust starts to rebuild in my chest, put back together by these two beautiful men.

"No," I say. "I know you wouldn't hurt me."

"Good. Now come on. We should talk this out in private. And it's freezing out here."

The entire elevator ride, he rubs his temples and takes deep breaths like he's trying to keep himself from crying or maybe from screaming.

As soon as we step into his apartment and the door closes behind me, he says, "Tell me everything."

"I'm not sure you want to know—"

"I do. I need details, Sara. You owe me that much." The words are accusing, but the tone is soft and measured, helping me feel at ease.

I nod.

"Was it Ramiro?"

With my eyes closed, I force myself to nod again. "Yes."

"Did you have sex?"

"No."

His relieved breath leaves him, and he smiles before taking another deep breath.

"Did you want to?"

My eyes fall with shame. "Yeah. I think so, for a second. I'm such an asshole, Devyn. I'm so, so sorry. I can't tell you just how sorry I am."

Devyn nods, then swallows hard. "Were either of you naked?"

"No."

Another smile. "What happened, then?"

"We kissed."

"That's it? You kissed? Stop it with the twenty questions, Sara. Please. Tell me what happened."

So, I do. I tell him about the promotion, and this man that I've just hurt so much stops to smile and congratulate me. I tell him Ramiro was the only one around to tell, and we were excited and happy and celebrating and that's when the kiss happened. It was frenzied and I don't think either of us was thinking straight. I tell Devyn all of this.

"He kissed you or you kissed him?"

"I kissed him first," Devyn's face falls and then he asks for every physical detail of that kiss.

It's hard, but right now I'll do anything he asks. If this is my purgatory for what I've done, then I'll walk through it. I explain in graphic detail everything about the kiss, or rather, make-out session, his eyes shut tight like he's trying to scrub the images from his memory the second they enter.

"Who stopped it?" he asks.

"I did. It felt right, Devyn, but it felt wrong. I knew it would hurt you, and I stopped it."

He stays quiet for long minutes. With no more questions for him to ask me, and no more details for me to offer him, we sit in the silence. Finally, he speaks. "Thank you for telling me," he says.

There's silence for several more minutes—the longest minutes of my life—while Devyn paces the length of his apartment several times, thinking, and I'm sure, finding his composure.

When he finally speaks, I feel like I can breathe again. "In some fucked up backward way, this experience makes me trust you more. Despite the kiss, you didn't sleep with him, and you told me about it. I've heard communication can make or break a marriage. Anyway, that's what my pa told me before he died. Cold feet would be common in the best of times, and you had already told me there were feelings there for Ramiro, so I'm not too surprised, to be honest. I've gone into this with eyes wide open."

"Devyn, I'm so, so incredibly sorry. You don't know how awful I feel for hurting you."

"I'm not angry, Sara. Just … disappointed."

That makes me wince. What's worse than anger? Disappointment. Disappointment is way worse.

"Do you still love me?" he asks.

"Yes," I say instinctively. I don't have to stop to think about it because I know I do love Devyn too. Too?

"And you also have feelings for him?"

I shut my eyes tight when I nod. "I don't want to, Devyn. But yes, I do."

"Then you have a choice to make. Him or me? I'm not the sharing type, sugar, and I highly doubt Ramiro is either."

I smile at the use of his nickname for me, like this is all up to me, but I guess it is.

"I choose you," I say almost immediately.

Devyn shakes his head, a sad smile forming on his mouth. "No. Take your time. Make the right decision."

"It's you, Devyn. I've already chosen you. I don't know what happened tonight, I went crazy or something. I wasn't thinking," I peer down at my engagement ring and twist it around my finger. "I don't deserve it, but if you want to move forward together, I'd like to still be your fiancée."

He pulls me to him then and wraps big comforting arms around me. "Well, then, let's go to bed, sugar."

We don't make love tonight. Instead, he holds on to me tightly, so tightly, it's like he's afraid of letting go lest I float away from his grip.

CHAPTER 29

Devyn drives me home in the morning since I didn't drive last night. As he always does when he's dropping me off, he walks me to the front door. Unlike every other time, though, I don't invite him in. He doesn't ask about the change, but I'm sure he realizes I need to keep him away from Ramiro right now.

Instead, he says, "I'm not happy that you're still going to stay here."

"I know. I'm sorry. We have a plan for my leaving that the boys already agreed to. I really can't change it up on them now. I'm sorry."

"I know, Sara. I know you have to stay, but it doesn't mean I have to like it."

I smile at him. "I promise nothing will happen again while I'm here."

He kisses me goodbye and has just turned around to leave when the front door opens. The sound of it makes Devyn turn to face me again.

Ramiro steps out holding a trash bag he's taking out to the bin. "Oh, hey—" he starts to say, but is cut off by Devyn's fist to his mouth. Ramiro stumbles back, letting go of the trash bag that falls to the ground, and cups his face, wincing with pain. "Fuck!" he growls.

"That's for last night, asshole," Devyn spits out, looming over Ramiro.

Ramiro straightens and looks between us, understanding dawning. His hands raise in surrender. "All right. I deserved that." Then he spits a bloody glob to the side.

"Yeah, you did," Devyn says. "And it didn't do you any good. We're still getting married, and when we do, you'll never put your hands on her again. Got it?"

Ramiro's face smooths out as he looks at me. I nod, confirming I'm still getting married, and his Adam's apple bobs when he swallows. A trickle of blood trails down his busted lower lip when he nods. This is not the first time Ramiro has bled for me, I realize now, remembering what Carolina shared about Brian. He wipes at the blood with the back of his hand, then looks at me straight in the eye. "You are?" he asks, but it's less of a question and more of a confirmation.

"We are getting married. And Devyn, I'd like for Ramiro to keep his invite, if it's okay with you. I want the boys there and they will have more questions if Ramiro can't go."

"I want him there too," Devyn says to me like Ramiro isn't standing in front of us.

"You do?" I ask, confused that he'd want the man I made out with only a week before our wedding to be present for our nuptials.

Ramiro is standing tall again, nearly matching Devyn's height, their eyes locked in a dare. "Yeah," Ramiro says bitterly, never once breaking eye contact with Devyn. "He wants me there to witness losing you to him."

Devyn smiles, and it's mocking, and it's a petty side of him I haven't seen, but I also understand that Ramiro and I have earned this side of Devyn with our betrayal.

I text Mandy and Sofia the following morning, begging them to cancel my bachelorette party. After what happened last night, I'm not in a celebratory mood. In some way, I guess I also don't feel like I deserve a bachelorette party. Not after how badly I hurt Devyn.

Mandy: No f'n way. We're going.

Me: Please?

Sofia: Do you know how hard it is to have a night out?

Sofia: I have someone covering at the bar.

Sofia: I actually found a sitter for Addy.

Sofia: I shaved my legs!!

Sofia: The stars aligned. We're going!

I roll my eyes. Sofia is not usually the one to guilt trip anyone into anything—that job belongs to Mandy most of the time. When I think about it, Sofia hasn't been able to pull away for much since having Addy, and her guilt trip is working. I type my next message more gently.

Me: What if you go without me?

Sofia: Not in a million years.

Mandy: I cleared Caro's schedule all afternoon so she could get out of work early.

Mandy: WE'RE going.

Me: Fine.

CHAPTER 30

Mandy goes to the bar to get us another round. Sofia rented out a section of a strip club for my bachelorette party and we have eight strippers for only four of us, which is a great ratio in my mind, several drinks in. Seven of the strippers are male, and I know Mandy asked for one female stripper for Sofia.

Sofia, who hasn't been with anyone since she got pregnant and had her daughter, is alight with mischief as she gets lap dance after lap dance.

It's Sofia, not Mandy as I had expected, who is enjoying this night the most.

When we arrived, Mandy handed me a stack of ones and fives that I've been tucking into boxer briefs all night as my tiara slides further and further down the side of my head until it's barely clipped on by the hair clips any longer.

The strippers are hot, and I'm giddy when I touch them. I spoke to Devyn to make sure he was okay with me having a bachelorette party after everything that happened and told him our plans for the night. I told him I could cancel, and we could go to dinner, but he shook his head and told me to go ahead. He said Ramiro and the strippers tonight will be the last men besides him I ever touch for the rest of my life, so I have a green light for everything except sex of any kind.

And I plan on taking full advantage of that green light because I'm too drunk not to.

When I look over at Carolina, she's sitting on one of the strippers. He sucks his finger in his mouth, draws it over his neck, and sprinkles salt on the same spot where it sticks to his saliva. Then he wedges a slice of lime between his teeth and hands Carolina her tequila shot. Sheepishly, and blushing, she takes it, licks off the salt from his neck, takes the shot, and with her mouth claims the lime wedge from his lips.

I've never seen Carolina do anything like this, and all I can think is 'Go, sister.' On my other side, Sofia is in a three-way make-out session with the female stripper and one of the other guys. It's Mandy I'd expect to do that kind of thing, but when I find her on the other end of the long table, she seems ... distracted more than anything.

I shrug and delightedly keep tucking bills into pair of glittery briefs after pair of glittery briefs.

I don't manage to get into much trouble after that, though I do manage to black out.

And the next morning ... the next morning is painful.

Which is, of course, why that's the precise moment to meet Devyn's family.

MRS. HOLLAND IS A SMALL WOMAN WHO LOOKS PUNY NEXT TO her son and daughter. She has the same shade of dusty blond hair as her son, but with a few white streaks in it. She is warm and inviting and takes me into her arms, thanking me for finally getting her son to settle down.

"It's me who should thank you, for raising such a wonderful son."

"And this pest here," Devyn says, "is Elise. My baby sister."

Elise takes me into a hug when her mom releases me. "I'm so happy to finally have a sister," she says.

"Thank you," I say.

Elise is tall and slim and looks nothing like her mom and brother. Devyn had shown me pictures of his dad before, so I know the dark brown hair and slightly round face are features she shares more with her father. "Are you okay?" Elise asks. "You look a bit green."

"A bit hungover," I admit with an embarrassed grin. "My bachelorette party was last night, and I'm afraid my girlfriends and I drank a bit too much."

"Yeah, Don Gustavo said Carolina had to call in sick."

"What?" I ask, completely incredulous. "She never calls in sick."

Devyn shrugs. "Guess you really raised hell, huh? Anyway, she stayed at Don Gustavo's, and he said he'd have her good as new with some pozole."

"Mmmm," I groan. "Pozole."

"I can't believe you didn't let us come yesterday so I could go to the bachelorette party too," Elise says with a fake pout.

"No way I'm letting my baby sister near a strip club."

Elise rolls her eyes, and it warms me to see their banter. "Some baby. I'm twenty-six!" she says with a scowl.

"Sure, pest. I'm still not going to facilitate your attendance at a strip club."

"I've been to a strip club before—"

Devyn covers his ears dramatically. "Don't want to hear it." When his hands come down, he says, "Don Gustavo said to go get you some pozole, so I'll go pick that up and let you ladies get to know each other."

While he's gone, I learn Mrs. Holland never remarried after

her divorce and she's a schoolteacher in El Paso. Elise is finishing up her master's in cyber security, and her undergrad work was in electronics engineering.

They ask me questions about my life, and expecting Devyn might have shared some of it already, I stick to the truth. I tell them about my parents and why they won't be present at the wedding, but that Don Gustavo is a sort of stepdad and he'll be walking me down the aisle this coming Saturday.

Mrs. Holland's hand squeezes mine when we're chatting over large mugs of coffee. "Well, you can call me 'ma,' dear," she says with a warm smile that brings a tear to my eye.

When Mrs. Holland heads to Devyn's spare bedroom to hang her dress and settle in, Elise corners me in the kitchen. I'm about to grab a soda from the fridge when she shuts the door and crosses her arms.

"I know my brother forgave you, so I will too. But if you hurt my brother again …"

"Oh," I say, closing my eyes. Devyn must have told her about the slip. "You know about—"

"Ramiro? Yeah. I know. Devyn is one of my best friends. You'd better not hurt him again."

"Elise, I never intended to hurt your brother. I love him. I truly do."

Elise smiles at me. "Good. He's crazy about you. You should hear the way he talks about you. About your future."

I smile at her. We don't get to talk much more because Devyn shows up with the soup, heats it up for me, and won't let me go shower until after I've eaten.

CHAPTER 31

After the makeup artist is done with my face, I take my robe off and step into the dress.

Sofia whistles. "You are going to stop Devyn's heart in that lingerie."

I laugh. "You mean the thong and garter?"

"Yeah. Lucky guy. He's going to have a great honeymoon. Where are you going again?"

"Virginia Beach. We'll wait for a big trip next year."

"Virginia Beach is great," Sofia says.

Carolina helps me with the back zipper, and Mandy and Sofia fluff the skirt for me.

"You look beautiful," Carolina says. She places my tiara on top of my head, and she's crying by the time she steps away from me.

"Don't cry," I plead. "You'll make me cry."

Mandy hands us all champagne glasses and raises hers for a toast. Our glasses raise to meet with hers, and before she sips her drink, she says, "May we all get laid tonight."

"Hear, hear!" Carolina says.

"At least we know for sure Sara will," Sofia adds, making me blush.

Sofia's hand goes to her heart. "Oh, look at the blushing bride."

I smack her arm playfully. "Will you stop it?"

Sofia snorts. "Fine. If you want, I'll just let Carolina make you cry."

I chug the rest of my champagne for bravery and set it down when a knock on the door turns our attention.

Elise pops her head in. "Okay to come in?"

"Yeah," I say, and smile when she steps in wearing a tux. She's taking her role as best man seriously. "You look great," I tell her.

She smiles at me. "You look beautiful," she says in return.

"Your brother hasn't escaped out a window yet?" I ask playfully.

Elise laughs. "He actually sent me to make sure you hadn't done exactly that."

Everyone laughs, but it's awkward. "Then please report to him that the bride is still in position."

"Ew. I'm going to pretend that wasn't as dirty as it sounded." With that, Elise is about to leave, and Carolina follows to close the door behind her, but when Elise turns the knob and the door swings open, Ramiro is standing there, his hand in a fist about to knock.

"Oh, hey," he says. "Could I have a word with Sara?"

Carolina turns to me for approval, and after I nod, she waves her hands for Sofia and Mandy to follow. As they all leave, Elise sends Ramiro a withering glare, likely assuming who he is, since I don't think we have introduced them yet.

His broad back is to me when he closes the door, and it expands with the intake of a deep breath. He turns to face me and palms his chest over his heart. "You're breathtaking, Sara."

I feel the heat rush to the apples of my cheeks again. "Thanks," I say.

"I had to see you before … uh, before—"

"Before I walk down the aisle?"

He smiles. "Yeah."

Then his smile vanishes, and his face turns into a shadowy, dark thing that worries me. "What is it?" I ask.

"I want to do something selfish."

"Okay …"

"I want to ask you—no—beg you not to marry Devyn."

He says it so calmly, like he's been thinking about it for a while. I want to assume he's joking, and I want to laugh, but he looks so serious, so tall and empowered by the suit he's wearing, I can't laugh. All I can do is ask, "Why?"

"Because I love you. Because I'm in love with you, and I think you love me too."

I step toward him and take his hand to lead him to a couch in the small sitting area of my dressing room. I maneuver the skirt of my dress so I can sit and hopefully not wrinkle it too much.

After setting the bouquet on the coffee table, I pat Ramiro's leg and keep my hand there for reassurance. "Ramiro, you are not in love with me—"

"I am—" he says.

I shake my head and silence him by raising a hand. "Let me finish." A nod. "I think you're fond of me, and maybe you do love me, but you're not in love with me. I think I know what's happening here. You're afraid of being with the boys alone for the first time, and I think you're desperate for things to stay the same, Ramiro, but you will do great. You'll do great because you're a good man, a good father, and you have a village supporting you, and that village includes me when I'm back from my honeymoon." At the word honeymoon, Ramiro closes his eyes. "You don't have to worry about losing me. You never will. I'm hopeful you and Devyn can put the past behind you, and with time, everything will return to normal."

"I'm not afraid of change. Don't pretend to tell me how I feel, Sara. I'm in love with you, damn it. It's one thing for you to sit here and tell me you love Devyn, and that you don't love me. I'm fine with that truth. But my truth is that I love you."

"I can't believe that—"

"Why not?" he asks with a tone of surprise.

I stand and grab the bouquet again. "You're right about one thing. I do love Devyn. And yes, I have feelings for you too, but I've done everything I could to stop them from growing and taking over—"

He stands now too. "But why can't you believe that I love you? Why can't you let yourself love me?"

"Because it's painful, Ramiro!" I shout, startling us both. I'm not the shouting type. In a more measured tone, I continue. "I'm sorry. I—uh, didn't mean to shout. To answer your question, because after my entire adult life of loving you, I wasn't your first, or even your second, choice. If you love me, I'm your third choice. Because I can't believe the entire time you were blinded by Carolina that you ever saw me. I was invisible to you. And Devyn … Devyn looks at me the way I used to look at you. The way I want to be looked at in return. It's too painful to think you love me, so please stop saying it."

"Oh, Sara, I'm sorry." He pauses to rub his head. "The last thing I wanted to do was make you cry on your wedding day."

I dash for a tissue and pat my eyes before my makeup is ruined. "I know. Listen, if you can't be here today, I understand."

His smile is tender when he squeezes my free hand. "I won't miss any of your big days if I can help it. I won't say it anymore if it hurts you, but I'll be out there with the boys. Okay?"

I sniffle and nod. "Thanks."

With that, he leaves, and shortly after, Don Gustavo is outside my dressing room. His eyes grow teary when he sees me. "Ready, mija?"

I smile. Mija. My daughter. What he calls Carolina. I nod with another sniffle and a smile. "Yeah."

Then I lace my arm through his.

INTERLUDE

At eleven-years-old, René Garcia Jimenez wouldn't have been able to express his feelings in so many words, but with the clarity that comes with age, maturity, and a lot of expensive therapy, thirty-year-old René can remember Sara's wedding with more perspective. He is, after-all, nearly the same age his dad was when he did the bravest thing René had ever witnessed.

Before the ceremony, Ramiro disappeared, leaving René and Oscar with Carolina on the front pew, representing Sara's family. They thought he'd be late, but eventually he showed up just in time for the ceremony, and René heard when Carolina leaned in his ear and asked, "Well? What happened?"

"Nothing," Ramiro said, and trained his stare on the altar. "She's going to be Sara Holland in a few short minutes."

"You're an idiot," Carolina said, loud enough for even Mandy, sitting just behind René, to hear, and making Mandy grunt.

"You are," René said in solidarity with Carolina. "Tía Carolina is right. You're an idiot."

Ramiro turned to René and blinked at his son. "That is very rude," Ramiro said.

René only shrugged. "She's supposed to be with us. She's supposed to be our mom. Not some other kid's."

Ramiro patted René's hand on his lap. "Sara will always love you and Oscar. She'll be your tía, like Carolina. You'll always have her in your life. She promised, remember? When has Sara broken a promise to you?"

"Ugh," René whined. "Not like that. She's supposed to be ours. Live with us. You're supposed to take her from Devyn. Like in the telenovelas."

Ramiro chuckled a little at his son's innocence. He'd known Francisca and Doña Pancha loved their telenovelas, and René and Oscar had grown up watching the soaps in their periphery. "Life doesn't work like that. And besides, she chose Devyn." Ramiro tried to reason with an eleven-year-old boy in whispers so the other wedding guests couldn't hear their conversation.

"Because you chose everyone but her," Carolina scoffed.

Now this comment, René didn't understand at the time, but now that he's older and he can understand the complexity of navigating adult relationships, not to mention having a better grasp of sarcasm, René knows exactly what Carolina meant: Ramiro had chosen Carolina. Then he chose René's mom. Not until Sara chose Oscar and René did it even occur to Ramiro to choose Sara. Or, so he thought, not having heard the conversation in Sara's dressing room before the wedding.

Carolina held René's hand, and they watched as Devyn stepped up to the altar. The music started, everyone stood, and Ramiro nudged both his sons so they'd stand too. The doors opened, and Sara looked like a princess on Don Gustavo's arm. Like a Disney princess if René had ever seen one, and he wondered if little birds and mice helped her get ready for that day.

In that moment, René felt a wave of sadness he couldn't comprehend in his young mind. She looked so beautiful, but she looked that way to leave them forever. Then the wave of sadness ebbed, and when it returned, it had transformed into sheer panic.

The panic in René's chest grew with every slow step Sara took. He tugged on Ramiro's sleeve to get his attention, and Ramiro tried shaking it off, keeping his eyes on the bride. So René tugged harder. "Dad!" he whisper-hissed. "Dad!"

Finally, Ramiro turned to look down at him. He ducked and whispered, "What is it? Do you need to go to the restroom?"

René shook his head. "No. You have to get her back!"

There was a desperation in René's voice that softened Ramiro's features. In René's mind, Ramiro wasn't taking this seriously enough. Shouldn't he be as panicked as René was?

Though he didn't understand the panic then, he now knows it was fear of losing a mom twice. In the year prior, Sara had turned into their mom. They weren't told that, and she never, not once, asked to be called Mom. That was never the expectation. She was meant to be temporary.

And yet ...

Even to this day, René shivers when he remembers that first Day of the Dead altar, and the whispered voice in his ear he'd sworn he imagined. A soft voice that sounded a lot like his first mom telling him Sara would keep him safe now. That Sara would take care of him and Oscar, that she'd help them remember their first mom. That Sara would love them like they were hers.

As an adult, of course René doesn't believe in ghosts, so he's reasoned it was actually a dream that happened after the ofrenda when he was already snuggled warm in his bed after Sara had tucked him in. But at the time, it felt real.

Sara was meant to be his mom, and Ramiro was about to ruin it.

"Dad," he pleaded, tears streaming freely now, shocking him and Ramiro both. "You have to get Mom back. *Please*," he begged in a watery voice. He wasn't talking about his first mom. He was talking about his second mom. The one he was on the brink of losing forever.

Oscar, who'd been listening, was clinging to Ramiro's other arm, chin trembling, and it wouldn't be long before he broke out into his own sob.

Ramiro only nudged René to sit down and wrapped an arm around him, tugging him close to his side for comfort. He squeezed his shoulder in reassurance, but René felt anything but reassured.

This was wrong.

So wrong.

A mistake.

As the priest spoke words that had no meaning to René at the time, he whispered pleadings in Ramiro's ear. "Please don't let her do this. Please don't let her leave. Please get her back for me." Then he started bargaining. "I'll be good always. I'll never get in trouble again. Please, just get her back."

It was a tantrum now. A full-blown tantrum like a toddler but measured in his whispers so he could keep his promise not to be bad anymore.

A whisper must have been too loud, because Sara's attention turned for a second, landing on the little boy clinging to Ramiro's neck. A thought passed between her and Ramiro, and Ramiro smiled at her, nodding, encouraging.

At seeing this betrayal, René wanted to kick and scream and throw a real tantrum, but instead, he resigned. He let go of Ramiro, brought his feet up to the bench where he was sitting so he could hug his knees and bury his face. He couldn't watch this. He clamped his ears with his hands. He couldn't hear this.

This was wrong.

Ramiro's soothing hand patted his hair, not forcing him to stop or to look up or to listen. A touch just as resigned as René felt.

And just when all hope was lost, René heard it. His whispered voice.

"Don Gustavo, Carolina, if I needed, could you take the boys and keep them for the weekend?"

"I have the weekend off," Carolina said with a huge grin. "I can stay at your place if it's easier for them to stay with their stuff in their rooms."

"Thank you," Ramiro said, and that's when René finally lifted his head to look at his dad with a questioning look.

Ramiro kissed the top of his head, then looked him straight in the eye. "I'm going to try my darnedest. Okay?"

"What?" René asked.

Ramiro smiled. "Like in the telenovelas." Then he winked at René.

René wiped his tears with the back of his hand and smiled, nodding at his dad. "Go get her, Dad!" But that time, he said it loud. So loud. So encouraging and so brave, it must have injected new bravery in Ramiro too, because when everyone turned to look at the little boy who had just screamed his encouragement, Ramiro sprang to his feet, and stood in front of the couple before they were fully wed.

DEVYN, SARA, AND THE PRIEST WERE ALL LOOKING AT RAMIRO now. Knowing the entirety of the wedding guests, staff from Sara's hospital, her boss Leah, the full workforce from the auto repair shop, and Devyn's family were all boring eyes into his back didn't calm his nerves one bit.

Sara had been right, though, and therapy had helped Ramiro understand he needed to start telling people how he felt. The alternative would be a life of hollow resentment and regrets that he earned himself. He couldn't let her go thinking she was his third choice because she never had been.

Even if she declined again, she had to know the truth. He had to try again. For his sons. For himself. Out of respect for the intense love he felt for her he'd be forced to take to his grave if she didn't walk out of this church with him today.

"Ramiro? What are you doing?" Sara whispered, still

holding on to Devyn's hands, her body twisting to look at Ramiro.

She looked breathtaking. Her updo cast a halo of blond curls framing her beautiful face, a thin tiara buried in the tresses. She was the perfect bride, if only she were *his* perfect bride.

"I love you, Sara. I'm in love with you. And I'm sorry, but you were wrong. You're not my second or my third choice. You're my only choice."

"Ramiro," she said, "this isn't the time to—"

"Don't you get it? It was supposed to happen this way. I was meant to wait for Francisca so I could have my sons. Your sons. They're ours. Together. It couldn't have happened any other way."

Sara's hands fell from Devyn's as she looked at her first true love. Her sky-blue eyes brimmed with tears when she looked at Ramiro, undecided on what to say next.

"Mi cielo. I know you love him," Ramiro pointed to Devyn. "And I'm sorry, man, but I have to try." Devyn nodded in response, composed, and holding his breath for Sara's answer, while Ramiro turned to Sara again. "But you can't lie to me and tell me you don't love me too. Now the question is, who do you want to make a home with? Build a family with?"

Behind him, Ramiro heard the soft footfalls of two little boys who sprang up to flank him a few feet back.

"Mom," René said, and Sara's tears spilled. "Please," René begged again, this time to his mom. "Come home with us."

That was the first time anyone had called Sara "Mom," and her hand pressed to her chest to calm a heart Ramiro knew must be swelling. He knew this because that's what it felt like the first time René called him Dad.

She shook her head, eyes bouncing over her guests, breath

coming in ragged, unsure of herself. Her entire body started shaking as she made up her mind.

She's going to marry Devyn, Ramiro thought. It's him. She was not sure how to reject the two little boys who just threw their hands into the fire for her along with his.

He took a deep breath, ready to turn around and leave with his sons. He closed his eyes for a moment to let himself imagine her saying yes. One second when he let himself believe he could have her and everything he wanted.

Through his closed lashes, a single tear fell. And he didn't care. He didn't care that Sara and Devyn saw the tear. That his sons saw him crying. He wasn't ashamed or embarrassed by his hurt. It was a tear for having lost Carolina to another love. A tear for having lost Francisca to another life. And a tear for having lost Sara to his own blindness and poor timing. He was simply resigned and vowed to also be accepting.

It didn't matter that he cried in public. Nothing mattered.

He'd lost her.

They'd lost her.

CHAPTER 33

He doesn't see me stepping down from the altar. His eyes closed, and holding his breath, I get closer to make sure I'm not imagining it. When I reach him, I see the trail of a single glimmering tear rolling down his tawny cheek. This must be a first for Ramiro Jimenez.

I let my hand float to hover over his face, and with one thumb, I clean up the tear. I rub my fingers together, inspecting them, feeling the wet on my skin, confirming it exists.

At feeling my touch, Ramiro's eyes fly open. He's completely startled.

He didn't think I'd pick him.

When his hand goes up to cup mine and presses it to the side of his face, he finally lets out a long exhale. "Sara?"

I smile at him and nod. "I'm coming home," I say, then I close my eyes with pain.

I've turned my back on a good man. A great man, even, but not my man. When I open them again, and turn around to say goodbye to Devyn, to apologize for hurting him, he's no longer standing next to the priest. I search until I find a set of doors closing behind his hunched back.

Fast footfalls follow in the same direction after him, and his mother and sister dash by in a flash of mauve-colored taffeta. Neither of them turns to look at me as they rush after Devyn.

When I look back at Ramiro, he's holding Oscar and René's hands as he says something to Don Gustavo and Carolina. The boys sit next to them, and Ramiro comes back to the aisle where I'm standing alone.

He takes my hand in his, and together we walk as fast as my heels let me out of the church, barely catching a glimpse of Rocio grinning with approval. Her words from the funeral echo in my brain. "Some things are just meant to be."

And then it dawns on me. She knew. She's always known.

I GET IN RAMIRO'S CAR, AND WHEN THE DOORS LOCK, THE WEIGHT of my choices drowns me in the small space. "What did we just do?" Oh no. I thought the panic attacks were a thing of the past, and I feel the edge of one starting to creep over me.

"Sara. Sara, look at me." We're still parked, and Ramiro holds one of my hands while he turns my face to look at him instead of out the window where I'm scanning the cars for a sign of Devyn.

"Sara, mi cielo, mírame por favor."

I grab the words before they go out the other ear and focus on them to ground me. Mírame. Mírame. Look at me? See me? Maybe it's a combination of those two meanings in one word.

Don't look out the window for Devyn, Sara. He is now your past. Ramiro is here saying, "Mírame. Mírame, mi cielo. See me, my sky."

I'm his sky, and he's my everything.

So, I do. I look at him and let the dams break. Tears for Devyn, the beautiful man I just crushed in front of all his loved ones, and selfishly, tears of happiness to get to be with the person I know in my heart was meant for me.

Mírame. My sky. See me.

Mírame.

My breathing slows a little as Ramiro peppers kisses over my knuckles.

It was never a choice between Devyn and Ramiro. In another life, one in which Ramiro didn't exist, Devyn and I were meant to be, but in this one, there was only ever one acceptable outcome, and that is Ramiro and me together, co-parenting our sons.

Our sons.

I'm a mom.

Not a tía.

They called me 'Mom,' and I didn't stop to think about it at the time because it felt so natural … necessary, even.

I should have listened to Ramiro before the wedding. I should have stopped all this before I publicly humiliated Devyn like that, but the pieces hadn't fallen into place. I didn't have the full picture in front of me until I saw Ramiro, in his suit, holding on to his two son's hands—our sons' hands—that every decision I ever took made sense.

And the choice, the only one I could pick, was them.

"Sara, it's okay," Ramiro reassures me. "It'll be okay."

I nod, breathing almost normally now, I can ask, "What now?"

Ramiro smiles wickedly at me and puts the car in reverse. "Now we go on a mini honeymoon. I'll give you a real one soon. I promise. But Sara, I have to have you."

I nod nervously, then squeeze his hand as we pull out of the church's parking lot.

CHAPTER 34

Different hands and different fingers were meant to be undressing me tonight.

I want this. I truly do ... but the desire is all jumbled up with regret and shame for what I've done to Devyn.

If there was a time to have a panic attack, right now is it. How ridiculous to feel inadequate at the fact that I'm not having a panic attack. Can it be a vicious circle? Going into a panic attack for not having one to begin with?

It's Ramiro.

His presence.

His reassurance and confidence in what he's done, in choosing me, in winning me, that finally calms me.

After Ramiro slides down the zipper of my dress to the base of my spine, he turns me around to face him.

I'm a little nervous. "Could we order room service? I could use a drink."

Ramiro laughs. "Champagne?"

"Maybe something stronger?"

He laughs again, a beautiful, amused grin painted on his deliciously full lips. "Are you nervous, Sara?"

I nod, wringing my fingers in front of me, then holding the bust of my unzipped dress to my chest before it falls down to my hips. "A little. I never thought that you … that we'd … you know?" God, what am I? I sound like an inadequate teenager instead of the strong woman I know myself to be.

He grabs the phone and calls the front desk for a bottle of champagne and some other things I don't pay attention to as I get lost in my racing thoughts. Then he returns to where I'm still frozen on my spot. Despite my request for something stronger, I know he wants us both sober tonight, and I couldn't love him more for it.

"You may have never thought we'd be here, Sara, but I dreamed about it," he says, wrapping an arm around my waist to pull me into his arms, proving he's dreamed about it by way of his thick erection pressed to my belly now.

"You have?" I breathe out.

He nods, then gathers all my hair to tuck it on one side, leaving half of me to feel the nakedness of my neck and shoulder as he tugs the dress down slowly. "Every night, Sara, I dreamed about this. Every night since you kissed me that first time. Do you know how hard it was? To have you in the room next to mine? Picturing you there, on the bed, lonely and cold, wishing I could warm you up with my skin pressed to yours?"

"Oh, god," I moan as I feel his lips trailing nibbles on the side of my neck.

"Do you know how many nights, with only one wall separating us, I jerked off thinking about you?" He nips the space between my neck and shoulder. "Thinking about holding you like this?"

"I thought about it too," I admit, finding my voice. My desire suppresses all reservations and guilt about wanting Ramiro. A wanting that I've suppressed for so long, it's rushing to the surface unchecked now.

"I love you, Sara. I don't ever want to have to keep that in again."

"Then don't," I say.

I'm pushing him away, taking off his suit jacket, getting ready to rip his shirt open, buttons be damned, when room service knocks.

"That'll be our champagne," he jokes when I groan in my desperation to have him.

He heads to the door, and a cart with champagne flutes, fruits, and assorted snacks is wheeled into our room.

Ramiro tips the gentleman who brought up our sustenance for the night and finds me again.

His touch is gentle when his fingers find my skin again. Too gentle. Too slow. Too tender.

Under his touch, my skin feels on fire, ready to explode with the pent-up tension.

He pauses to pour us drinks, never once peeling his smoldering gaze away from me. Still holding my dress up barely with one hand, I head over to him and take my glass from him. He chuckles when I chug the champagne like it's cheap beer. I set the glass down and fill it to the brim once more and repeat the process. He barely has a sip of his before he's on me again, pressing me to the wall, making out with me, the champagne taste strong between our tongues.

He kisses me almost viciously. I can't breathe, and I don't want to. I never want to come up for air. I could live with Ramiro's lips glued to mine, his fingers tangled in my hair.

When he tugs on my updo and makes me grunt, he pulls his mouth away, and instead presses his forehead to mine. His fingers unfurl from my hair and move to caress my jaw. "I'm sorry," he whispers.

"Why are you sorry?" I ask.

"Got carried away. Didn't mean to be so rough—"

"Ramiro, look at me." I duck a bit to find his eyes. "I'm not made of glass. I won't break."

"That's not what—"

"It is. Listen to me—"

"Sara—"

"I trust you. More than I've ever trusted anyone. And I need you to trust that I'm telling you the truth. I need this to be rough. I don't want to be robbed of my preference for primal sex. I can't give away that power. Do you understand?"

Ramiro studies me carefully, pupils dilated still from his arousal. "I think so. You want rough sex? That's what you like?"

I smile encouragingly at him. "Yes. Sometimes. I enjoy making love too, but right now, in this moment, I want you so bad, all I can think about is devouring you. I can't be tender right now. And I don't want you to be tender either."

I want to explain that I'm reclaiming my power, that I don't want to be a victim for the rest of my life, but I don't want to invoke bad memories. Instead, I plead with my eyes for him to understand, anyway.

The brown in his eyes scorches to coal when they darken, and in one swift movement, Ramiro yanks the bust of my dress from my grip, exposing my breasts. The dress catches on my hips and doesn't go any lower.

He skates one hand down my dress, and sneaks it under the skirt, caressing my leg on its trail to my center.

He sucks in a breath when his hand catches at my thigh. "You're wearing a garter?"

I swallow hard then nod. "Yes."

"Fuck ..." He groans out, then lifts the skirt so he can see what his hand felt first.

The grip on my thigh is harsh, like he's testing if the roughness is okay, and I moan with the pleasure of his rough handling of my body. That makes him smile, and he finds the lace of my thong, tugs it to the side, and buries his face.

My wedding gown is simple, but still, there's enough material that I have to help him hold the scrunched-up skirt, so I can't grab the back of his head like I'm dying to.

I want to pull him harder to me, guide his mouth over my pussy where I need him.

I peer down at him, kneeling before me still in his slacks and dress shirt, while my dress is scrunched around my waist, his head lightly bobbing as he teases, licks, and sucks my clitoris. My legs shake with the pleasure he's delivering and the pleasure of the sight of him on his knees for me.

I whimper when he pulls away, making him chuckle. "Keep holding your dress," he says.

I lick my lips when I nod, and I obey. I keep my position propped up by the wall, holding my dress up so he can have a full view of my pussy while he stands and undoes his buckle. The sound of the zipper draws my eyes down to below his waist, and I watch as he pulls out his penis. His incredibly large, veiny penis. My legs quiver, both in anticipation of pain and pleasure.

"So, the sweet, young bride likes it rough," Ramiro says, twisting his fingers in my hair to pull my head back, exposing the flesh of my neck to him. He draws his teeth down the delicate skin there.

I thrust my hips forward, forcing his erection to press against my pussy. The lace of my thong is soaked through and Ramiro grunts at the rough feel of it on his velvety length.

He forcefully grabs my thighs and helps me wrap my legs around him so he can position himself at my entrance. He tugs the lace to the side again, and in one harsh stroke, he's inside me.

So incredibly, stretching, stretching, and when I can't imagine he could go any deeper, he pushes in more. I clamp around him, legs crushing him around his waist, nails digging to his massive shoulders, and I suck in a breath. He stills for a moment while the realization of what just happened hits us both.

We didn't even take a second to think about a condom. I peer up at him through my lashes, and the way he's looking at me tells me he's thinking the same thing. We let the question linger unsaid, then he kisses me again, biting my lower lip, and we let ourselves forget the recklessness. So much carelessness in one night.

For two people who have gone through so much, and having so many responsibilities in our daily lives, being reckless feels … right. Like how it's supposed to be.

Ramiro fucks me against the wall like he's trying to demolish it with my body. It's rough, just how I asked him, but I know he needs this too. He needs to know that I trust him, that I'm strong enough for him now.

And fuck if it doesn't feel amazing. Every punishing thrust, and every finger digging into my thighs pushes me farther and farther into the hazy ecstasy of an orgasm.

Those rough hands that wield tools, fix things, and work out problems every day, explore my body with the same fascination, learning how my body works so he can make me undone and put me back together.

If we could only have a mirror near us, I'd love the sight of us. Him still dressed as he pounds into me, and me with my dress around my waist, my garter around one thigh, heels still on my feet. I let go of his shoulders so I can rip open his shirt and feel his skin.

I finish peeling the shirt off him, and he lets go of me for only a second—long enough to free his arms from it and toss it on the floor next to us. He presses his body close to mine, and groans when my nipples meet with his chest.

"You feel amazing, Sara," he says in a raspy voice that hardly sounds like him.

"Yeah, like that. Harder," I say, and Ramiro obliges.

His thrusts grow harder, and his belt buckle starts hitting my clit at the exactly right spot. I shudder when I come around him, and Ramiro lets out a growl so primal, I feel it from my chest all the way to the base of my spine as he comes right after me, filling me.

Spent, he works to catch his breath, and I lower my feet back to the ground. It takes me getting on my tiptoes, even in my heels, to reach him for a lengthy, wet kiss that makes me almost dizzy.

He pulls out of me, and I finish shimmying out of my dress. I'm about to walk into the shower when he stops me.

"Where are you going?" he asks.

"Shower."

He smiles darkly. "Oh, I'm not done with you yet."

"What?" I ask as he takes off his shoes and peels off his slacks.

Fully naked, he charges for me, then scoops me into his arms, and takes me to the bed.

"You don't really think I've had enough of you, do you?" he asks as he looks down at me and stops my answer with a hungry kiss.

I'm dripping with his cum and mine when he glides into me once again. I smile up at him. "You're still hard," I tell him.

"You make me so fucking hard," he whispers.

Incredulous that he stayed hard after coming, I get lost in his body again. Now that I'm not holding myself up to him, relaxed on the bed, I can pay attention to every inch of his naked body, every section of hard muscle.

And this time, he is tender, because I think he needs this too.

As much as I needed to not feel like a glass doll, he needs to feel loved. I understand he needs to feel like this is real, like we're together, like I love him. So, I kiss, and nibble and taste, and we make love for so long, his forehead starts dripping with sweat onto my eyes. I reach for the corner of the bedsheet and wipe his brow with it. He smiles sweetly before delivering a tender peck of gratitude on my lips. I wrestle him to get on top, circling my hips to angles that plunge me into heaven. Our bodies are slick with perspiration, and it's hard to find a good grip. My hands slide over his pectorals, down his abs, not finding a good spot to stop and hold on.

"Mi cielo," he says. "I love you."

CHAPTER 35

I stop moving. He has tears in his eyes as I look down at him. "I love you too," I say and clench around him until his eyes roll to the back of his head.

His thumb reaches for me, finding my clit and circling it to the same rhythm of my hips until I come again, and I do come. I come until he finds his own release and growls with it just as he did by the wall.

I stay seated on him, stunned, and in disbelief that despite two orgasms, he's still mostly hard inside me. I wait for a few moments, wanting to feel him softening inside me before pulling off him and luring him into the shower with me, but he never does.

He smiles up at me. "How about that shower?" he asks.

I nod. "We need it." We both look down at our bodies, wet and flushed like we've been in a sauna. My hair is wet and matted to my neck, and I desperately want to wash it.

It's not until we're in the shower together, and Ramiro is massaging my scalp while he washes my hair, his erection still bobbing, heavy and semi-hard between his legs, that I decide to ask two questions that have been bothering me for a while. In the shower, he has nowhere to go until I'm done, and he can't avoid this conversation.

Manipulative on my part? Perhaps. Maybe I should give him more credit. He has, after all, invested a lot with therapy to work on opening up. He's done the hard work on himself and earned all of my trust. Then there's the part of me that can't risk it, so I choose this moment. "Why do you call me your sky?" I ask.

Ramiro turns me around to face him, then continues massaging my scalp as he answers. "Because you're my everything."

A pause.

I think about that for a moment. It's a pleasant thought, if a bit scary, to be someone's everything. It's also natural, though. Ramiro, Oscar, and René are my everything, so I can certainly understand the feeling.

I clear my throat. "How long have I been your cielo?"

His hands freeze in my hair, and he lets out a long breath. "Almost since I met you."

"Excuse me?"

"I've liked you a lot longer than you can imagine, loved you even—"

"But Carolina—"

His dark brow arches. "You, more than anyone, should understand what being in love with two people is like."

"Wait, what?" I shake my head and wash out the shampoo from my hair quickly so I can straighten when I look at him again. "You loved me?"

Water droplets roll down his face like phantom tears. "I suppressed loving you. It felt like being unfaithful to Carolina—"

"But fucking every woman in sight during that time didn't feel like being unfaithful?"

"No."

I scoff. "No?"

"No. I didn't have feelings for them."

"Then why, Ramiro? Why, when you finally decided to move on from Carolina, why wasn't it me? Why was it Francisca?"

He shuts off the water and wraps a towel around my shoulders. "Let's get dry and comfy, yeah? I'll tell you everything you want to know."

Reassured by his promises of truth, I follow his lead in drying and getting under the covers, both of us still naked.

"I was fucked up after Carolina."

"I remember."

"When I came back from Florida and had to see her almost daily, I was going insane. The drinking picked up. The endless stream of women—"

"I remember that too," I say dryly.

"Then one day, I was at a bar close enough to home that I didn't want to get a ride-share, so I walked home since I couldn't drive. I must have been more drunk than I thought because I never got home."

"You blacked out?"

"Yeah. First time in my life. As often as I was drinking then, I've never really enjoyed being that drunk. But anyway, that night it went too far, and I passed out on someone's front lawn on my way home."

"Francisca's?"

He nods. "Francisca's. When she woke me up, I thought about what Carolina would have done in that situation. She would have yelled at me, pulled me up by my ear and shoved me in my shower, clothes on and everything. With cold water. Definitely cold water, then yelled at me some more."

"Like a big sister," I say with a smile.

Surprisingly, Ramiro smiles too. "Like a big sister."

"That's not what Francisca did, though?"

"No. She was gentle and spoke softly, knowing I likely had a headache. When she grabbed my hand, she was so gentle. She led me into her house, and Oscar, René, and Doña Pancha ate eggs with hotdogs, and Francisca served me pozole for the cruda."

I smile. Francisca loved to heal with her food. She had that in common with Don Gustavo.

"Weren't you still in love with me, though?"

"I've never not loved you, Sara. But in that moment, I wanted nothing to do with Carolina or Don Gustavo. I almost didn't go back to work with him. I couldn't bring myself to date her little sister and be around her all the time. It wouldn't have been fair to you. And in front of me was this gentle woman, taking care of me. And for once, I didn't feel inadequate, or like I didn't belong, or wasn't good enough. The way she looked at me Sara, like I'd hung the moon … I needed that after Carolina."

"I see," I say, trying to understand.

"If I could go back in time and change things, date you instead, I wouldn't do it. I'd still be with Francisca because that's how I got my sons."

As much as I don't want to admit it to myself, Ramiro makes a lot of sense. I squeeze his hand in mine. "You're right. The time had to be right for us."

It's then he barks out his laughter. "You think the best time was on your wedding day to another man?"

My face blanches. "Oh god. Don't remind me. I need to talk to him, to explain—"

Ramiro cups my hand in his. "Not right now. I need this weekend to be just us. I want time to get to know us as a couple. Time to explore your body. Learn what you respond to, what you like. I don't want to think about anyone outside this room."

"You want a honeymoon," I say.

"No. This weekend is not our honeymoon. When I take you on our honeymoon, it will be somewhere beautiful, for several weeks where I can have you naked as often as I want. It won't be over in just a few days."

My brain misfires when he says this. He said "when" we have our honeymoon. "When?" I ask in a shaky breath, replaying his words in my head.

"Si, mi cielo," he says, and kisses me. Tenderly, with his tongue parting my lips in an erotic way that opens my mouth and body to him. "*When.* One day soon, I'm going to ask you to marry me, and you are going to say yes. And our wedding reception won't be this stuffy small wedding either. We'll invite the entire block, and Tavo's Auto Repair staff. And we'll wait for Leo to be on leave so he can be my best man. Every person I've ever known will be present the day I claim you as mine. And we'll have Mariachis, an endless taco bar, and we'll have Sofia bring kegs of beer—"

"I love tacos and beer," I say with a goofy smile.

Ramiro kisses my temple, pressing a soft chuckle to that tender spot. "I know. And we'll dance all night and celebrate our new life together. And you won't run off with anyone else. The boys will stay with my parents for a month, and we'll go to Mexico.

"Mexico?" I ask excitedly. "I've always wanted to go."

"And you'll blow them away with your Spanish. Don't think I haven't noticed how fluent you've become. I'm so proud of you, Sara."

"One day soon, huh?"

"One day soon."

I bite my lip thoughtfully. "Can I ask you one more question?"

Ramiro chuckles. "You have a lot of questions."

"When did you know? That you loved me?"

Without a second of thought, he says, "When you pronounced my name right for the first time."

I lift a little, resting my elbow on my pillow and propping my head up so I can look down into his eyes. "What?"

"When Carolina introduced you to me, you tried to roll your 'R's' and couldn't. You tried about twenty times, and I think it got embarrassing for all of us, but you were so determined."

"I remember," I say, my cheeks flushing with heat at the memory. "I started taking Spanish lessons with Don Gustavo shortly after that. Carolina was hardly around during med school, and I think my lessons gave us both a purpose."

Ramiro nods. "Anyway, a few months later, you found me working out at my garage, and Don Gustavo had asked you to drop off some dinner for me because my parents were out of town. When you said my name that time, you rolled your 'R's' perfectly."

"I was so proud when I finally learned to do that. It took months, Ramiro."

He brushes a strand of hair from my eyes and pushes it back. "I know. When you rolled those 'R's,' the sounds shot straight through my groin. Remember, I asked if you could put the food in the fridge for me?"

I shake my head. "It was so long ago."

"Well, I did. I couldn't stand up, and I had to place my gym towel on my lap because I got so hard."

"Oh. That's lust though, not love."

"It was both, Sara. And it scared the hell out of me."

"I think I understand."

"That's all in the past, mi cielo. We're together now."

"One last question, I promise."

Ramiro barks out a laugh. "I don't believe that for a second."

"Do you still love her? Carolina?"

He shakes his head. "I would never have proposed to Francisca if I did. It's true what they say. Time heals all."

"And Francisca?"

"I'll always love the memory of her. I loved her. I'm sorry. You think you can share my love just a little bit?"

"Of course. I wouldn't want it any other way. It will be good for the boys to know that you will honor her memory."

"They do," he says, and kisses my temple.

"Thank you for answering my questions."

He kisses me again, and when I tell him I want to text Carolina to bring us a change of clothes because I can't walk out of this room in a wedding dress, he takes my phone and shuts it off. "Tomorrow," he says, and climbs on top of me again.

All day, and all night, all we do is fuck rough, and make love sweet, and we pause to order room service and eat, with a few naps here and there. When we fall asleep, either Ramiro will wake me up, sometimes with his cock inside me, sometimes his fingers, or his tongue, or I'll wake him up, with my mouth sheathing his hardening erection.

A full weekend of getting to know each other intimately—of eating each other, of pure bliss.

On Sunday morning, when eventually we're forced to ask Carolina for clothes, and I crack the door to the room open to grab the duffle bag from her, she is grinning like this is the happiest moment of her life, but also mischievous like she's caught me with las manos en la masa.

I don't let her crack any jokes because I don't want her to ruin this perfect weekend of mine and instead shut the door in her face after grabbing the bag. All I hear is her bark of laughter as she walks down the hallway.

We're getting dressed, planning on checking out of the hotel and returning to our lives, when the weight of our actions crashes down on both of us.

Even so, Ramiro's jaw is set with resolve and that gives me courage we've done the right thing.

"Ramiro, we didn't—" my voice breaks.

"We didn't what?"

"We didn't use protection."

"Oh, that. No, we didn't. I haven't been with anyone since Francisca, and we both got tested before we started seriously dating."

"Right. And since Brian, I've only … with Devyn, and—" I swallow, watching the pain flash across Ramiro's eyes. "We always used protection, though I'm confident in his past safe sex practices. I'm happy to get tested again, if it makes you feel better."

The muscle over his left jaw clicks, and his Adam's apple bobs up and down. He takes slow steps toward me and cups my lower belly in his palm. "I thought you'd be afraid you're pregnant."

I shake my head. "I have an IUD."

He smiles, his eyes glued to my belly. "I wouldn't mind if you were pregnant."

Even though I'm standing perfectly still, I stumble somehow and lose my balance enough that I have to hold on to his arms to stay upright.

"You want to have kids?" I ask, but it comes out like a screech.

He nods. "I'd be happy with just the boys and us, but if you ever carry our child, I'll be very happy about that too."

His voice is so serious when he speaks, I hate that I'm laughing when I answer. "That would put a significant dent in the vision you have of our wedding and honeymoon, don't you think? No tacos with beer for me if I'm knocked up in my wedding dress."

He chuckles and meets my eyes again. "That's why you're mi cielo. You make me smile and laugh, even in the most serious of moments. In the darkest of times, you bring the light with you. It's remarkable, Sara, for someone who came from so much darkness, and who's been through so much, that you can continue to carry this joy and share it with everyone around you. That you continue to smile, and laugh, and love."

With that, he grabs my hand, and we open the door of our love bubble and step into the hallway, ready to face the consequences of our actions—and our future.

Together.

EPILOGUE

TWENTY YEARS LATER

Mexico and France are tied with only two minutes left in the second half. In a last-ditch effort to avoid a penalty shootout, number thirteen, the Mexican national team's most talented striker, gets dangerously close to his target when number four, a French defender, elbows him aggressively to shove him back, earning number thirteen a penalty kick.

Not since the eighties has Mexico gotten so much as close to the quarterfinals at the International Cup, and not once has the nationally beloved team won. And here we are. At the final match. The weight of the world—not to mention the eyes—are all on number thirteen as he readies himself for the most important moment of his life.

His agent, and the entire world it seems, begged him not to play for the team that was thought of as doomed never to win an International Cup. Especially not when he had lucrative offers to play from both Germany and Argentina.

But to number thirteen, there was only ever one option. His mother would put on the green jersey and use face-paint to meticulously draw the Mexican flag onto the apples of her cheeks for every single televised game. She only ever rooted for one team, and number thirteen wanted to gift her the International Cup win she never got to see in her lifetime.

He cut his hair before the season started, and it's a bit hard to pick him out without his signature low man-bun he used to roll at the nape of his head. Luckily, the number thirteen is easy enough to spot, and so is the hyphenated name above the number: Garcia-Jimenez.

Half a world away, I know Don Gustavo is glued to the screen despite the time difference. I can picture them all: him, Carolina, Hector, and their daughter Marisela, likely all in pajamas, holding hands and readying themselves to jump up in triumph.

Don Gustavo is likely sending a quiet prayer up to the heavens.

I smile at the thought and wish our entire family could have joined us for this once-in-a-lifetime experience. On one side of me, Ramiro is squeezing my hand a bit too firmly, but I'm sure I'm squeezing back with equal force. To my left, an eighteen-year-old Astrid is holding my other hand as she holds in a breath, her cheeks puffy and turning a shade red with the strain of the air inside them.

I whisper in my only daughter's ear. "Breathe—I don't want to be stuck with all boys."

Astrid, with golden-brown skin, a shade somewhere between mine and Ramiro's, and his dark brown eyes and inky black hair, giggles next to me and gulps for air. Everyone in our row is just as tense as we are, and this is the quietest the massive stadium has been for the entire game.

Number thirteen's brother couldn't be here today. As much as our workaholic son wanted to, he couldn't pry himself away from work, and gave up his ticket for the International Cup final's game to his baby sister.

We watch as René takes several steps behind the ball, puffs

up his chest with a gulp of air, and on the exhale, he breaks into a jog. His right leg swings back, then forward, aiming right, but at the last second, aims toward the upper left corner of the net instead.

Believing his initial aim, the goalie throws himself right—leaving his left entirely open.

The ball swooshes against the net, and the crowd explodes with its collective roar.

Ramiro jumps, screaming "Goooooooooaaaaaaaaal" on one side of me, while Astrid does the same on my other side.

"That's my son! That's my son!" I scream at everyone around us who will hear me past their own shouting, pointing at René, though really, I'm just pointing at the field.

The man standing behind me taps my shoulder, and I turn to face him.

"Number thirteen? That's your son?" He asks in Spanish, pointing to the field himself.

I beam at the stranger. "¡Sí!"

The stranger leans forward and offers me his hand. I take it, shaking it, and he cups it in the other.

"Thank you," he says, "for giving us the gift that is your son."

I laugh a watery laugh through my tears of joy. "I'll tell him a fan said that."

The man smiles, then turns to take one of his buddies into a hug, the celebration continuing.

The penalty kick tilted the balance of the game in our favor, and with only two minutes left in the game, there's no way the opposing team will manage to turn the score again before the game is over.

TEQUILA IS POURED ALL NIGHT AT THE HOTEL BAR, AND THIS TIME, the celebratory shot doesn't taste bitter. The shot goes down smooth as butter.

And since the drinking age in this country is eighteen, even Astrid is allowed a shot of tequila.

Her dad pours two shots in front of them. They salt their limes, and she follows his lead. Then he bites the lime, and shortly after, slams the shot back.

Astrid does the same and Ramiro's daughter ... well, she doesn't make a face. Doesn't wince. Doesn't clear her throat. Advice from her aunt Sofia, no doubt, on what to expect, and how to behave during her first-ever tequila shot.

Smiling, Ramiro pours her a half a shot for their second drink. This time, they cheer to René before they take the drink.

René went out to celebrate with his team after giving us all big hugs, instructing Ramiro to give the squirt—Astrid—a celebratory drink but then cut her off, and promising to have breakfast with us in the morning.

We decided to make this a bit of a family vacation, win or lose, and it only stings that Oscar can't be here with us.

He's changed so much since he was a little boy. I miss my old buddy, and I hope one day he'll come back to us for good. In the meantime, I get to see him every November when, no matter what, both my boys make their way home for Día de Muertos when we honor Francisca and Doña Pancha, who we laid to rest next to her daughter when her time came.

At the very least, once a year, my little family comes together in its entirety.

My very own family that we built together.

My ultimate dream come true.

After dinner, Ramiro and I walk Astrid to her hotel room before heading to ours for a shower. He promised me a romantic night of dancing before coming back to do wicked things with my body—his words, not mine.

With Astrid finally going off to college, we are about to become empty-nesters, and my husband has declared his intentions fully.

A second honeymoon is how he's described it.

I poke my head in the bathroom where Ramiro is showering, his body outlined past the steam on the glass shower door. Despite the years, Ramiro has kept his high muscle mass. Often training with René and having to stay fit to practice with him while he was in high school was his original excuse, but I know that lifting is his self-care technique—one which his counselor, whom, yes, he still sees, fully approves of.

The only change in him is that he's grown out his hair into a short inky-black cut that is just now starting to get a little salt in the pepper.

My mouth waters, and I almost want to beg him to forgo dancing and have his body instead, but we deserve a night out. I know I still get to have him when we come back. "I'm going to see if Astrid borrowed my favorite lipstick," I call into the shower.

"Okay, baby," he replies, and I head over to Astrid's room.

After I knock twice, Astrid opens her door.

"Hey mom," she says. "What's up?"

I glance down at her in pajamas and pink slippers that do not go at all well with the full face of makeup she's put on since we dropped her off. I hand her a stack of bills.

"What's this for?" She asks.

I smile knowingly at her. "If you plan on sneaking out tonight, take your cell. Stay safe."

"Mom!" she screeches in protest.

I roll my eyes. "I know my daughter," I say and snicker.

It wasn't always easy for Astrid, growing up in a house with not one, but two over-protective brothers and an equally over-protective father. I was often her co-conspirator and helped her sneak away for her first boy-girl party, her first date—so many firsts.

"And here," I discreetly shove a square package in her hand.

With a furrowed brow, she turns her hand over, looking at the package.

"Mom! Really? Condoms?"

"Just stay safe if you do," I tell her. "Not that you have to—but just in case. Have them in your purse."

"Kill me now," Astrid says with a moan and runs her hands over her reddened face. "You are so embarrassing!"

It takes everything in me to keep a serious expression. I've had the talk with her many times—the first time when she turned thirteen and one of her girlfriends from school started dating. "Listen, kid," I tell her. "You don't tell your father I give you condoms, money, and getaway plans, and I won't tell him you snuck out your window on your birthday and stayed out all night."

"Mom! You knew?"

I take Astrid in for a hug. "Si, mi amor. Mothers know all." When I let go of her, I boop her nose with my index finger. "And don't you forget it." With one last squeeze around her tall frame, I pull away and head back to my room.

When I open the door, I find Ramiro wearing dark slacks, and a deep gray dress shirt he's rolling up to his forearms. He must have just applied his after shave because I can smell him the minute I step inside.

I close the door behind me and lean on it, my eyes skating down his body and landing on his fly. The minute they land there, I bite my lip.

"You keep looking at me like that, we're not leaving this hotel room," he tells me darkly.

I peel my eyes upward to find his. "Then my plan is working," I say with a massive grin.

His own grin is crooked, his eyes menacing, offering a warning as he stalks to me and takes me into his arms for a bruising kiss. When we pull away, he says, "Did you get the lipstick?"

"What?"

"From Astrid. You said she had your lipstick."

"Oh," I say. "No. We must have left it at home."

"Good," Ramiro says.

I giggle. "Good?"

He nods. "You're the most beautiful when you aren't wearing any makeup."

"¡Mentiras!" I say.

He shakes his head. "I'm not lying, mi cielo."

"You're not?"

Another shake of the head. "When you're like this, fresh-faced, and your lips are red and swollen from kissing me, your sky-blue eyes pop. I've never seen a more beautiful face, mi cielo."

'My sky.' After all these years, I'm still his sky.

And you know what? Since the day we got married, I never had a single panic attack again.

The End

KEEP READING

Want to read a bonus steamy scene between Sara and Ramiro? Visit Ofeliamartinez.com/freebooks and read what they do on their first day as empty-nesters—as well as what became of Devyn after all these years.

If you're ready to start on Sofia's story, you can now read Hiding in the Smoke, the first book in the Industrial November on Tour rock star series. Keep reading for an excerpt.

ACKNOWLEDGMENTS

I dedicated this book to the allies. In my personal circle, these include my beautiful beta readers and Ofeliati members, Jenni and Shannon. These allies also include the lovely Becky and Leah from the Buzzing About Romance podcast and the beautiful community they've created with their hive. They are inclusive, warm, and welcoming. I've always felt the space they made for me in their book club and in their lives.

My circle of Allies also includes my beta reader and author Friends Michelle McCraw (who is a master of diversity inclusion done right and writes steamy STEM romance with smart characters), Carla Luna (who I count as a Latina friend even if she's hesitant to accept the label feeling so disconnected to that line of her heritage (I claim you!). Her romcoms are like an ice cream when you need to soothe the soul).

Leading to the fall of 2022, there was much public discourse on authors' responsibility and how we represent marginalized communities, especially Latine communities—my community.

I remained mostly silent about this topic on social platforms.

In large part, I remained silent because if you care to know what I think about bigotry or how my Mexican-American (Chicana) community is represented in print; you need to look no further than in the pages of any of my books. In them, you will find a high-achieving doctor who is also a cancer researcher, a professional athlete fighting for her life, a business owner who sends money home to support her mother and grandmother, and a gloomy undocumented high school graduate at a crossroads, who falls in love with music for solace. They are all either successful or on their way to success.

Their Latine friends are good people. Their Latine parents are good people. Their Latine neighbors are good people. Some of the characters speak Spanish. Some don't. Some do, but badly. None of them denounce their heritage or disparage it in any way. You will never find a Latine character in my books who embodies any of the negative stereotypes some non-Latine authors have the audacity to write. My characters reflect the world I live in.

I stay quiet because I have written hundreds of thousands of words carefully planned to fight stereotypes and bigotry. My pen is my sword, and writing is my theater of war.

Remember, the single most subversive action an artist can take is to make our art. It is up to the reader to interpret the art and engage in discourse. I've done my job as an author. For many of us, it comes at a high cost. Carving away space for our voices is difficult. But I do it for you, the reader. So when my work contributes to emboldening you to stand up against bigotry, I couldn't be prouder of you. But that is your job—your theater of war. Know that I'm cheering you on, and I'm so incredibly proud of you.

So be kind to those in the community who stay silent. We have our reasons. Be kind to those who are raging with anger and lashing out. We're all exhausted and hurting. Some of us collapse inward, and some of us explode outward, but it's all coming from a place of exhaustion and frustration. We're all battle-weary because we've been fighting this much longer than the reader community at large has been aware of it.

I want to give a big shout-out to Jessica Arrieta, the reader warrior who always has, and I suspect always will, continue to fight for the dignity of the Latine community in the United States.

It was entirely by happenstance that this book, released in

October 2022 (but that was written in early 2022 and planned in 2020), features a white female main character. I hope I did that with care, avoiding any stereotypes of American white women. Sara approaches learning about the culture of her adoptive family with an open mind and a lot of respect and love —in turn, that is the same level of respect and love the Latine community around her bestows on her. And, of course, she falls in love with a Mexican-American prince charming. I write the world I want to live in—the world I surround myself in with my circle of allies.

I would be amiss if I didn't thank Ashley and Genoveva, who both beta-read this book and gave me amazing feedback—you both know I write with only you, my Latina readers, in mind.

Big thanks also due to the editors at Midnight Owl Editors. Your team is amazing, and I couldn't do this without you.

Lastly, to my partner, best friend, and biggest ally, Robert. Though you never understood the dream, you fueled it with your encouragement and love. Thank you for putting up with me having no days off and never shutting up about my books. And for the snacks.

Mostly the snacks.

I love you.

ALSO BY OFELIA MARTINEZ

The Heartland Metro Hospital Series

Carolina & Hector's Story: Remission

Valentina & Rory's Story: Contusion

Izel & Logan's Story: Incision (Novella)

Camila & Leonardo's Story: Palpitation (Novella as part of the *Heroes with Heat and Heart Vol.2* anthology)

Sara & Ramiro's Story: Sensation

The Industrial November on Tour Series

Sofia & Brenner's Story: Hiding in the Smoke

Lola & Karl's Story: Running from the Blaze

Erica & Friedrich's Story: Scorching to the Touch

Anthologies & Collections

Diagnosis Amor Vol. 1: Heartland Metro Hospital Collection

Camila & Leonardo's Story: Heroes with Heath and Heart Vol 2

HIDING IN THE SMOKE

HIDING IN THE SMOKE EXCERPT

ONE: SOFIA

On most days, it's feast or famine at *La Oficina*—my bar. But tonight is surprisingly steady and mellow, so I can't hide a face-splitting grin when my two best friends show up with one of their coworkers from the hospital, and I actually get to hang out with them.

I don't even go over to greet them before heading to the kitchen to put in their order that I know by heart. My best cook, Martín, glances at the order and his own grin grows wide. "Carolina is here?" he asks.

I nod. "So is Sara," I say.

"*¿La comelona?*"

I laugh, but nod again. "You know what that means."

"You need the salsa," he says all businesslike.

The *Salsa* is Carolina's mom's recipe and a fan favorite on the menu, which means we run out on most days. Martín always hides a secret stash for when Sara comes by because she sulks if we're out and don't save her any.

I head to the table where I can already tell from Carolina's furrowed brows—and from Sara looking everywhere but at her friends—that they are arguing about something with their coworker Mandy.

"How about you, Sofia? Are you free tomorrow night?" Mandy asks with hope in her eyes. She presses her palms together in front of her chest like a prayer and juts her lower lip into a pout.

"Oh, no. I don't know what you three are fighting about, but I know I don't want to be dragged into it. I just came to see what you want to drink."

Carolina and Sara call out their drinks, and I repeat them to make a mental note of the order. "A beer and a Horsefeather. Coming right up. You, Mandy?"

Mandy relaxes her shoulders and shakes her head. "No, I'm fine. Thank you."

Joe, my bartender and manager, is busy, so I go behind the bar to pour the drinks myself. When I get back to the table holding a tray of food and drinks, they eye me with conspiratorial smiles spreading across their faces.

Oh, no. This can't be good. Carolina, Sara, and I have been best friends for a while now. Ever since Carolina, a doctor, helped me without charging me when I needed stitches. We became instant friends. Sara was a bonus—a sort of package deal—since she's practically attached at the hip to Carolina. She is a nurse at the same hospital, Heartland Metro.

My bar sits conveniently in front of their emergency room entrance, so I see them quite often. And when those two women get together and look at me like they are looking at me now, I know they have something up their sleeves. Something I'm not going to like.

I set the platter, filled with zucchini blossom quesadillas fanned out into the shape of a flower, in the middle of the table. My cooks, Rubén and Martín, are artists, and they didn't forget the salsa. Sara nearly starts drooling and is the first to dive in, followed shortly by Mandy and Carolina.

"What?" I ask and take a seat next to them.

"We think you should go with Mandy," Carolina says, chewing on a bite of quesadilla, her thick, black brows shooting up along with her smile.

"You should totally go," Sara adds in her signature bubbly voice that has grown on me over the years.

"Go where? I have no idea what you three are talking about."

"Mandy has tickets to the *Industrial November* concert tomorrow night," Carolina says, turning her attention to Mandy, who is flashing me a toothy grin.

"I do! I called the radio station and got front row tickets and backstage passes. Can you believe it? I never win anything. I'm still on a high from it. But I have no one to go with me, and I really don't want to go alone."

I blink at Mandy. I barely know her through Carolina. Mandy is her research assistant at the hospital and a kick-ass artist, but we've never really socialized on our own. I'm not sure we have much in common. To be perfectly honest, I've avoided her. Mandy is super-hot, but she is also Carolina's favorite research assistant, so I never dared spend time with her alone. Carolina would never forgive me if I did a number on Mandy.

"What about your cousins?" I ask. I know she is close friends with her two cousins.

"Tlali and Izel both have to work tomorrow. They get out way too late to make it to the concert."

"I'm sorry, Mandy. Wish I could. But Friday nights are the busiest around here. It will be hard to get away."

"Come on," Carolina says. "You're too much of a workaholic. When was the last time you took a night off?"

"Are you calling the kettle black there, Dr. Ramirez?" I ask Carolina. Her brows furrow because she hates it when I call her by her professional title.

Carolina crosses her arms, annoyed. The truth is, I haven't seen much of either of them. Carolina's career has taken a bit of a stumble, and she is nursing a broken heart—caused by the same guy who messed with her career. Sara, too, had a tumultuous relationship with a scumbag who beat her to a pulp only a few months ago. Both women threw themselves into their work at an alarming pace.

I know people deal with heartbreak differently—I probably would do the same—but I'd be lying if I said I don't begrudge them for hardly being around anymore. It takes a miracle for me to see them these days. I'm sure it is their guilt of not being around as much that has them pushing Mandy and this concert on me. As if I have no other friends. I mean, I don't, but that's beside the point.

"Look," Carolina says. "I know you like *Industrial November*. I also know Sara and I have been a bit absent—"

"A bit?" I scoff, but I smile because I can't be too mad at them.

Carolina raises an eyebrow at me. "Fine. A lot absent. We just want to make sure you don't fall into your tendency to *only* work."

"Tell me," I say to both Carolina and Sara, "why, exactly, aren't either of you going with Mandy?" I raise my eyebrow right back at Carolina, even if my brows aren't as spectacularly thick and sculpted as hers.

Sara hangs her head, her blond tresses falling over her face like a curtain she hides behind to avoid any and all conflict, and Carolina has to answer for the both of them. "We're working."

I bite my lip, trying to suppress laughter. They can't get out of work, but expect me to?

"Look, I know we're total hypocrites, but we are slaves to our schedules. We can't take off on such short notice. You, on the other hand, are your own boss. You can do anything you want, even close if you have to," Carolina says.

I shake my head. "I can't close."

"Can't Joe handle it on his own?" Sara asks, looking up at me once again.

I glance over at Joe. He's been my bar manager for a year, and I have yet to leave him alone on a weekend night. I don't doubt he'd be able to handle it, but I'm not sure I'd have any fun worried about the million things that could go wrong. I've built my business from the ground up. It's successful because of all the hard work I put into it.

Mandy, for her part, is looking at me like I'm holding her new puppy. Talk about peer pressure. I roll my eyes.

"You're the *Industrial November* super fan, Carolina. I know their music from it popping up on some of my playlists, and I like them well enough, but I couldn't name a song if you had a gun to my head."

"I know. Trust me," Carolina huffs. "It's killing me that I won't get to meet them."

Rolling my eyes again, I look over at Mandy. "Let me talk to Joe. If he's okay with it, and we can get at least one backup waitress to come in, then yeah. I'll go with you."

I take my place back behind the bar—my favorite spot to be. I worked hard to give this place—my baby—an edge that felt like *me* without being kitschy. *La Oficina* is a modern bar with a moody feel, including exposed brick walls, tall, black-framed windows, dim lighting, and black and white photographs of my favorite Spanish rock bands. The likes of *Café Tacvba, Maldita Vecindad, Molotov,* and *Panteón Rococó* adorn my walls. *Industrial November* isn't amongst their ranks in my heart, even though they are the world's most listened-to band.

I don't admit to my friends that if the tickets were to *Café Tacvba,* I'd jump at the opportunity and close the bar faster than Mandy could say *Hot Potato.*

"What was that all about?" Joe asks, breaking my thoughts.

"Mandy wants me to go to the *Industrial November* concert with her tomorrow."

"No way! You get to go? I'm so jealous. I'm not too ashamed to admit that I actually wept when I couldn't get tickets. They sold out within an hour."

"I'm not sure I'm going. It's our busiest night," I say to him because he clearly hasn't considered the ramifications for him if I were to take off.

"Hey, if you don't go, please say I can have your ticket."

"What part of 'it's our busiest night' are you not getting?"

"Sorry, boss," he says. "But you really should go. I don't think I can work for a woman who, when given a chance to see the best band on the planet, declines. I'd have to question your judgment."

If Joe weren't married, or Mandy weren't quite as forward as she is, it wouldn't be inappropriate for them to go together. But given the realities, it's me or no one.

"Are you sure you can handle it, Joe? Like, really handle it?"

"You haven't given me a chance to prove myself yet. This might be the perfect opportunity."

"Okay. If you can get Tracy to come in tomorrow night, and you swear you'll text me the minute you need me for anything at all, I'll go."

I don't much care for our backup waitress Tracy, but she's gotten us out of some trouble in the past.

"You won't regret it, boss," he says. "Oh, and before I forget, David Price called again today. He really wants to buy the place?" Joe asks, with a slight look of concern straining his face.

"Joe, I'd never sell the bar."

"Next time he calls, want me to tell him to go to hell?"

I laugh. "No. He's still a colleague. Be professional. He'll get the hint one day."

When I get back to the table with the girls, I only smile at Mandy before she jumps up and hugs me. She doesn't even give me the chance to tell her I'm going.

"It'll be amazing, you'll see," Mandy squeals. "Drinks are on me. All night tomorrow night."

"Nope. Not drinking," I say. "I'll be driving." I grin at her.

"You don't mean . . ." Mandy trails off and covers her mouth from the gasp she let out. Seriously, what a drama queen.

When I nod, Mandy jumps again and hugs me tight one last time. "I get to ride Bonnie? No freaking way. It's going to be the best night ever."

When I sit with them, Mandy announces she has to go home and get ready for the next day. I watch her leave the bar with a pep in her step, her calves accentuated by the red pumps she's wearing.

When I look back at her, Carolina tilts her head to the side and crosses her arms. When her right eyebrow floats up, and her perfect lips form into a scowl, I know I'm in for it. "What did I do now?" I ask, annoyed. This is what she wanted. Isn't it? For me to take her assistant to the damned concert?

"Mandy's straight," Carolina deadpans.

"I know."

Sara interjects before any further questioning. "It looks like you two are going to be arguing for a while. I'm going to hit the hay. Caro, I'll get you next time?" Sara says and leaves me alone with Carolina.

"Please don't put the moves on her," Carolina says when we're alone.

"I wasn't going to—"

"It's your MO. Whenever you have the mood for a woman, you wow her with Bonnie, then take her to bed, and it always ends with the poor woman's heart broken."

I do my best to look offended. "My god, you're paranoid. I don't only take *lovers* for a ride. I thought it would be fun for Mandy. That's all."

"You promise?" Carolina asks.

"What's it to you, anyway?"

"I care about Mandy. You're both important to me. I'd hate to have to pick sides here."

The thing is, Amanda "Mandy" Gomez is very attractive. She is short, barely five-foot-three, and her frame is slender in a muscular sort of way that's always been catnip to me on a woman. She always makes me smile because she basically lives in high heels, trying to be just a little bit taller, and it's adorable. Her cool-toned, light-brown skin brightens with her broad toothy smiles that can cheer anyone up. But I'd never go there. She's a big part of Carolina's life, and I respect those bonds.

"Look, Mandy's hot and all," I finally admit. "I'm not blind, and I'm only human, but you know I don't date. I wouldn't jeopardize any friendship for a fuck. It's not that important." I don't say out loud what Carolina already knows. I don't do relationships. Period.

"I'm going to trust you here—"

"Have I ever given you a reason not to?" I ask my friend.

Carolina eyes me warily and takes too long to respond.

"And if you remember, it was you and Sara who pushed me to take her to the stupid concert," I add.

"Okay, I'm going to let go of the fact that you just called my favorite band 'stupid.' But you're right. You can't win tonight, can you? I'm sorry. I've been in a mood."

My eyes soften when I take a moment to study Carolina's tired features. Her eyes are sunken, and she looks a little worse for wear. "I know. Hey, how are you doing—*really* doing?" I ask her, worried about my stubborn friend trying to pick up all the pieces of her life by herself when she doesn't need to do it alone. She has friends, damn it.

But I also get her. I'm just as fiercely independent as she is, if not more.

"Not ready to talk about it," she says. "Besides, I have to get going. Early morning tomorrow. Close out our tab?"

"You got it."

Joe walks over to me at the register. "Tracy said she'd come in."

"Good, cuz I already told Mandy yes."

"You won't regret it, boss. Nothing will go wrong tomorrow night."

Famous last words, I think.

When it's nearly closing time, I walk over to the last straggler, who's been checking me out all night but has been too afraid to talk to me. He is tall, handsome, and well-built—a little burly—just how I like my men.

"Can I get you another drink?" I ask him.

"Nah, but maybe close out my tab?"

Once I hand him his credit card, I place my elbows on the bar counter, letting my cleavage swell over my tank top. "So, Nick. You gonna ask me out or what?"

Nick blinks quickly. "How'd you know my name?"

I point to his hand. "Your credit card."

"Oh."

"You've been checking me out all night." I lick my lips slowly as I stare him dead in the eye—my favorite flirting move. My luscious lips are my favorite part of my body, and whenever I lick them, it makes men crumble, if I do say so myself. "We're closing now, so you could say you've missed your chance."

"Oh. Have I really?" Nick chuckles nervously, scratching his jaw.

"Yeah, sorry. But if you'd like to fuck, my place is close by."

Nick does a doubletake. "What?" His mouth falls open.

"Hey, I'm sorry if I misunderstood. I just thought you—"

"No. You didn't misunderstand . . ." he hastens to add.

"So," I say. "You're interested in going to bed with me tonight?"

Nick nods. "Very."

I lean in closer until I can feel the heat of his breath. "Okay. I have rules."

"Okay," he says, looking at me—a mischievous smile curving his mouth. "What are they?"

"One night and one night only. No repeats and absolutely no sleeping over. Are those acceptable terms?"

"Fuck yeah," Nick says and slams down the rest of his drink.

"Oh, and you have to be sober," I add.

Nick smiles. "I only had two drinks. I'm completely sober."

Joe smirks at me and shakes his head as he leaves the bar. Undoubtedly, he heard the exchange, but he's used to me taking customers to my place and doesn't bat an eye—anymore.

I lock up *La Oficina*, and Nick trails me home.

HIDING IN THE SMOKE EXCERPT

TWO: SOFIA

There couldn't be a worse place to be than at the front row of an *Industrial November* concert. Hell would be cooler. I made the mistake of not looking into the band's live shows before showing up at the concert.

The arena is packed to the brim with screaming fans, and apparently, the lead singer, Brenner Reindhart, has a thing for pyrotechnics. Much like the *Pink Floyd* laser show, *Industrial November* also attacks their audience with a light show, only they use real fire. I will be surprised if those of us at the front leave with our eyebrows and eyelashes intact.

Fire erupts from below, from the sides, and even outward over the audience's heads—at a safe distance, but still close enough for the scorching heatwave to graze our skin. Midway through the concert, their microphone stands light on fire. At one point in the show, when they play "Metal Red Day"—their most popular single and the song I am most familiar with—the singer places a thick helmet over his head that sprouts a massive mohawk made of fire. I have to admit it now—I'm impressed.

This is the concert that turns me into a fan. Experiencing their music live is an entirely different experience than hearing it over my headset. Though the same is true for probably any rock band, there is a spectacular visual element to *Industrial November* that elevates their show to a form of performance art.

They don't rely on the visuals, though. The music is just as powerful as their studio albums produced with sound engineers. I can see how it would be easy to slack on the musicality when fans are clearly here for the spectacle, but they do both, and they do it well.

I do feel a bit out of place. Everyone all around me knows the lyrics to every single song. If only they sang in their native language—German—I'd probably be in better company. But as is my luck tonight, every single song is performed in English.

All four members of the band are exceedingly handsome—tall, muscular specimens. Brenner is the tallest, though perhaps the least attractive of the four men on stage. His face isn't classically handsome, but more a type of beastly sort of ugly-handsome with a strong jaw and slightly wide nose. His straight, black hair falls to his forehead with every head-bang, and he pulls it back with one hand, slicking it into place with his sweat. He is drenched with sweat after the first three songs and exudes the type of virile sexiness that I've always been attracted to in men. He moves on stage like a brute, with powerful thighs, firm steps, and one of the broadest sets of shoulders I've ever seen.

Midway through the concert, when Brenner takes off his shirt, revealing chiseled abs below a barrel chest, I am done for. To put it plainly, the heat emanating from the concert isn't only coming from the fire.

As the audience's energy winds down after an impressive four-hours, and the band turns to their slower songs, Mandy rests her head on my shoulder. She's tired from all the jumping, screaming, and singing of the night. As she leans on me, Mandy sways to a rock ballad she informs me is called "Bed of Eyelashes."

That's the moment when Brenner sweeps me away. His deep

voice carries a power in the hard metal songs, but I never expected he would be able to carry that over and actually sing. His voice in the rock ballad borders on operatic. It flows like authentic Mexican hot chocolate, silky smooth and hot with a hint of spicy. I know then that I'll go home and listen to all their albums, hoping I'll find more ballads there.

Then it happens. I can't believe it when he does, but midway through the ballad, Brenner Reindhart, the one and only, lead singer of *Industrial November*, locks eyes with me. I'm not singing along like everyone around me, and he shakes his head lightly as he smirks between lines of the chorus. He locks his gaze on me for the entirety of the ballad after that, effectively serenading me.

I look around and behind me, wondering if I'm imagining it, and he's actually looking at someone near me, but when my gaze lands back on him, he shakes his head and points, nodding, almost as if to say, *Yes, you, stupid*.

"Holy, hell," Mandy says when the song is over. "Did you see the way he was looking at you?"

"I didn't just imagine that?" I ask her.

Mandy grins, turning me by the shoulders to face her. "No. You didn't."

I've been to my fair share of rock concerts, and not once have I seen anything close to what *Industrial November* does when the show is over. They exit the stage, and the crowd stomps their feet until they return for the encore. All four men come back out, line up in a straight line, grab hands, and take a bow. The concert is heavy metal, performance art, and theater all rolled into one. It's pure art.

"Ready to go backstage?" Mandy asks.

When we get backstage, Mandy and I are escorted to a room packed with other fans and groupies. I find a spot on a couch and take a seat to check my phone, which I now realize I haven't done all night. I frown. I got so lost in the music, in the magic of the singer. Brenner Reindhart actually made me forget about *La Oficina* for four hours.

Three missed text messages from Joe await me.

Joe: *Tracy was a no-show. We are short-staffed.*

Joe: *Never mind. Don't worry. I was able to get Ileana to come in. Enjoy the concert.*

Joe: *Did you not get change for the register?*

I rub my temples. Joe's never had any issues like this before. He is probably nervous and, I'm sure, figuring things out on his own. Not that it eases my nerves any.

The door opens, and all the women in the room, including Mandy, jump to their feet, if they aren't already standing, as the bass player walks in, followed by the guitarist. Two security guards flank them.

"Hello, ladies," the guitarist says with a wide smile. He has the look of a golden, blond god as he opens his arms wide for two women to fall under his wings and fawn over him.

"That's Karl," Mandy says. "And that one over there, the brooding, muscular one with the beard, the bass player, his name is Fritz. We should go over and say hi."

"Why don't you go ahead? Get their autographs or take a selfie or whatever you want. I have to deal with Joe."

"Everything okay?" Mandy asks.

"Yeah. Go on. Enjoy what time you can with them. When I'm done with Joe, I'll join you."

Mandy shrugs, and I can almost see her skipping toward the two band members—surely her high heels are the only thing stopping her. I still can't believe she wore those shoes on Bonnie. I had to hand it to her, the woman was committed to her high heels.

It is a little tempting to go meet the band now that I have a better understanding of what they do, but they are so outnumbered by fans, I imagine any real conversation likely won't take place.

Instead, I decide to take my seat once again and text Joe about how to access the safe and get the change he needs. Joe and I are in the middle of that text conversation when someone sits next to me, but assuming it's Mandy again, I don't pay much attention.

"Why aren't you tripping over yourself to meet Karl?" a husky voice says.

"One second, please," I say without looking up.

Me: *Were you able to get into the safe?*

Joe: *Yeah. Got it. Sorry to have bothered you. I got it from here.*

Me: *Are you sure?*

Joe: *Yeah. You're distracting me now.*

Me: *I have every faith in you.*

Whoever sat next to me clears his throat, grabbing my attention for real this time. "Um, sorry about that. Work." I shrug apologetically as I tuck my phone in my back pocket and turn my attention to the man speaking. I have to do a doubletake to realize who is sitting next to me.

Brenner Reindhart.

I look around the room, and the groupies are all still huddled around Karl, plus a few around Fritz, along with Mandy. Had no one noticed Brenner walk into the room? I sure hadn't. But he would be hard to miss, being the tallest person in the room. Or did they just not care?

"So?" Brenner asks.

"Um—so what?" My heart starts to race, and I can't believe I'm having a hard time forming words.

I always imagined that if I ever met someone famous, I wouldn't be a fumbling moron like everyone else seems to be. I also am not the super-fan of *Industrial November* that Mandy is, so it catches me by total surprise when my brain stops working in front of Brenner Reindhart. His chocolaty-brown eyes bore into me, and I melt under his gaze. Brenner exudes a virility that overtakes my senses, and I decide it is that—and not his rock-god status—that attracts me to him.

He asks again, "Why aren't you over there with the other groupies dying to meet Karl or Fritz?" His voice carries the slightest hint of a German accent that sounds so sexy from his lips, I almost liquefy into the couch.

Words come out chopped, and time slows around me. "Oh, I'm not really a fan . . ." Crap. That's not what I meant to say. My eyes widen with panic, and I clasp my hand over my mouth.

Brenner throws his head back with laughter. "Well, this is a first." He rubs his fuller bottom lip with his thumb, keeping his eyes locked on mine. "So, if you're not a fan, what are you doing backstage?"

"That came out wrong," I offer. "I guess I'm a new fan of the band, but tonight's the first time I've been to one of your concerts."

"Oh?"

I point to Mandy. "That girl over there, Mandy, she won tickets from a radio station and invited me."

"So she's the fan?"

"I really didn't mean to say I wasn't a fan. I, um—I like your music."

My phone dings again. I close my eyes and count to ten. I am going to kill Joe. "I'm so sorry. Really, it's work."

I barely have my phone in my hand when Brenner speaks again. "You Americans are so rude. Always glued to your phones or work—or both."

My jaw drops, and I can only stare at him. What the hell? "Excuse me?" I say, my voice clearly laced with disdain.

"Get back to your *work*." Brenner stands and walks over to where Fritz and Karl are standing as Mandy runs over to my side. What an arrogant ass. To think I found him handsome and talented. Though, from what stereotypes I hear about musicians, especially front men, they are all arrogant. I shouldn't have expected anything less, not even after he basically serenaded me in front of thousands of people.

His rude comment and prompt dismissal cure me of any celebrity-induced blindness I may have had.

"Ohmygawd, ohmygawd, ohmygawd," Mandy whisper-screams at me and squeezes my forearm like a boa constrictor. "You aren't going to believe this!"

"What?" I ask, prying her hand from my arm before she bruises it.

"They want to come over to *La Oficina*! Karl said he wants to party, but the band didn't want to go out because they don't feel like dealing with fans all night."

"You think they won't have fans at *La Oficina*? I'm pretty sure they'll get recognized anywhere they go."

"Yeah, but you have that private party room. I told them I know a bar with a private room and discreet staff, and they could go there. Karl is all for it. Fritz agreed. Please tell me it's not booked tonight."

"No, it's not, but—" Mandy stops listening to me then as she turns to give Karl a thumbs up.

"Mandy, focus," I say. "I think Brenner and I got off on the wrong foot. I doubt he'll want to go to my bar—"

"Oh, they said he probably won't go. He rarely goes out drinking with the band."

Leave it to Mandy to know all the inner workings of a band she met only minutes ago.

"I don't know," I say. Rock bands are notorious for property damage and rowdy behavior. *La Oficina* isn't that kind of bar, and I don't want it getting the wrong reputation.

My typical customers are hospital staff or the families of patients. They come to celebrate new babies or near-death recoveries. Sometimes they come to mourn. But all of it is a mellow sort of vibe—the local watering hole. I always knew what kind of ambiance I wanted my place to be, and high-profile expensive clients don't quite fit the bill.

"Come on!" Mandy whines. "Think about it. You'll make a killing from them alone."

Mandy makes an excellent point, and I'm not renting out the private room tonight, so I am fresh out of excuses for her.

"Let me text Joe so he can get things ready—"

"Really? This is amazing! I'm going to party with *Industrial November*!" Mandy all but squeals.

I shake my head at this strong, beautiful woman reduced to teenage antics as she fangirls over the German band. "Tell them to use the back entrance. I'll leave empty boxes they can lift to cover their faces and carry them into the private room so no one will see them go in. They'll pass for staff."

"You're brilliant!" Mandy gives me a peck on the cheek and is about to run off when I stop her.

"Hey, we should get going. I need to be there to help get ready for them."

Mandy shoots me a wicked grin. "No worries. I'm going with the band."

As I speed-walk to Bonnie, I text Joe about the private party, leaving out the details about who exactly our VIP guests are. I don't need another fumbling idiot beside me. If I wait on the private room, no one else in the bar needs to know who is there. I'll let Joe know at the end of the night before they leave so he can meet them.

When they arrive, Mandy beams at me as she goes into the private room, followed by the band members, who all carry in boxes and successfully enter the bar under the radar. So successful is my brilliant plan that I don't catch that one of the men carrying a box is Brenner Reindhart—the ass. I don't notice him until I go into the room to take drink orders.

The private room has six tables, and they are packed with the band, their security detail, and various groupies, including Mandy. The only band member not present is the drummer—Adrian, I think.

"What can I get you all to drink?" I ask, ready to start jotting down orders.

"Just get us a bottle of vodka and a bottle of tequila for every table. Waters for everyone too," Brenner says, not looking at me.

"I'll have a beer," Mandy adds.

"And a beer for the lady," Brenner says, smiling at Mandy, letting his eyes linger on her. "All on my tab," he adds, still looking at her. He never turns to look at me during the exchange. When he lifts his credit card in the air and waits for me to grab it without so much as a 'thank you,' I decide I'll be over-charging him out the ass for his arrogant entitlement. I can't believe he had the gall to call me rude when he behaves like this to waitstaff.

When I return, clutching a tray of water glasses and shot glasses, the mention of my name stops me in my tracks outside the entrance to the private room.

"So, what's the deal with that girl who came to the concert with you?" the voice I recognize as Fritz asks. "The hot one with the short black hair. The one who took our order."

"Sofia," Mandy says. "She's a friend. I kind of dragged her out tonight."

"But what's her deal? She single?" Fritz asks with interest, making me smile. Maybe the night isn't a total dud. Fritz is hot in his own way, even if he doesn't have Bren's dangerous voice.

"Aww, man, you claiming dibs on the hottie? Didn't even

give a guy a chance," says another man, who I'm pretty sure is the guitarist.

Then Brenner's thunderous voice rises over everyone else's. "You all sound like idiots. You can't claim dibs on women."

Someone laughs, and I think it might have been Fritz. "Looks like dad already claimed dibs," he says, and I can picture the grin on Fritz's face even without looking at him.

"I hate it when you call me that. And I'm not calling dibs. I wouldn't call dibs on an insignificant waitress," Brenner answers.

"That's not cool, man," Fritz says. "Who cares if she's a waitress?"

"Yeah," Karl chastises. "Nothing wrong with being a waitress."

That does it. I walk into the room, my hands shaking so much the glasses tilt and water sloshes, nearly spilling over the rims. Mandy must see murder in my eyes—and I can't deny I'm seriously considering turning the tray upside down on Brenner Reindhart's head—because she calls out to me to grab my attention.

"Sofia! Hey. Thanks for the drinks."

Her loudness draws everyone else's attention in the room, and Brenner looks at me for the first time. In his defense, he grimaces and slides a bit down in his chair.

Good. I hope he is embarrassed.

Mandy begins offering an explanation, "Actually, Sofia isn't—"

"Done getting all the drinks. I'll be right back with more. Mandy, can you come help me, please?"

"Um, okay."

Joe has the vodka and tequila bottles ready to go with buckets of ice by the time I get back to the counter, Mandy trailing behind.

"What was that about?" Mandy asks.

"Don't tell them I own the bar."

"Why not?" she asks.

"If that pretentious ass thinks I'm a waitress and that he gets to look down at me because of it, I don't want him to change his tune. I will never see him again after tonight. Let's just get through the night and leave me out of it."

"You promise you won't pour a drink over his head?" Mandy asks sweetly.

"I promise I'll do my very best."

HIDING IN THE SMOKE EXCERPT

THREE: BREN

I insulted Sofia, our waitress, not once but twice. The first time at the meet-and-greet backstage, when I flat out called her rude to her face, and the second when I put down her profession just now, and I'm almost sure she heard me.

I'm almost certain of it because her icy glares send shivers down my spine the rest of the night, and when I sign for the bill, I pay about twice what I usually do. Given we are in Kansas City, I expect the bill to be less than at a major American City, not more. I can't fault her for padding the bill, though. I've been a total ass.

I've tracked her all night, hoping to find a moment to explain myself and apologize, but she's a slippery one. In my defense, after the concert, I was exhausted. At thirty-four, I am the eldest member of the band and the front man. I need to keep up with the younger guys, but I also need to deliver our overly ambitious performances. When I saw her sitting there alone, I couldn't believe there was a woman as hot as her not kissing Karl's or Fritz's feet. An excitement I hadn't felt in a long time bubbled in my chest, and I had to talk to her.

It doesn't help matters that she is perfect. Her raven-black, short hair falls in straight tresses around her perfect, heart-shaped face. She is wearing black jeans and a black t-shirt. Despite her simple outfit, her body is fucking killer. The instant I saw her sitting by herself, my cock twitched. Then I got close, and she bit that perfect full bottom lip of hers as she typed on her phone.

I wanted that perfect mouth on me—anywhere.

Then she kept her attention on her stupid little phone and texted away. And I'm Brenner fucking Reindhart. I'm not used to women dismissing me. Sure, I'm not the first one the women go to, but once Karl, Fritz, and even our drummer, Adrian, pick, I get the same kind of attention from their castoffs.

Usually, it doesn't bother me to be last pick. Karl, Fritz, and Adrian are still looking for the next hottest groupie for the night. But I want something real. Something more. And I think women realize that when they get to know me.

But after Sofia's cold shoulder the rest of the night, and the effects of the vodka taking over, I grow increasingly more pissed at her indifference. Does she not care who I am?

Now we're waiting for the bar to empty out so we can leave unnoticed. Once Karl keeps ignoring a gorgeous redhead, she saunters over to my table.

"Hey, you're the lead singer, right?" she purrs. Then she tosses her red hair over her shoulder.

"Yeah. Please, call me Bren. Nice to meet you."

"Bren." She giggles as she says my name.

This is always the most infuriating part. Waiting for people to adjust to who I am. It takes some longer than others to see that despite it all, I am just a guy. Same as any other.

"I'm Amber," the redhead says. She bites her lip, and that gesture forces my thoughts to Sofia as she had bitten her own lip earlier in the night. What the fuck? Why am I still thinking about her?

"So, it's getting late," Amber says. "You thinking about heading out soon?"

"Yeah. The bar is already closed. We're just waiting for it to empty out so we can go."

"Want some company tonight?"

For some unfathomable reason, my instinct is to say no. I want no one if I can't have Sofia, but as I scan the room, she's nowhere to be seen. Besides, I've been such an ass to her, I'd probably have a better shot at her throwing a drink in my face than wanting to spend the night together.

"You know what, Amber? Yeah. I'd love some company."

Almost the second I close the door to my hotel room, Amber's miniature dress comes off, and she stands there in her underwear. She drags me by the hand until I sit on the bed, and she straddles me to grind on me.

"Brenner Reindhart. I can't believe I'm in Brenner Reind-hart's bed." She keeps giggling, and the sound is like the screech of audio feedback.

She also keeps saying my full name, and I have to resist the urge to roll my eyes. When she kisses me, I feel nothing. She is beautiful and hot and exactly my type, and there is absolutely no reaction from my body.

Amber keeps grinding over my groin, waiting for a reaction that never comes—pun intended. "Everything okay?" she asks after her ministrations end up fruitless.

"Sorry. Bit tired. And distracted."

She stops moving for a moment. "What are you thinking about?"

I don't lie to women, so I became apt at workarounds a

long time ago. "Don't worry about it," I say and press my lips to hers. I close my eyes and think about Sofia and Sofia's lips only. My pulse quickens and redirects blood to my dick, stirring it alive. I dart my tongue into her mouth, and she purrs in response.

As I harden, she picks up the pace of her grinding over my jeans. Then she cups the shaft through the fabric and pulls away from my lips. "Oh, there you are, Brenner Reindhart."

The sound of my full name in a voice that isn't Sofia's pulls me out of the fantasy, conquering my brain. The voice is too high and chirpy to be Sofia's. Sofia's voice is seductive and honey-thick. My eyes fly open, and it's Amber, the redheaded groupie, grinding against me—not Sofia. I stand, nearly tossing Amber off my lap, but I steady her to her feet.

"Sorry," I say. I scan the room until my eyes land on her dress. I pick it up and hand it to her. "I guess I'm more tired than I thought. Do you need money for a cab?"

Amber's nostrils flare, and she huffs. "No. I don't need money for a cab."

She hastily gets dressed again and storms out of my room, slamming the door behind her.

What the fuck was that? Why can't I get an insignificant woman out of my head? We barely met, hardly talked, and it took thinking about her to get a hard-on. I've never, not once in my life, had a difficult time with that.

Kicking Amber out was a mistake. My erection presses against the zipper of my jeans almost painfully. I had already taken a shower before going to the bar, but I know if I want a shot at sleep, I'll have to shower again before bed.

After shedding my clothes, I jump into an almost-scalding shower, letting the water ripple down my body. I hang my head, letting the strong water pressure beat at the back of my neck, and I shut my eyes, thinking of her.

Sofia's thick lips wrapped around the head of my dick. Her tongue licking the length of me. I wrap my hand around my hard-as-steel shaft and squeeze with thoughts of Sofia on my mind. I stroke myself, picturing her mouth in the place of my hand.

Seconds pass before my load erupts from me, and my body tenses. I open my eyes, disoriented to time and place. I need to stop thinking about this woman.

Dreams of Sofia lull me into the best sleep I've had in a long time.

We have a day of rest in Kansas City before we move on to our next tour destination, and I'm determined to apologize to her, so I show up at the bar from last night. I don't expect her to be there, but I can ask someone for her phone number.

It is two in the afternoon when I arrive, and per the hours on the door, they won't open for another hour, but I see movement inside, so I try the door. I turn to my security guard, Andreas, before going in. "Wait out here."

Andreas nods.

I enter the bar and freeze when I see her. Even from her backside, I can tell it is her. My eyes glue to her slender frame as she stays busy taking chairs off the tops of tables and placing them on the floor. She has the body of a super-model. Why the fuck is she waitressing?

"I'm sorry, we won't open for another hour," she says. "Lola, you forgot to lock up when you got in this morning!" Sofia calls out, though I can't see anyone else.

"Sorry!" A voice drifts into the room from elsewhere. Then the same woman yells something in another language —Spanish, I think—and Sofia yells back, also in Spanish.

Sofia is smart, I think to myself, and I smile. That is such a turn-on.

"Um, actually, I was hoping to speak to you," I say.

Sofia spins around, and her breath hitches as her posture stiffens.

She has a uniquely rare beauty that almost leaves me speechless. I can't tell if her heritage is American, American Indian, Hispanic, Asian, or a combination of those things. But the sound of her voice in Spanish carries a sensuality to it that I shouldn't be thinking about, especially after I jerked off to thoughts of her last night.

"You," she says, her eyes narrowed. "I don't see what we need to talk about."

I clear my throat. "I owe you an apology. Last night—I acted like an ass. I'm sorry."

Sofia uncrosses her arms. "I appreciate that. Apology accepted. Anything else?"

"See, you accept my apology, then you're short with me."

"So?"

"So, it makes me think you don't really accept my apology."

"Look, I appreciate you making the trip. You apologized. I accepted. I'm not sure what else you want from me—"

"Dinner," I say, surprising us both. That was not my plan.

"What?" she asks, stunned.

What the fuck did I just do? I swore I'd apologize and get on with my life, my next tour destination, forget all about the waitress named Sofia. "Yeah. Dinner. I'd like to make it up to you and explain why I—"

"It's really not necessary, Brenner—"

"Please. Call me Bren. All my friends do."

Sofia cocks her head to the side with interest. "We're not friends." She keeps her hands busy pulling more chairs off tables as we continue our conversation. It doesn't escape me I'm trailing her like a puppy. *Pathetic.*

"I'd like to be. Please. Just one dinner."

"Even if I wanted to, I can't." She spreads her arms as if she were showcasing the room. "I work tonight."

"All right. How about a nightcap after?"

The woman who matched the voice in Spanish from earlier materializes, interrupting our conversation.

"Oh, sorry," she says. "Am I interrupting?"

The woman, if she can be called that because she looks like a teenager, is short and wears her blond curls in a mess of a bun like a bird's nest on top of her head.

"No, Lola. It's fine. This is Bren. Bren, meet Lola. She helps out a bit around here."

Lola can't bring her eyes to meet mine, but I don't think she recognizes me, so I step forward and offer my hand, but she only shakes her head and apologetically shows me the cleaning gloves covering her hands.

"I'll get out of your hair," says Lola. "Just, are we out of this?" she lifts a spray bottle of cleaning fluid for Sofia to see.

Sofia shakes her head. "We should have some. Try the cabinet in the office."

"Okay. It was nice to meet you," Lola says and keeps on working, not interrupting the few times she walks by us again.

"So, where were we?" Sofia asks.

"Nightcap."

"Bar closes at two in the morning. Bit late, don't you think?"

"You're really making me work hard here, aren't you?"

"I'm not trying to—"

"Night cap, morning-cap, call it whatever you want. Just have one drink with me."

She looks past me out the window, a question in her eyes as she takes in my security guard.

"That's Andreas. My security."

Her eyebrow quirks up.

"Purely a precaution."

Sofia's posture relaxes, and I can see the minute her resolve wavers. "Fine," she says. "One quick drink. Here."

"Perfect. I'll be back at closing."

Once the last of the staff leaves, she pours us two shots of tequila and places the bottle between us. She takes a seat next to me and leans on the bar, cupping her cheek in her palm as she waits for me to talk. She looks tired.

"Look," I say. "I was a fucking asshole last night. Not that it's any excuse, but I was exhausted—"

"You're right," she says. "It's not an excuse."

"No. It's not, but please, hear me out. I was tired, and the texting thing . . . well, it's a pet peeve of mine. I shouldn't have bitten your head off about it, though."

"Don't forget that you also insulted me for being a waitress—"

"You heard that, huh?" I ask.

Sofia nods, but there is a teasing glimmer in her eyes. She picks up a lime wedge between her fingers and brings it to her mouth to lick it once.

When I recover my senses after watching her tongue dart out and slide over the flesh of the fruit, I speak again. I smile because I'm fairly certain her licking that lime wedge was her intentional flirting. "I didn't really mean to insult you. If I'm sincere, I thought you were really hot—still do. When Fritz and Karl expressed interest, I admit I put you down, but I did it to try to get them to stop sniffing around you like hounds."

"So you don't know me, and you're displaying possessive behavior?"

"Again, I was an ass, and I'm sorry."

"Possessiveness is really unattractive, Brenner."

My full name on her lips grates at my ears. "Please, call me Bren."

"You said that's what your friends call you."

"It is," I say.

"We're not friends."

"I'm hoping we could be."

Sofia fills our shot glasses a second time and sips on the tequila, not once making a face, which I'll admit impresses the hell out of me. She leans forward, and I have difficulty keeping my gaze on her eyes and not on her cleavage. Then she licks and bites her lower lip, and my dick stirs alive. This woman is going to be the end of me.

"Is that what you want from me, Bren? To be friends?" Her voice is low and sultry when she delivers the question.

"No, actually. If I'm honest, that's the last thing I want to be." I rub my bottom lip with my thumb. I can almost anticipate the feel of her lips on mine.

"What do you want, then?" Her eyes are hooded when they freeze on my lips.

"More," I say.

For a moment, Sofia considers my one word and all the implications we both know I placed in that one syllable. We let the silence stretch for a long moment, but it isn't uncomfortable. I could stare at her rare beauty for hours without exchanging a word and die a happy man.

For some reason I can't explain, I feel light around Sofia.

Women have used me in the past. For press, or to make a quick buck on my name. Normally it takes me a long time to trust a woman. But Sofia is different. I don't know for sure that I can trust her, but my gut is telling me I can, and I need to find a way to spend more time with her. I'll take crumbs from her if that's all she offers me.

Finally, she breaks the silence. "I can't give you more."

"Why not? I know you don't know me, but I'd like for us to get to know each other."

"Even if we got to know each other, and you were the perfect man, I don't do more."

"Okay . . ." Shit. This isn't going my way at all.

"I'll admit I'm surprised. The last person I'd expect to be looking for something serious would be the lead singer of a famous rock band, but—"

"Who said I'm looking for something serious?" I try to backpedal.

Sofia leans back and crosses her arms in front of her, deepening the distance between us so she can study my face. "It was implied, Bren."

"All I'm proposing is that we spend some time together."

She bites her lip while she considers her next words. "You mean it?"

I nod.

"Fine. Here's the deal—if you want it," she says. "One night. No strings. No repeats. No sleeping over."

I blink. What the fuck did she just say? I'd hoped for lunch the next day, and she has turned it into something much more indecent.

"One night?" I croak out, incredulous.

"One fuck. That's it. That's all I can offer. Take it or leave it."

"I'll take it," I say, because really, who in their right mind says 'no' to this woman? I'll woo her later, and she'll take back her conditions. I just know it.

She grins devilishly at me. "All right. Let's go."

"What, right now?"

"Want to risk me changing my mind?"
"Definitely not."

Keep reading Sofia and Bren's story in *Hiding in the Smoke*. You can get your copy on all major ebook retailers.

Ofelia Martinez writes romance with Latinas on top. Originally from the Texas border, Ofelia now resides in Missouri with her partner and their dog, Pixel.

This is Ofelia's fifth book.

She loves good books, tequila, and chocolate. She proudly shares a birthday with Usagi Tsukino. When not writing, you can find Ofelia making visual art.

Visit OfeliaMartinez.com to learn more.